Praise for the Rendezvous Series

"An entertaining, vivid portrait of frontier America as seen through the eyes of an impressionable youth"
—*Booklist* on *So Wild a Dream*

"Blevins's sweeping vision of the American frontier is just plain irresistible."
—W. Michael Gear and Kathleen O'Neal Gear,
authors of *People of the Thunder,* on *So Wild a Dream*

"Win Blevins is my hero. . . . *So Wild a Dream* reads like spare prose poetry, limning vulnerable, yet heroic human characters against the untrammeled frontier of the early nineteenth century."
—Loren D. Estleman, author of *The Branch and the Scaffold*

"Blevins possesses a rare skill in masterfully telling a story to paper. He is a true storyteller in the tradition of Native people."
—Lee Francis, associate professor of Native American Studies,
University of New Mexico, on *So Wild a Dream*

"*So Wild a Dream* is a fabulous beginning of what promises to become a classic series that will be on college reading lists in history classes studying the fur-trade era."
—*Roundup Magazine*

"The glory years of frontier life, fresh and rich."
—*Kirkus Reviews* on *Beauty for Ashes*

"A rousing installment in a fine epic of the American frontier."
—*Publishers Weekly* on *Beauty for Ashes*

"Loaded with action, drama, vivid descriptions, and colorful historical characters, this is a whopper of a Western yarn."

—*Publishers Weekly* on *A Long and Winding Road*

"Blevins has done his research and knows the mountain men as well as anyone could—to read this tale is to get a true sense of what their ordeal and adventures must have been like."

—*Library Journal* on *Dancing with the Golden Bear*

Also by Win Blevins

Stone Song

The Rock Child

ravenShadow

Give Your Heart to the Hawks

DATE DUE

JUN 2 3 2015	
NO 1 2 '19	

Dreams Beneath
Your Feet

A Novel of the Mountain Men

WIN BLEVINS

A Tom Doherty Associates Book

New York

This is a work of fiction. All of the characters, organizations, and events portrayed in this novel are either products of the author's imagination or are used fictitiously.

DREAMS BENEATH YOUR FEET

Copyright © 2008 by Win Blevins

A Forge Book
Published by Tom Doherty Associates, LLC
175 Fifth Avenue
New York, NY 10010

www.tor-forge.com

Forge® is a registered trademark of Tom Doherty Associates, LLC.

ISBN 978-0-7653-4486-1

First Edition: December 2008
First Mass Market Edition: December 2009

Printed in the United States of America

0 9 8 7 6 5 4 3 2 1

To Meredith,
who is my California home
wherever we go

Acknowledgments

A series of six historical novels requires a lot of expertise, and I got it from good colleagues and knowledgeable friends. Dale Walker, my editor, has been as wise and helpful as always. He has been an enormous source of support for more than a decade. The Honorable Clyde Hall of the Fort Hall Reservation has been my guide, both professionally and personally, in matters of the culture and spirituality of Native peoples. Dick James has shared his encyclopedic knowledge about mountain men. Many Native friends and fellow writers have helped me along the way. Thanks—I'm indebted to you all.

Thanks to Dean Koontz for permission to quote from his excellent novel *Life Expectancy*.

Every day throughout this writing, my wife, Meredith, helped as only the best of mates can. My love, respect, and gratitude for her are boundless.

Ours is a story mad with the impossible, it is by chaos out of dream, it began as dream and it has continued as dream to the last headlines you read in a newspaper. And of our dreams there are two things above all others to be said, that only madmen could have dreamed them or would have dared to—and that we have shown a considerable faculty for making them come true.

—BERNARD DE VOTO

In *So Wild a Dream*, challenged by the half-breed Hannibal, Sam follows his heart west. After traveling to St. Louis with the con man Grumble and the madam Abby, Sam goes to the Rocky Mountains with a fur brigade and begins to learn ways of the trappers and the Indians. At the end he is forced to walk seven hundred miles alone, lost and starving, to the nearest fort.

In *Beauty for Ashes*, Sam courts the Crow girl Meadowlark. Helping Sam attempt a daring feat to win her hand, her brother is killed. Seeking reconciliation, Sam goes through the rigors of a sun dance, and Meadowlark elopes with him. Her family takes her back by force and kicks Sam out of the village. But Meadowlark runs away to join Sam, and at the trapper rendezvous they are married.

Dancing with the Golden Bear launches Sam and Meadowlark to California with a fur brigade. After terrible hardships crossing the desert, they reach the Golden Clime and the ocean. But Meadowlark dies in childbirth. On a harrowing journey across the Sierra Nevada and the deserts beyond, Sam passes through the dark night of the soul.

In *Heaven Is a Long Way Off*, Sam returns to California for his daughter, only to discover that she, her uncle Flat Dog, and her aunt Julia have been kidnapped. Sam brings off harrowing rescues and makes a wild escape on a river in flood. On the way back to the Crows, he becomes deeply involved in rescuing teenagers from slavery. Finally he returns his daughter to her village and finds his rival waiting to kill him.

At the beginning of *A Long and Winding Road*, the sisters of Tomás, Sam's adopted son, are married and shortly afterward kidnapped by Indians. Father and son swear to rescue the women. The search takes them deep into Navajo country, then far north to the trappers' rendezvous on the Green River, to Bent's Fort, and at last back to Taos, New Mexico, and a surprising confrontation.

Part One

One

SAM MORGAN HEARD his partner, Hannibal, get up and step to the dead fire. Morning by morning, they took turns rising first, using cold fingers to get a little flame going and start some coffee.

First light would come along within a few minutes. They both had an instinct for first light, and it would arrive with the first sip of coffee.

Sam savored the warmth of his buffalo robes and the pad of his folded blanket coat under his head. In the aspens the mare Paladin and the other horses chuffed from time to time, clomped, and dreamed of a country free of horseflies.

Sam inventoried these familiar camp sounds. He could tell his mare from Hannibal's gelding Brownie and from the packhorses by her step alone. In the other direction he heard the Henry's Fork River. He listened to the pouring of the coffee water and the ping of the pot hung on the rod above the flames. He reached out and touched the cold barrel of the Celt, the flintlock rifle he inherited from his father.

One familiar part of Sam's world was missing. This past winter his pet coyote, Coy, aged sixteen, walked out in the snows and never came back. Walking was difficult for the old coyote, and Sam was sure that he had gone deliberately, knowing that his time had come.

Sam missed him. As a pup Coy saved Sam from a prairie fire, and they had been together day and night for a coyote lifetime.

Making the coffee, Hannibal MacKye chuckled at himself. He and Sam had traded for a few beans before they left Fort Hall on this hunt, but they'd been making brew from the same grounds for two weeks now.

Toasty in his bedroll, Sam waited for the first two words of every morning, "Coffee's hot." Then the men would squat across the fire from each other and sip the flavored water without a word. Since they had ridden together for nearly two decades—trapped beaver, lived with Indians, rambled from the plains to the peaks to the Pacific—they had their routines. Their way was a little silence on waking, a span of time untouched by talk.

Suddenly Sam knew something. It just popped up, like a bubble from the mud bottom of a pool. He wiggled his back and bottom against the ground, and the thought was still there.

"Coffee's hot," said Hannibal.

Sam shifted around, scrambled to the fire, and held his cup out for the pale brew. The silence was amiable, as always, but Sam was holding back.

He waited until they'd finished the first cup of coffee, his tongue dissatisfied with the taste, his belly grateful for the warmth. He looked at his partner and had thoughts that hadn't occurred to him in years. They were a truly strange pair, an Indian and a white man partnered. Who would guess, looking at them, that Sam, the white man with white hair and blue eyes, had been taught to read by the Indian? And that Hannibal, half Delaware and educated by his classics professor father, was fluent in Greek, Latin, and the philosophies of the world? Who would guess, really, what they had in common?

Sam couldn't have named it, himself, and Hannibal wouldn't. They loved the myriad and intricate ways of these mountains, here a spring, lower down a beaver pond, beyond that a wide meadow with a solitary bull elk feeding at its edge. Above the meadow a green reach of lodgepole pine, leading to a low divide, which framed the intense blue unique to the mountain West. From there a sighting of a hundred miles of lava plains, ending in a horizon of sawtooth peaks. They also loved the exhilaration of running buffalo and the heart-in-throat glimpse of a huge salmon leaping up a waterfall.

They were intrigued by Indian people and all the subtle byways of meeting them with proper ceremony, trading with them, being guests in their villages for days or weeks. Avoiding another tribe, even fighting against some. Sam had married into the Crow tribe and lived the tangle of having a red family.

Maybe the biggest attraction, the single, great, mind-blinding opiate, was the way that beauty and danger teeter-tottered. Every mile ridden, every trap set, every buffalo hunted, every stretch of desert crossed, every river forded was a dazzling diamond—and the facets of these jewels were wonder, hazard, miracle, excitement, and death. However hot, cold, or tired a mountain man felt, no matter how full-bellied, well-loved, or ready to hoot and holler, no matter how hungry, thirsty, or bowel-running scared, he always felt alive.

As Sam and Hannibal sipped their coffee, they knew such stuff, but they didn't talk about it. They were too busy living it.

Sam looked at his friend and his mount—his hunting trail family. He pushed his eyes over to the single pack of beaver they had, a pitiful taking for their entire spring hunt. Up and down the west side of the Yellowstone Mountains they'd trekked, up and down the valley of the Henry's Fork. Other trappers stayed away from this country, because of the danger of coming face-to-face with Blackfeet. After so many years Sam and Hannibal would have missed the danger if they didn't smell it, and they were glad to have this country to trap alone. Once it was prime. Now it was paltry, but the best of what was left.

The irony was that the scarcity of beaver didn't matter. They started hunting the creature for its fur, which made the best hats. Except that over the last few years, silk hats became the style. A way of life done in by a whim of fashion.

Sam swallowed the dregs and chewed the grounds. Even that way, the coffee had no taste.

The way Hannibal was grinning at him, Sam knew his friend had the same experience.

It was time. "I got a thought," said Sam.

This thought of his would change their plans. Last night they'd agreed that today was the time to start downriver toward Fort Hall.

"I want to go to the Smokes," he said.

They went to the Smokes each year, but at the end of the fall hunt, not the spring hunt.

Hannibal said, "Why not?"

So the Smokes it was. Just that easy.

Two

THEY UNSADDLED IN the Smokes late that afternoon, with all the long twilight of a spring day before them. They hobbled the horses and munched on dried meat. Sam checked the ties of red cotton that held last autumn's sweat lodge together, and the footings of the limbs. He pursed his mouth, uneasy. "They're good," he told Hannibal, "but I want to build a new one."

"I'll hunt."

Sam cut a baker's dozen of green willow branches, tore new strips of red cloth, and constructed the lodge in the shape of an upside-down bowl. He gathered a couple of dozen lava rocks for tomorrow's ceremony.

Dusk came the way water darkens white paper. Hannibal slipped into camp with an elk on a packhorse, and they hung it high. A low fire and soft talk held off the dark until they got into their bedrolls.

The last thing Sam remembered was the smell of the Smokes. It was named for a handful of sulfurous springs that gushed from the seam where the mountain met the meadow. The first fifty paces or so of each creek ran hot, and the narrow valley was soupy with steam. Doing a sweat lodge here at the end of each trapping year was one of Sam's rituals.

The next morning he didn't eat, just downed plenty of water. He and Hannibal built the fire and set the lava rocks on to heat. They covered the lodge with their blankets and buffalo robes. Sam built an altar, filled his pipe with tobacco, and set it facing the lodge.

Hannibal helped with this much and then started cutting the elk into over-sized strips to dry. The sacred pipe and the sweat lodge were Sam's red road, not Hannibal's. This understanding between them was as comfortable as everything else, and Sam found satisfaction in performing the ceremony alone.

When everything was ready, he carried a dozen rocks into the lodge with a shovel, stripped, and entered.

He performed the ceremony as the Crow medicine man Bell Rock had taught him years before. He burned cedar on the rocks. In the darkness of this womb of the Earth he prayed, pouring four dippers of water slowly onto the lava, pinpricking the black air of the lodge with fiery moisture, the breath of the rocks. He uttered the traditional prayer of the first round and then chanted a song in the Crow language.

Hannibal stopped cutting and listened to the song, for music was one of Sam's gifts.

Between rounds Sam smoked the sacred pipe and with the smoke sent prayers to Father Sky. He carried in more rocks, to roil up the heat. He poured a round of seven dippers, another of ten, and the last round without counting. He prayed.

All sweats were good—he felt a rightness in them. But this time he was searching for something. He didn't know what, and it didn't come to him.

Sam performed another sweat that afternoon, again good, again with something missing.

When a valley opened toward mountains to the west, as this one did, twilight came early and lingered long. Sam helped Hannibal finish butchering the elk. They performed other tasks, ate their supper of dried meat, and talked of this and that. Sam's last words before sleep were, "I'll sweat again tomorrow."

"Sure."

Three

NAMELESS.

An hour before dawn Sam saw himself walking, stepping forward ceremoniously, slowly, into the steaming clouds of the Valley of the Smokes.

He was perfectly aware, in reality, that he was comfortably tucked into his robes and across the fire from his partner. Yet this other experience, this walking—it was more real than real.

Without words he knew—*I am seeing beyond*. Years ago, during the sun dance he gave, he had seen beyond.

Now he stepped, hesitantly, through the valley, blinded by mist. He was searching for something, and he had no idea what.

A jolt of fear surged in his blood. *Something I will never find*. The mist invaded his nostrils and filled his body and it was fear, wild, crazy fear.

He stood still and groped with one hand for something to hold on to. Fog wafted through his grasping fingers.

He brought back a memory. Several summers ago, at rendezvous, he had been taken over by a feeling this strong and strange. After hunting, he had walked to the edge of a cliff to spot the easy way down to the camp.

Suddenly, the feeling took over his body. It was a weakness in his knees, a yearning to take a single step forward into the empty air.

He leaned back against this inner force. Still the wild lure of walking into air held him. He shook. Finally, he threw himself backward onto his back and bottom.

Then he found his feet and his sanity and walked back to his horse. He shuddered, shook the feeling off, and for years thought no more about it.

Stop. Don't remember. Be here in this seeing beyond.

In the Valley of the Smokes he padded forward, feeling disoriented, stupid. *I am looking for something, but what . . . ?*

He was half-blind, half-deaf, wandering. . . .

A huge snake appeared in the air in front of Sam, coiled. He had never seen a serpent like this. It was blue as a sapphire, and not smooth but faceted, like a gem. Even in this fog each surface gleamed, as though radiating its own sunlight.

Sam felt no pang of fear of the snake. It hadn't come forward to strike him. It cocked its head and looked into Sam's face.

Sam thought, *It is a messenger,* and now he felt fear wriggle up his back.

The snake squirmed, and flake by flake its facet-scales began to pop off its body.

Sam had seen dried husks of rattler skin hundreds of times in the West. He had always supposed that snakes let go of their old skins without noticing, whole, as an entire scab drops away without a pull.

That was not happening to Snake. He sent mighty spasms up and down his body. The scales bubbled up on his flesh like small blisters. Up and down his length the surges ran again. Amazingly—it was beyond amazing—each new scale was a gleaming new color, red, yellow, green, orange, or purple.

As a few scales dropped off, a hundred new ones blistered. Snake was turning into a sunburst of colors before Sam's eyes.

Suddenly Snake drew Sam toward his own yellow orbs, divided by one black slit. Something in the look said . . .

Sam tried to see into the slit. He tried to ease his spirit out of his body and enter. . . . Fear quaked him, and he drew back with all his might.

Snake disappeared.

And Sam?

Stunned, disoriented, Sam shook in his robes. He reached around himself with his ears for the night sounds of camp and could not hear them. Wherever he was, it was not the Valley of the Smokes.

For a stabbing moment he thought he'd lost something important, something had drifted away like the steam of the hot springs. Then he remembered with a pang. Something nameless.

He wanted to be back on the earth, on the ground in his bedroll. An unaccountable nostalgia swooshed over him like a wave running up the sand, and he wanted the Yellowstone country. He loved this place. He decided to find it by reminding himself, like counting on his fingers, of some of the particular spots he loved. There was a lake in the heart of Yellowstone country that flowed toward the Atlantic Ocean from one end, to the Pacific from the other. A mountain studded with petrified stones, which always brought to Sam a sense of wonder. Another mountain of obsidian, good for making sharp blades and for trading to Indians. Yellowstone Falls, both lower and the upper, which seemed to Sam perfectly magical, gestures of a god bored by the practical and entranced by grace. Sometimes Sam imagined walking through the bottom of these long tumbles of waters, beyond the visible and into a trembling darkness.

The nameless feeling sloshed cold against the walls of his chest, but his mind knew no words for it.

Sam looked at the sky now and saw its stars, so clear they looked like clusters of shiny horseshoe nails. At lower altitudes they always seemed far duller. They revealed themselves only to people who rode high enough to see their truth.

Suddenly, he had a nutty idea. He would reshape the stars with his eyes. He would place them where he wanted and make words of them. Since he'd learned to read in his twenties, he'd grown very fond of it, and he even carried a volume of the verses of Lord Byron in his possible sack. The book was so much fun he could stand the word "Lord" in front of Byron.

Now Sam bent his mind hard to the task and pushed the stars around the sky until they formed words. He couldn't hold more than one word at a time in his mind, though. He couldn't tell what the words were, and none seemed to be the right ones. The nameless held itself aloof from words. He would start one word—he tried to shape "alone" from one herd of stars—but it seemed wrong. Then he'd rub it out in his mind, just like using an eraser on a blackboard, and start again.

He tried to make "hard times." Those words sure spelled out the last couple of years. But the stars began to get fuzzy. He realized they weren't nearly so bright. He didn't have much to spell with.

Instead the stars said something to him. They turned into tiny animals. He could barely make out the shapes, but clearly they were humped buffalo, long-necked cranes, slinky coyotes, spry ants, and all the other animals of creation. And they started marching off. Step by measured step, they began walking off the black slate of the sky. They would need forever to empty out that slate—the stars were almost numberless, like the animals—but there they were, the vastest of herds, moving on.

Just then he heard Hannibal get up and step to the dead fire.

The stars were gone, and Sam didn't know the nameless.

He heard a clank from Hannibal. Sam was half in a magical world with a blank sky and half in the ordinary world. He squirmed. He opened his eyes and looked at his partner. He didn't dare glance at the dark sky. He rooted himself here on the ground in the steamy valley.

Then he smiled at himself. Aha. Eureka. Whatever words applied—words were Hannibal's specialty. *I still don't know what the nameless is. Don't understand myself or the world. But by God I know what to do.*

He rolled over in his blankets, away from Hannibal.

Sam felt stuck. He wanted to talk to Hannibal and he couldn't. Hannibal was the wisest man Sam knew. Sam was hoping to work his way to the banner Hannibal said he rode under, *"Rideo, ergo sum"* (I laugh, therefore I am).

But Sam couldn't talk about what he saw beyond except to a medicine man. The tradition was that you did a sweat with him and told him what you had seen. It was like what Sam understood of the confessional, sacred and to be shared with no one.

The medicine man didn't give absolution, and he might not give interpretation. A few questions, some hints, and a suggestion that only the seer could understand the vision, that would be all.

Sam wondered if he would get to things the right way with a Crow medicine man again, ever.

He sat up. He had to say something, even if it violated morning coffee silence.

"I can't name it," he told Hannibal, "but I can do it."

Hannibal raised a questioning eyebrow.

"Let's go get Esperanza," Sam said.

Hannibal waited for his partner.

Sam sat up in his robes. "We both know the truth. This trapping life, it's finished. We know what comes next. Let's get my daughter and head for California."

Hannibal ran some thoughts through his mind, but he felt the need to speak only one.

"All right," he said. He handed Sam a hot cup, poured himself one, looked across the rim of his cup at his partner, and said, "How are we going to keep the Crows from killing us?"

Four

FROM THE FIRST "Get along" Sam felt hard-minded about the job ahead of him, and he was impatient with everything that got in the way.

They stopped by Fort Hall to pick up their mail and buy some presents. Half-broke or not, they couldn't go see Sam's daughter and his in-laws without presents. The factor at the fort also gave Sam a long-awaited letter and an important package.

Then they rode east in a restless silence over the Salt River Range as fast as they could and into the valley of the Siskadee. Sam didn't trouble to think or remember consciously. His memories were music tapped out by the horses' hoofs.

Sam had written his life on every piece of this country. He'd been in the first trapping party to cross the Southern Pass and wander into the beaver heaven of the Green River Valley. That was Jedediah Smith's 1824 outfit, the first to winter with the

Crows. Bedazzled youngster that he was, Sam fell in love with Meadowlark. The next winter he came back and courted her, won her heart, disgraced himself, and eloped with her.

Sam rode and felt the days of his life in the morning's dawn and the evening's sunset, in the curve of the river, in the swaying of Paladin's back at an easy lope. Paladin herself, a gift from Meadowlark's uncle Bell Rock, was now Sam's saddle horse of seventeen years, the binding of his comradeship with Meadowlark's dead brother Blue Medicine Horse, still his fleshly connection to the family.

Sam couldn't fall asleep at night without Meadowlark coming to him in touches, glances, warmth of body next to him. The hold of their eyes was the dancing of soul mates.

He pulled the blanket of sleep over his memories before they got to what happened. The lovers eloped and married. They went eagerly to California, because Meadowlark yearned to see the great-water-everywhere. They were incredibly happy. At Monterey she died in childbirth.

He brought his daughter back, after big troubles, to the Crow village east of the Yellowstone country where she belonged. The chief, and the child's grandparents, told him to get out and stay out. He did, twelve long years ago.

Daylight brought Sam back to the here and now. He and Hannibal swam the Siskadee—in May the river was at flood tide—and pushed their way up the Southern Pass. They made primitive bivouacs at night, doing nothing but throwing down their bedrolls and hobbling the horses. No need to speak.

Hannibal had watched for twelve years as Sam lived the hard terms of his exile from the Crows. Each year he had trapped and traded and had adventures. Each July he saw Esperanza at rendezvous, because his brother-in-law Flat Dog was kind enough to bring her. But Esperanza never treated Sam as her father, not really. She was no American. Her first language was Crow and her second language Spanish, her mother Julia's native tongue. Esperanza's world was Crow, her habits Crow, her thoughts Crow.

Hannibal also knew Sam felt the loss of more than his daughter. He lost the Crows as his people, the Kit Foxes as his warrior society, the path of the sacred pipe and the vision quest as their shared religion.

The tribe gave him no choice. So Sam set his heart against the pain and with Hannibal made another life, winters lazing in Taos, autumns and springs wading creeks full of beaver, in summer rendezvousing with friends and Sam's fragment of family. Together Hannibal and Sam made two trips to California to buy horses, drove them back to the mountains, and made good profit selling them.

Sam seemed happy—hell, they were young men on the adventure. But he seldom talked about Esperanza.

As they started down South Pass, not far from the village now, Sam kept his mind clear and refused to worry. He watched the ridgelines for movement, for signs of game or enemies. He gave himself to the task at hand, minding his mare Paladin and his second mount.

He refused, even at night in his blankets, with every chore down and every precaution taken, to think about the words he was going to say to his brother-in-law and sister-in-law, who had raised his daughter. He didn't ponder what they might say in answer. He forbade himself to imagine what Esperanza would say.

Life was not his to control. He was doing what he saw he had to do.

Knowing what occupied his partner's mind, Hannibal angled his own to the practical. How the devil were they going to ride into the village of Chief Rides Twice and not get shot? And back out?

ON THE POPO Agie River they picked up the trail of the village. Near the big bend of the Wind River they spotted it in the distance through their field glasses. The village bustled with people and dogs, and women were covering high wooden racks with slabs of buffalo meat, laying them broadside to the sun to dry.

"They just finished with the hunt," said Sam.

After each cold winter in the high valley of the Wind River the village traveled to these buffalo plains and made meat for the summer. Bones swelled with flesh again. The elderly gave thanks for surviving another season of cold and hunger. The young men made plans to win honors in ventures against their enemies. Because bellies were full, it was a good time.

Sam and Hannibal looked at each other. "Nothing else for it," Sam said.

On a rise above the village they dismounted and waited in full sight. The sentries came quickly. Immediately Sam saw that they were teenagers, too young to remember him the last time he entered this village. He told them in the Crow language, "I have come to see my brother-in-law Flat Dog." Sam sounded a lot calmer than Hannibal felt.

The lead sentry nodded, and one of his companions rode back toward the circle of tipis. He met Flat Dog halfway there, coming at a gallop.

Flat Dog leaped off his moving horse and handed the reins to a sentry. Flat Dog grinned broadly and strode forward. Only Sam and Hannibal could see the slight quiver in his stride. The Crow gave Sam a Taos greeting, a clap on both shoulders and a buss on the cheek. "Welcome, Brother-in-law."

"Welcome, friend," to Hannibal, and an *abrazo* for him, too.

"Your daughter is well, Julia well, the children well," said Flat Dog. These words were as much for the sentries as for Sam and Hannibal. The young guards drew back and let them ride toward the village.

Fifty paces out Flat Dog's voice lifted up the song of their warrior society. "You dear Foxes, I want to die, so I say." Sam joined in immediately. This was his declaration, his shield. "I am a Kit Fox," it announced. "I am a Crow warrior."

Hannibal's eyes ate up everything. Because his friend was

banned from this village, Hannibal had been here only once, a dozen years ago. He remembered Rides Twice but had no idea what the chief's brothers and nephews looked like. Their hands would wield the weapons.

Sam, you dumb bastard, how could you have killed the chief's only son? Hannibal knew and understood perfectly—he had watched it—but the creepy crawlies along his spine weren't thinkers.

The women stopped their work of drying meat and stared. Children quit playing and gaped at the strangers. The old men watched through lidded eyes. Some of the young men reached for their bows or their war clubs. But all stood still, frozen by the song and its announcement in their language, "I am a Kit Fox. I am one of you."

Sam's face was the picture of concentration and devotion. A part of him, Hannibal knew, still longed to be a Kit Fox among his comrades.

Flat Dog led them to his tipi. As they staked the horses next to the lodge, Sam saw Esperanza walking up. Her steps were hesitant and a little crooked. "Papa?"

She was beautiful, her hair auburn, eyes brown, skin the color of cream stirred with powdered chocolate. Sam held out his arms to her. She put on a face of confidence, stepped up to him forthrightly, and offered her hand to shake.

Sam shook it. He was so tickled that she would try out a whiteman custom that he didn't tell her that ladies don't shake hands.

Pleased with herself, she stuck out her hand also to the man she called Uncle Hannibal. He bowed over it, and she made a funny face.

Flat Dog said, "Let's do this inside."

Ducking through the tipi flap, Hannibal took a last glance and thought, *I feel naked here.*

Five

SAM WAS GLAD that Crows were not people to plunge straight into questions, because he felt funny about the answers. He gave Julia the sack of coffee beans he'd brought as one of her gifts. She stepped outside, visible through the open flap, to build up the fire and make the hot brew.

Few words, many smiles. Sam's vision swam a little. Daughter, brother-in-law, sister-in-law. Relatives, companions, people he'd faced death with. Flat Dog and Julia's two boys must be somewhere around, probably off playing kids' games or with their grandparents.

Sam fished in his possible sack, brought out the box sent by Grumble, and handed it to his daughter. She looked surprised. He enjoyed bringing her a gift each summer and thought it opened Esperanza's heart more than she acknowledged.

She slid off the wooden lid.

"It's called a marionette," said Sam.

It was a carved wooden horse, each part painted brightly in red, green, blue, or lilac, with strings going up to a hand control. Esperanza looked at it, mystified.

"Let Hannibal show you," said Sam.

She handed it to him, and he dangled the horse from the strings. He showed her how to make the head and tail move. Then he made the horse walk across the dirt floor, using motion of the head and tail to make it look more realistic. Everyone knew his skill in training real horses, and he handled this wooden creature deftly.

Esperanza squealed and clapped her hands. "Papa," she said, "it's wonderful."

"You're welcome." Sam always felt strange that his daughter spoke English with an accent that was somewhere between Spanish and Indian.

"Let me try," she cried.

As Julia passed out cups of coffee, Hannibal coached Esperanza.

A half-dozen times she tried to make it walk and on the last time sort of succeeded. "I need to practice," she said.

"Papa, I don't have your present finished yet." Their custom was to exchange gifts at rendezvous, and the family wouldn't have left for the annual trade fair for another week or so. "It's very special, though—may I show you?"

"Sure."

She went to the parfleche behind the buffalo robes where she slept and got out three pieces of rawhide, each about as long as her arm. Two of them were stained. "See, I made this one blue and this one red. The other one's going to be yellow."

Julia said, "She spent a lot of time making those vegetable dyes."

"When I get it done, I'm going to braid the strands into a hatband for you. Watch." Quickly, Esperanza wove together an inch or so of the strands, just as she would braid her own hair.

"Beautiful," said Sam. "I'll love it."

She took his hat off and wrapped the rawhide strings around it, tails dangling properly behind.

Sam looked his love at her.

"I want to go show the marionette to my friend Porcupine, all right?"

"Sure."

She jumped up and bent to go out the flap. In the low doorway she saw the breechcloth and the wrinkled, veiny legs of an old man. Then, dipping down, the angry face of the chief.

She stopped cold and looked back at Flat Dog. "Papa?"

RIDES TWICE STEPPED in without a word, followed by a nephew and a grandson. The uninvited entry was a statement: *To hell with courtesy, to hell with your home, to hell with your family— I am the chief*.

The old man still had the bearing of a warrior, though now the effort showed. His face, on the other hand, was ruined, skin crevassed, mouth twisted with bitterness, eyes dark with fury.

I caused this, thought Sam. He took a deep breath, and the moment of the duel hit Sam again. He had stunned Red Roan by using Paladin instead of a weapon, first knocking his opponent's horse down with the mare, then riding directly over his foe. Finally he jumped from Paladin's back, kicked Red Roan to the dust, straddled him, and jammed the point of his knife against the man's throat. In front of his father, Rides Twice, Red Roan asked to die and Sam granted him his wish.

Now Esperanza circled away from the chief and his relatives and slipped in between her two fathers. No one else stirred. Rides Twice and his companions were unarmed, except for their looks of hatred.

Rides Twice glared at Sam. "White Hair," he said, "you are not welcome in this village. If your horses are staked here tomorrow evening, we will kill you."

Rides Twice couldn't have killed more than a mosquito, but his relatives would.

"My guest will stay," said Flat Dog, "as long as he likes."

A challenge thrown in the face of a challenge.

Rides Twice glared at Sam and shut everyone else out. "We will kill you."

He ducked down and out of the tipi, his nephew and grandson at his heels.

"Papa?"

"THEY MEAN IT," said Hannibal.

"Yes," said Flat Dog, "but it won't happen in my lodge."

Sam was stunned. He couldn't credit what he'd just heard. Flat Dog would no longer be able to live in this village, near his parents. "I've put you all in danger."

"Wait," Julia said. "Something important." She got up and went out. Sam, Hannibal, and Flat Dog just looked at one another. Esperanza buried her face in her hair.

In moments Julia came back with her other three children, Azul, who was twelve or thirteen, Rojo, nine, and Paloma, six months. The infant was named for the Santa Fe woman who had been a great friend to all of them and Sam's longtime lover, Paloma Luna. Now the brood was close to the mother.

Sam and Hannibal spent several minutes fussing over Paloma. A new niece, that seemed fine. Sam was touched that her name was Paloma.

He looked around at this family, his only family, and saw that he had to risk it all. He put his hands on each side of Esperanza's head. She looked into his eyes.

"I am going to California to live. For good. I came back to ask you to go with me."

Esperanza burst into tears, jumped up, and ran out.

Six

SAM'S MIND RAN in wild circles.

Everyone else dived inside his own head, trying to sort things out.

It was Hannibal who finally spoke. "The beaver trade is done."

Julia answered, "Flat Dog and I think the same."

Flat Dog pitched in, "Maybe this year's rendezvous will be the last one."

"California," said Sam in a mesmerized tone.

Hannibal put in, "Why don't you read them the letter from Grumble?"

Adventuring in California, Flat Dog and Grumble had forged the bond men make by risking their lives together.

Sam started to pull the letter out.

Flat Dog interrupted. "We need to tell you." He looked at his wife.

Julia put a hand on his shoulder. "Flat Dog and I have talked about it. We already decided to go to California."

Sam felt like he'd fallen off a cliff.

And then he soared.

SAM WAITED FOR Flat Dog's words.

His brother-in-law breathed in and out. Actually, the two felt more like brother friends, relatives by choice, than brothers-in-law. Flat Dog looked at Sam, it seemed, with resignation in one eye and pleasure in the other. "I have agreed," he said. "We were planning to say good-bye to everyone here, meet you at rendezvous, and go to California.

"Now we have some things to take care of first."

Suddenly Julia jumped up and darted out—she had a panicky feeling about Esperanza. But the mother found her daughter in front of the neighboring lodge, talking passionately to Porcupine.

"Come home," Julia told her daughter.

Hearing her tone, Esperanza came.

Julia eased everyone with the comforting routine of supper. They spoke little, and of nothing important. Minds were whirling, facing the important problem.

"I'm going to Porcupine's," said Esperanza.

Julia considered. Esperanza's life as she knew it was ending. *Talk to your best friend, yes.* "Come back early," Julia said.

"Then I'm going to stand with the young men."

"Not tonight."

Esperanza glared at her mother and went out.

Sam realized his daughter was courting. This was the Crow way. Teenage girls stood by their family lodge, and young men visited them, one at a time.

The adults shrugged at each other.

"Anyone special?" asked Sam.

"Two young men," said Flat Dog. "Good ones. Well, good as they get at eighteen or nineteen."

Julia said, "Read Grumble's letter to us." She spoke English but didn't read it.

Sam unfolded the pages, which had been opened, read, and refolded over and over. Grumble's annual epistle, though addressed to Sam, was intended for all of them. Grumble had helped Flat Dog escape prison in Monterey and had helped Julia give birth to Azul during a storm on the banks of a raging river.

For years Sam had traded letters with Grumble and Abby in a roundabout way. Grumble gave his letter to the captain of a ship headed for Fort Vancouver. Then it made its way with one of the fur outfits to Fort Hall, where Sam picked it up and handed his to the factor for the return trip.

Sam read the letter out loud:

at Yerba Buena
Christmas Eve, 1838

To my dear friend Sam, and all friends and family—
Abby and I would express our pleasure in your adventures and successes, except that we do not know of them. We received no letter from you this year. We're confident that you wrote one, but these methods of sending correspondence are so unpredictable. Our hearts are sore at your absence.

When Sam ran away from his home back in Pennsylvania, Grumble helped him make his way west. Sam worked a flatboat, and Grumble lived by working cons small and large. Abby joined them at Louisville, and when they got to St. Louis she and Grumble opened a business that offered liquor, gambling, and women. Peddlers of vice, though, must always stay one jump ahead of trouble. They ended up in the capital of California, Monterey, in the service of the same sins.

We were lucky, however, to get some news. A man (no gentleman certainly) named Pegleg Smith came into our establishment in Monterey, indulged in the vices we sell, and grudgingly told us that you are well. That is little, but in the circumstances much.

On to the principal matter of this letter: Abby and I urge you to remove permanently to Monterey. We are in the clover here and wish most heartily for you to share in our good fortune.

The Mexican government's seizure of the lands of all the missions has changed everything. Now the government grants these fine holdings to ranchers, which in turn draws settlers. Abby and I wondered, at the time, what impact the settlers might have on us. Now we know. They have made us rich.

Last spring an Englishman named Anthony Strong, a ship's captain who had stopped here several times in his global circumnavigations, located in Monterey and built a grand hacienda on the hills behind the bay. He was immediately captivated by Abby, and surprisingly, she seems to be equally taken with him.

Fortunately, she was discreet in revealing her personal history, and in the end he swept her away to his home. I attended the wedding happily.

Strong is an active man and cannot resist investing in lands, including those once owned by the mission, which you know well, and others in the Carmel River Valley. The latter are so fertile that, without doubt, Strong will eventually be an emperor of agriculture as he was a captain of the sea. In sum, in the prime of her life Abby has become a grand lady. She deserves it.

I am just as fortunate. Incredibly, I possess the Mission Dolores itself, the one on San Francisco Bay. (Abby helped me purchase it and is my silent partner.) You will guess how I savor this irony—first an altar boy, then a con man, and now the proprietor of a mission. Even more grandly than that, I have converted the holy building into what is commonly known as a low dive. Instead of consecrated wine and bread, I traffic in liquor, gambling, and whores, naturally of the highest quality. My bar traffic exceeds that of the former communion altar. If Don

Antonio and Doña Abby are the apex of respectability, I am the eminence of roguery.

The mission is next to the village of Yerba Buena (though people talk of renaming the little pueblo San Francisco, after the Bay), and near enough to the presidio to supply the yearnings of the soldiers.

However, I miss Monterey. Yerba Buena is too remote for me. As the capital, Monterey draws the great ships and the multitudes of sailors, ripe for plucking, and I am addicted to its marvelous mélange of cosmopolitanism and natural beauty. Within a year or so I will sell my business here and rejoin Abby in Monterey.

Here is the news that most affects you. Abby has asked her husband to make grazing land available to you on very favorable terms, and he has agreed. You have often remarked that those Carmel hills are ideal for a horse-raising enterprise. Now they are offered.

I sent this news to your son Tomás as well, and he reports that he intends to remove to this fine land next winter. For him California is simply a new province of his native country, and one he likes.

Sam and Tomás had an on-again, off-again relationship since Sam adopted him twelve years ago, so this was good news.

Altogether, I am confident, no prospect could be finer for you.

Americans are settling here in numbers and are welcome. Many of the Mexican dons look forward with pleasure to the day when California will be American.

Oh, wanderer! Put away your life of danger. Give up your wild Indians, cold creeks, and dangerous river crossings. Come to California for the life of leisure. Come to Monterey, where American, Mexican, and Indian can live together amicably, and indeed become one people.

Abby sends her love, and I my esteem. We hope to look upon your face in the coming year.

> *Your entirely disobedient, but affectionate, servant,*
> *Grumble*

Sam, Flat Dog, Julia, and Hannibal looked at each other with stupid grins.

"The mission breakup . . . ," murmured Julia.

"Lots of land available," said Sam. *And land cheap to me,* he thought.

Julia was lost in the past. She loved the mission in Malibu where she grew up. When she ran away to be with Flat Dog, it was the Mission San Gabriel that offered her the sacrament of marriage and sanctuary against the rage of her father.

"No wonder Americans are settling in California fast," said Hannibal. "Land easy to get, oceans of grass, and no winter."

They looked at each other foolishly, wanting to mouth the good news of the letter over and over.

Sam asked Julia, "What do you think about Americans filling up the country where you were born?" *You, the daughter of a don.*

"I am ready to go back," she said. "Don't misunderstand me. I have been here twelve years, and I have loved it. This life seems to me like a romantic idyll, a life in one of the fairy tales my mother used to read to me. I love the country and the Crow people.

"Yet I came here for one reason only. I love this man beyond the ability of words to say. Such a love is a gift of God. I would have followed it anywhere.

"Now, though, it is time for me and the man I love to take the best care of our children. I want more for them."

Sam thought again, *I can't believe my luck.*

"The children must be raised as Catholics," Julia said. "Esperanza and Azul were baptized, Rojo and Paloma not yet. None of them has made a first communion. Also, I want Flat Dog back in the church, and myself."

Silence circled through each mind.

Flat Dog put in, "You and Hannibal will do well training horses for saddle and harness."

"The three of us could do well," Sam said, "very well."

"The main thing is," said Hannibal, "it's going to be different for mixed-blood people. When they eliminated the missions, they struck down slavery. The Spaniards and the Indians are already mixed, thoroughly. The Americans are marrying Spaniards and Indians both. It will be the first place where race won't matter, the first place on the whole planet, really."

Sam said, "My dad always said Americans started out to make a country free of the old ways, a New World. Back in the States, we failed. California is going to be it."

Seven

"I NEED TO talk to my daughter," said Julia to the men.

She ducked out and confronted the flirting pair. "That's enough for tonight," she told them.

Esperanza said, "Mo-other!"

Everyone inside ran funny eyes at each other. Waiting and eavesdropping was odd.

"Come inside."

The two of them came through the flap.

"Treat me like a grown-up," Esperanza said to her mother's behind.

Julia took her place next to her husband behind the fire. When Esperanza was seated, Julia declared, "Our family, plus Sam your papa, Uncle Hannibal, and Tomás, we're all going to California. We'll live right near each other."

Esperanza turned her head sideways to her mother, Sam thought, like a bird spotting danger and ready to fly off the branch.

"I want you to go grow up in the church. To have books. To wear fine dresses. I want a better life for you." Julia fixed her daughter's eyes. "You must read, and know something of the great literature of the world."

Julia turned her head to Sam. "You don't know it, but Esperanza has a gift for reading. I have one book in Spanish, *Lives of the Saints,* and she has read it twice this last year."

"Mom—"

Julia interrupted her. "I want you children to live in a world with candles, wagons, crops, dinnerware, clocks, and stoves and windows. I want a life for you in civilization."

"I want that for you, too," said Sam.

His daughter turned her jumpy eyes at him. Up she stood again, and out she went.

Julia called for Azul and Rojo to come in. She sat Paloma on her lap. When the older kids sat down, Julia spoke to them again about what was going to happen and answered their questions.

Sam thought, *My daughter acts like a young American or Californio woman, rebellious and strong willed. Azul and Rojo behave like Crows, quiet, eyes down in front of their elders.* Right now Sam could do without anyone's rebellion.

Later Sam lay in his robes and watched the lavender at the top of the tipi turn to dove gray and black. To him the simple ways of this land were magic. Occasionally, whispers of his daughter and her suitor reached Sam's ears, but he didn't pay attention to the words—he knew the meanings. He was still very much awake when Esperanza slipped into her blankets.

As Sam drifted off next to his daughter, he indulged in fantasies of training horses with her on the great grasslands of Monterey Bay. She was a first-class rider and worked well with horses. He would give his daughter a fine life—she would eventually be the owner of a fine rancho. As soon as he got her away from Rides Twice's village.

Toward dawn something strange happened. For the first time since Sam was a kid, he dreamed of flying.

Eight

EARLY THE NEXT morning, before Julia had the coffee ready, Flat Dog stood up and said, "I have things to arrange."

"I need to sweat with Bell Rock," Sam said.

"Damn," said Flat Dog, "I wish you were more scared."

"Rides Twice gave me until this evening," said Sam.

"You trust too much."

After a moment Hannibal asked, "Want me to come with you?"

Flat Dog shook his head no and left, his face set hard.

"Esperanza," said Sam, "I want to talk to you about your future—"

She bolted out the door behind her Crow father.

Sam, Hannibal, and Julia looked at each other. "Flat Dog will figure out how to get you out of this village alive," Hannibal said.

Since the alpine morning was crisp, Julia made a fire inside the lodge. She put last night's stew on to reheat. It had frozen in the metal pot. Adults and children ate out of cups.

Though the boys said nothing, their body language was wretched.

"Go outside and play," Julia instructed.

The adults talked idly of this and that, everyone's mind elsewhere. The lodge started feeling oppressive to Sam. The thick walls of buffalo hide kept the light out. One patch at the top where the poles stuck out let through a little sunlight and air, too little.

Hannibal said in a silly tone, "Is it safe for me to go out to pee?"

Julia said seriously, "You, yes, but not Sam."

"I went out before first light," said Sam.

Flat Dog came in about noon and got some food. "Bell Rock and some relatives will build a lodge by the river," he told them. He nodded with his head toward the bank nearby. Too close to the village, but . . . "We'll wait for dark."

Past the deadline.

Sam handed them the other gifts he'd brought, a hackamore ornamented with silver for Flat Dog and a bolt of bright red cotton for Julia. In civilization buffalo hides were an expensive rarity. Among the Crows simple cotton cloth was a luxury.

Esperanza popped in. She acted polite now, eyes averted modestly, and took her seat across the center fire from her two fathers.

When she spoke, it was in Crow, and that alone was a statement.

"By coming to this village you have risked your life for me," she said to Sam. "I am stirred in my heart by that. You did it for my sake, or what you see as my sake. Still . . .

"You, Mother and Father." Sam noticed the term being applied to Flat Dog. "You have raised me. You want the best for me. But . . ."

She took a big breath and let it out.

"I am old enough to marry." She let those words sit in front of everyone.

It was true—Crow girls did marry as soon as they became women. Meadowlark had been older than most, sixteen. "I have made a decision. I will stay here and live with my grandparents. This is my home. These are my people."

Sam burst out, "Esperanza—"

She interrupted her real father, looking straight into his eyes. "Soon I will have a Crow husband, and soon after that Crow children."

Head carefully down, body language soft, she left as abruptly as she came in.

Nine

THE GROWN-UPS LOOKED at each other with long faces.

Flat Dog changed the subject. "The sweat lodge will be ready in a couple of hours."

"Just me and Bell Rock," said Sam.

"And a few of us to walk you there."

"No one will strike at a man going to a sweat lodge."

Flat Dog nodded, but he was always careful. He went on in a firm voice. "We have a plan." He explained it.

"Seems reasonable," said Sam.

"No other choice," said Hannibal.

"Esperanza?" asked Sam.

"You kidnapped one member of our family," said Flat Dog. "You can kidnap another."

Sam had taken the longest chance of his life, it seemed at the time. In the face of her entire family's refusal, he abducted Meadowlark. Luckily, a few days of married life convinced her.

Flat Dog looked at his wife. "We're going to take her if we have to tie her to a pack saddle."

Julia nodded and said, "Tomorrow morning."

Flat Dog stood up to get his daughter. When he opened the flap, he met Gray Hawk bending down.

FLAT DOG'S FATHER and mother, followed by Esperanza, circled the lodge clockwise behind the seated family. Hannibal and Sam scooted over to make room for them behind the dead fire.

It took Sam's breath away. *Gray Hawk and Needle, the parents of Meadowlark, are sitting down with me.*

"Would you like some coffee?" said Julia, extending a cup.

Gray Hawk and Needle took it in silence. They sipped in silence.

Gray Hawk sat for an extraordinarily long time without a word, staring into the fire. Then, stunningly, he looked straight into Sam's eyes. "Joins with Buffalo . . ."

Sam was shocked that Gray Hawk addressed him by his proper Crow name.

"Joins with Buffalo, Needle and I no longer blame you. Our son made a young man's mistake. Our daughter . . . She was headstrong, and chose her own fate." He lowered his eyes, hesitated, and looked back at Sam. "We forgave you long ago."

"Thank you," Sam said.

Gray Hawk gazed off into the shadows of the lodge.

"I've come here to remind you of something. Others here need to hear it for the first time, especially Esperanza."

He looked into Sam's eyes. "You remember, nearly twenty years ago, a medicine woman came to you and spoke of what she had seen beyond."

Owl Woman, now dead, so that her name could not be spoken.

"Shall I repeat the message she brought, or do you want to?"

Sam closed his voice and remembered as though hypnotized. "She said she saw Crow people—all the Crow people—floating dead in a lake. It was where the waters divide between the great ocean to the east and the great ocean to the west. Past the ghostly corpses in the water rode white people, hundreds and thousands of white people. They rode and rode and never saw the dead human beings."

Sam let a big breath out. His audience—Owl Woman's audience—was rapt, not only Gray Hawk and Needle, Flat Dog and Julia, and Hannibal, but Esperanza.

"She told me then, 'Though you are a good man, the coming of the whites is the end of the Crow people. Our way will die. I cannot express my sorrow.'"

They all looked at one another, wondering.

Gray Hawk broke the silence. "I have come to your lodge today to say what this medicine woman would say. I urge all of you to go on. You, Flat Dog, your wife, your children. Go with Joins with Buffalo and his friend. Go to the edge of the world to the west where the ocean is. Life is moving west. Here it is dying.

"My wife and I will stay here. But you are young, and must go—find a new way to live."

He fixed his eyes on Esperanza. "Above all, you must go. Your parents are Crow, American, and Californio. You are the new way. To the west life opens to you. Here awaits death."

Ten

ESPERANZA HATED EVERYONE looking at her, waiting. She took some time to think about her words. Finally, she said, "It is my life. And I will live it in this village."

"Where will you live?" asked Gray Hawk.

Esperanza stared at her grandfather, shocked. Then she hid her gaze properly, and her panic. This was unbelievable.

"Grandfather," she said, "Grandmother. Will you permit me to live with you?"

The wait for their answer was intolerable. Finally, it was Needle who said, "No, Granddaughter."

"Then I'll live with Porcupine."

"Granddaughter, I'm sorry," said Needle. "I know she is your best friend. But we will ask her parents not to take you in."

Esperanza's mind spun, looking for ways out. She thought of her uncle Little Bull, but he and his family lived in a village far to the east, beside his wife's parents. And Little Bull would not go against Flat Dog, or against Gray Hawk and Needle. She saw no escape.

Esperanza began to weep. She hoped that in the half-light of the lodge, with her head down and her hair in front of her face, no one could see her tears.

Gray Hawk said, "Owl Woman saw. The world is changing."

Silence. Then Gray Hawk went on. "You must go with your father and mother to California. Your two fathers."

Gray Hawk's face was composed, but Sam saw the agony in his eyes. The man produced four children. Within a few days, when Flat Dog left, he would have no child in this village and only one in the entire tribe.

Now Needle was weeping openly. "Granddaughter, this is painful for us. We will never see your children."

Esperanza looked up into Needle's face. It was implacable. *This betrayal, my grandmother turning against me, it is the worst of all.*

Esperanza jumped up and dashed out of the tipi, sobbing. She walked around the village, the circle of lodges that always faced into the rising sun, the world where she had grown up, the world of everyone she cared about.

She began to calm down. She turned outside the circle and walked along the path where the women came to the river for water. She sat on the bank and looked at the moving ripples, the dragonflies hovering above their surface, and the shadowy fish beneath. She watched the last of the day's light flicker up and down on the little waves. Now she knew what she had to do.

Eleven

BETWEEN THE ROUNDS of the sacred sweat lodge Sam told Bell Rock what he had seen beyond, all of it. His sense of searching for something nameless that he would never find. The appearance of the glistening, blue snake popping out of its skin. The writing in the skies. Sam held back only a few details, keeping them for himself alone, as was proper.

Without a word Bell Rock asked his assistant to close the lodge door, and they filled it with steam, prayers, and songs again.

When the door was flung open, Bell Rock waited for the cool evening air to ease in. Then he said in his metallic voice, "You've seen beyond before."

Sam nodded. "You know both times."

Twice before Sam had asked Bell Rock to help him comprehend his own vision.

The first time he hid from a prairie fire in the carcass of a freshly butchered buffalo cow. The cow saved his life, and a few days later Sam had a dream of crawling back into that bloody darkness and feeling that he merged with the buffalo, that they shared the same blood and breath, that they were a new creature, a samalo.

Bell Rock explained to the young trapper that he had seen beyond and gave him the name Joins with Buffalo.

The second time was when Sam gave a sun dance. There he followed his oldest enemy, the serpent, down a tunnel. When the snake turned and threatened him, he seized its body and tied it into Celtic love knots. He still remembered the laughter inside when he realized what he'd done.

"What is your question here?" said Bell Rock.

"I want to know what the nameless thing is."

"You are haunted by that?" Bell Rock's eyebrows arched in skepticism.

"Yes," said Sam.

"What you saw the other two times, did it fit handily into words?" Bell Rock was backing up, reminding Sam what he knew.

"Not really," he said. He corrected himself. "Not ever."

"Summing it up in words would make it smaller in some way, leave some important parts out."

"Yes."

"Sometimes, though, words point to the beginning of a path. So now I will give you one word. 'Home.'"

Sam opened his mouth to discuss that and—

Bell Rock held a hand. "You already know," he said. Then he cried, "Close the door."

The assistant covered them in darkness again, and immediately the steam burst from the hot rocks.

ESPERANZA WENT INTO her parents' lodge, her home until now. Eyes down and speaking to no one, she got her favorite blanket, the white one with the slender red stripes. Then she took her place outside of her parents' door. For the last few months, she had done this every evening, as was the custom of Crow girls of an age to be courted. And every evening two or three young men came and stood with her. She let one of them, only one, wrap himself in the blanket with her, Prairie Chicken.

She'd known Prairie Chicken for only a year, since he came to live with his mother's brother, Axe. Right away she liked him because of his big, thick chest and arms, like a bear. At first some of the other kids teased Prairie Chicken because of his name. The prairie chicken cocks did a really funny mating ceremony where they stood around in a circle, spread their tails, and quivered. As she got to know him, though, she was attracted to him. He could copy the call of almost any animal, and he was always paying practical jokes on the other teenage boys—he was really funny. She liked his big body, too—to her it was manly.

The only company Esperanza wanted tonight was his.

WHEN BELL ROCK said, " 'Home,' " Sam's skin shuddered. Before he could speak, Bell Rock called for the sweat lodge door to be closed.

Bell Rock poured this last round fiercely hot. Sometimes he spoke of pain as a sacrifice to the spirits.

He prayed fiercely but did not mention what Sam saw beyond or his ability to understand it. He sang fiercely. When he asked for the door to be flung open and then all the hides taken off, Sam was exhausted.

Bell Rock spoke almost as an attack. "Why does a snake shed its skin?"

Sam answered immediately, "I guess it's to start new, but that's not the way I feel."

Bell Rock waited.

"I just feel confused."

Bell Rock nodded. "What is the nameless thing you seek?"

"I don't know."

"Where is your home?"

"I haven't had once since my dad died. I couldn't stay around my bossy brother. I thought I . . ."

"What?"

"I thought Meadowlark and I would make a home in this village, but . . ."

They both knew that story.

"I've never been able to make a home for Esperanza. I never made a home for Tomás." In their dozen years together, when they weren't irked at each other, Sam and his adopted son had roamed the mountains with Hannibal.

"Where is your home?"

Sam surprised himself with the answer. "I sort of feel like this whole country is my home, the Yellowstone to Taos. I also feel like I'm losing it."

"I was born to a home," said Bell Rock. "So is every Crow. So were you, but you threw it away." He gave a lighthearted smile. "You whites are funny people."

Now Bell Rock turned serious again. "Maybe Flat Dog is a funny white man, too."

Sam looked at him curiously.

"Flat Dog is losing his home, throwing it away. After more than thirty winters."

STANDING BETWEEN HER Crow father in the tipi and her real father in the sweat lodge, from time to time conscious of their voices, Esperanza kissed Prairie Chicken passionately. She had kissed him often enough and plenty of times told him to keep his hands to himself. Not that she didn't like the way his hands felt. Tonight she had a surprise for him.

Out of the corner of her eye she saw dark shapes moving from shadow to shadow. She flinched—men sneaking up on Sam?

Then she heard Bell Rock's voice, which always sounded like steel striking steel, and realized that her American father, the medicine man, and their helper were coming back from the river, wrapped in buffalo robes.

She buried her head in Prairie Chicken's neck.

Sam recognized Esperanza's blanket and eyed the young man she was embracing, a husky fellow. He asked himself, *What is her home?*

Inside the tipi the three from the sweat lodge sat by the fire and accepted the bowls of food Julia had saved for them, the meal traditionally given to the man of medicine after a ceremony. They ate in courteous silence. When they'd finished, Flat Dog said, "We leave in the morning."

Bell Rock rolled his eyes in the direction of Esperanza. "With her strapped onto her pony?"

They all smiled. That was how Sam took Meadowlark out of this village all those years ago.

Sam mulled on it. Damn rude to interrupt courting, but some things were more important than manners. "I'm going to go out and talk to her."

Hannibal and Flat Dog spoke at once. "No."

Julia and Needle made murmurs of agreement. "Too dangerous."

"She's just saying good-bye to Prairie Chicken," Flat Dog said.

"Well, hell," said Sam.

They looked at each other across the small fire. The night was cool and the lodge half-lit by the low flames. These were men who liked to act. Waiting for a girl to make her decision galled them. Staying in this village was dangerous, and that galled them worse.

Hannibal got out a treat he'd brought all the way from Santa Fe—cigarillos. They all lit them. Bell Rock offered the smoke to the four directions—tobacco was sacred, no matter the form—

and Sam followed suit. Then Sam struck up a conversation. He didn't want to seem to be trying to overhear Esperanza and Prairie Chicken. Instead he trotted out some ideas.

"At rendezvous we can pick up some others going west, maybe."

"Good to have a stronger party," said Flat Dog.

Hannibal blew a couple of smoke rings. Azul and Rojo giggled.

"Same at Fort Hall," said Sam. "I'll bet Joe Meek and Doc Newell will come along."

"Do we have to take the missionaries, too?" asked Flat Dog.

"Maybe if they pay us a lot to keep them alive," said Hannibal.

Protestant missionaries had turned up at the last several rendezvous, headed for Oregon to save red men's souls. The missionaries were such greenhorns that they put a traveling outfit at risk.

They were also part of the big problem. They kept sending messages back to the States: Send more people. Blacksmiths, carpenters, wheelwrights, coopers, women, children, people to settle a new country.

"Easier now to make a living as a guide than a trapper," said Sam.

"This," said Bell Rock, "is Owl Woman's vision come true."

Sam and Hannibal looked at each other. They had never foreseen white people tramping all over Crow country.

"Which trail then?" said Hannibal. The route to California cut off from the trail to Oregon on the Snake River plains, crossed to the Humboldt River, and followed it to the Sierra Nevadas. It had been traveled seldom, and never by women and children.

"I think the Oregon road," said Sam. "Here's why. The best horses in the world are Appaloosas. Riders love the way they look, too. So I have an idea. . . ."

WHEN EVERYONE WAS sleepy, Flat Dog said, "I guess we're not in favor with Esperanza right now."

"I'm sure she went to her grandparents," said Julia.

The fire was faintest embers. Azul, Rojo, and Paloma were sound asleep. Even Hannibal had rolled up earlier. Sam lay down and thought, *Things are going to work out after all.*

Twelve

ESPERANZA NOTICED THE light through her eyelids but didn't open them. She drew the morning air into her nostrils, truly noticing it for the first time in her life. She felt fresh and frisky, deliciously new. She squirmed with pleasure.

She could hear the deep, slow breathing of the sleeping Prairie Chicken. She turned and put her head gently on his shoulder and stretched a leg over his. She didn't want to open her eyes yet. Why look at your old life when you are a leaf in the wind of a new world? She pictured the mist on the river and listened to the faint stir of the cottonwood leaves. Then, slowly, she let her mind run up and down the pictures of all she and Prairie Chicken did with each other during the night, feeling them with fingers of memory as though they were silk.

The loving, that was a whirlwind. It was strange at first, but fun when she began to catch on. She was eager to try it again—

she knew she could fly a lot higher. Prairie Chicken had known just what to do, and she wondered about that . . . Funny, she had intended to be the one who swept him away. That wasn't how it worked out.

She chuckled to herself. It felt so good. Her parents and grandparents—they thought they would manage her life! Amazing. Outrageous. And now she could say, "To hell with you. I am in charge."

Certain things could be said with punch in English but not in Crow. That one felt good: "To hell with you."

ESPERANZA AND PRAIRIE Chicken got their ponies from the herd and rode up into the mountains. The sentries saw them leave together, and it would cause talk, but she didn't care.

She wanted to ride to a little lake she knew. She'd only been there once, with her family. She and Prairie Chicken would splash and play in the water and then warm each other up on the sand. Or maybe they would heat each other up first, then jump in the cool water and go back to the fire of their bodies.

They would spend the day hungry. She couldn't get food without getting caught. The lake and her feelings were a lot more urgent than hunger.

Prairie Chicken didn't say much. She liked a man who would do and not talk. She thought of him again as a bear. Next month he would go on a vision quest, and perhaps the bear would become his spirit animal.

At the lake they went through the cycle of doing, then splashing in the water, then doing again. Prairie Chicken was fierce and playful by turns, and Esperanza could barely match his passion. She was happy.

Lounging on the bank in the glow of romance and the exhilaration of her daring, she said, "I want to tell you a story about my mother. She ran off with my American dad just like we're doing now. Well, they prepared more, took a travel lodge and food to stay for a while. The point is, she ran off with him. A love match, like us."

Prairie Chicken looked at her oddly.

"The main thing is, she did what she wanted, she took the man she wanted."

Esperanza mused on it a little. Meadowlark, the mother she'd never known, had also run off to California because she wanted to see the ocean. That was the tale both her fathers told. She reminded herself, though, that it wasn't the ocean that killed Meadowlark, it was a fever.

Esperanza turned on one side toward Prairie Chicken. "Life can be short," she said. "You have to do what you want to do." She rolled over on top of him. "What I want is you."

She began to demonstrate exactly how she wanted him.

Prairie Chicken said, "I want you, too."

After a long while, when they were lounging back again, he gave her a big, dumb smile, tucked a few stray hairs behind her ear, and said, "Porcupine told you, didn't she, that she and I are getting married?"

FLAT DOG, HANNIBAL, and Bell Rock went on a hunt for Esperanza. Sam stayed in the lodge and steamed. To calm him down, Julia let him help with the task of making moccasins. She was sewing several pairs for everyone—it would be a long trip.

Sam didn't mind doing women's work. He'd made or repaired moccasins plenty of times.

"They'll be able to track her," said Julia.

Sam nodded and stitched.

"You can't help thinking about when you and Meadowlark did the same thing."

"That was my doing alone."

"You still think that?"

Julia and Meadowlark had been friends at Los Angeles Pueblo.

At the time, Meadowlark was with child, and Julia was arranging her own elopement with Flat Dog.

"I feel for Esperanza," said Sam.

Julia looked at him across a sole she was cutting from deer hide. "And how about for Prairie Chicken?"

Sam wanted to muster a smile, but he couldn't. "It was awful. We had a short honeymoon there in Ruby Hawk Valley. It was lovely. Not just passion. We talked for the first time about her brother getting killed, and . . .

"The fourth morning I stepped out of the lodge at dawn to get water and looked straight into arrows, lances, and war clubs right close up. Some of her relatives had forced Flat Dog to lead them to us, said they'd let me live if he helped. Took me back to the village with a rope around my neck.

"After that they never let me see her. Before long I realized I had to get out of the village. It was a long time, weeks, before she and Flat Dog suddenly came riding into rendezvous."

"A young girl's passions rage." Julia's had carried her on a flood tide away from her wealthy family and into Flat Dog's arms.

"Yeah. Including Esperanza's, I guess. Are we doing the right thing?"

"I hope so." Julia took a moment to finish a moccasin. "I think so." She looked carefully at her work and then into Sam's eyes. "The whole world is changing."

The door flap lifted, and Esperanza ducked into the lodge.

Sam and Julia stared at her. The look on her face made them hesitate to speak.

"I'm ready to go," said Esperanza. "California. The sooner the better."

Without another word she marched around the fire, lay down on her blankets, rolled up, and turned her back to everyone. Julia sat down behind her and put a hand on her shaking shoulders.

Thirteen

THIRTY OR FORTY male voices sang, "*Iaxuxkekatū̃'e, bacbi'awak, cē'wak.*"

Hannibal thought it was magnificent, and he was hardly scared at all.

The warriors were Kit Foxes, members of a warrior society, and this was their initiation song. "You dear Foxes, I want to die, so I say."

These men came to Flat Dog's lodge on their horses and formed a wall of protection for Sam Morgan, Joins with Buffalo, who was himself a Kit Fox. As were Flat Dog, Gray Hawk, and Bell Rock. The village had other warrior clubs, such as Lump-woods, Big Dogs, and Muddy Hands, but the Kit Foxes were large and influential. They would ride in a throng out of the village, Sam in the middle. It was more than physical protection. It was a statement that anyone who attacked Sam, anyone who violated this brotherhood, would bring on himself the enmity of all the Kit Foxes.

This was the doing of Flat Dog, Gray Hawk, and Bell Rock. They had needed only to remind the Kit Foxes of the time Sam brought honor to the club and the village by making the sacrifice of the sun dance, and then by counting coups on several of the Headcutter enemies and stealing many of their horses.

Hannibal looked at Sam's face. He sang as enthusiastically as any of them. He had loved being a Crow once. Now he was going away from all that, for good. Hannibal could only imagine the churn of conflicting feelings in his friend's heart.

They reached the edge of the village, but everyone kept singing. Gray Hawk rode on one side of Sam, Flat Dog on the other. Tears streamed down Gray Hawk's face. Tears at the loss of his only daughter to death? Of his son to California? Of his grandchildren? All of those, Hannibal supposed. Hannibal admired him. *You are doing the right thing.*

The men rode on slowly, ceremonially.

Behind them Julia managed the move. She, Esperanza, and Needle took the lodge down. Julia supervised the loading of the family's belongings and made sure the boys did their share. All except Needle mounted their horses. Julia led the pony drags, and Azul brought his father's other horses along on a lead.

By the time she was ready to ride, she hadn't been able to hear the men's singing voices for quite a while. She asked herself again if Sam was safe and again answered yes. A mile or two outside the village the Kit Foxes would wait for the rest of the family, and all would ride together and make camp well up the Popo Agie River. That was the plan.

She looked at the village where she had lived for more than a decade, where her children had grown up. The boys were excited to be going to rendezvous, as they did every summer, and they wanted to see California. The thought of never seeing their relatives here again, never playing with their friends—Julia knew they didn't understand, not really.

She looked around for a last time. Then she clucked, and the family moved out.

THE ENTIRE PARTY made camp that night at the sinks of the Popo Agie. It was a peculiar place, and Sam liked it. Here the river suddenly dived under the ground, into a limestone cave. After about a quarter mile it rose up again and formed a large, calm pool. The pool reminded Sam, somehow, of the peace and ease he felt when he was waking up slowly and gently, his mind rising from the bottom of sleep to the light.

This evening Sam sat by the waters. The highest peaks caught the last of the sunlight, a bright edge of rosy gilding on the ridges and summits. This valley was bathed in light blue, which would soon be dark blue, and then black.

Hannibal sat down next to Sam.

"*Rideo, ergo sum,*" said Sam. "If only I could *rideo.*"

Hannibal laughed for him.

"The Kit Foxes have decided to ride on up to the divide with us," Hannibal said. "I think they just like being on the move better than lounging around camp."

Sam watched the light shimmer on the water. A dragonfly drifted sideways. He took a deep breath and let it out. "Hannibal, do you ever miss having a home?"

"Never thought about it. Wanted to see the world." Hannibal had roamed far and wide. At John Bill Pickett's circus, he got a big sample of humanity. Working as a trader, sometimes in the clover and sometimes hungry, he'd walked and ridden from Philadelphia to the Pacific to Mexico City and had lived at a score of places in between.

"You still like wandering?"

"I guess."

Sam studied the still waters for a long moment. "I think I'm done with it."

"Yeah. Maybe we both better think about Flat Dog."

Sam looked through the half darkness at his friend's face.

"He's all torn up. His whole life in one village, close relatives, same set of friends, same mountains making the horizons. That time he went to California with you hardly counts. The way he sees it, fate took him there to meet the woman he loves, and he brought her back as quick as he could. Also the sweat lodge, the sacred pipe, the sun dance. And now he's leaving all that. Permanently. We cross that divide tomorrow, he's out of the Crow world for good."

Sam flinched. "I thought about Esperanza, not a bit about Flat Dog."

"And we've all had our minds on keeping you alive."

"Maybe I better talk to him about it."

"Keeping him in mind is enough, I think."

Sam noticed that the clouds were collecting close on the peaks. Might be some rain.

"You don't think about having a home?"

"I guess I do."

Sam wished he could see his partner's face better.

"Woman? Children?"

"Maybe. There is something about the word 'home' feels good."

"California would be the only place."

"Here's the truth, though. You have to *make* a home. Old times, people were given a home and that was it. This New World is different. You have to make a home for Esperanza, for Tomás, for yourself."

Home, Sam thought. *What I hunt for in my dreams and never find. The nameless.*

Part Two

Fourteen

LEI PALUA SAID, "Keep your goddamn hands off of me." Every word she spoke, except the oath, was in the Hawaiian language.

She whacked at Delly's hands. "Boy!" Lei called out.

"Back off!" Kanaka Boy said sharply to him. Delly leaned away and got to his feet. "Fire's too damn hot anyway," he said. He was also Hawaiian, built stout as a whale. Walking away, Delly threw a leer back at Lei, hinting that this wasn't finished.

Boy reached for Lei, but she scooted away. They had a deal, but he took little interest in enforcing it. Tonight was the dangerous night, because Boy had told the men they could drink the whiskey to the last drop.

They had just finished a three-week roundabout, as Boy called it. Boy had set up his own stills—Hawaiians made good booze. They'd gotten a big lot of whiskey brewed up and kegged in their camp. In his usual way, Boy took a dozen or so of his men and rode out among the Indian villages, trading them liquor or, more accurately, trading them drunken orgies.

Lei hated the roundabouts. The Indians gave Boy almost anything he wanted for the whiskey and went on a binge. It was sickening. Men and women alike swilled until they were staggering and stupid. Before the men passed out, they managed to mount wives other than their own. If a woman resisted, and that was uncommon, she usually got raped. Lei had seen a man rape his own daughter, who shrieked the whole time. She had seen one brother kill another.

Boy and his men usually did what they called joining in the fun. Lei stayed sober, and scared.

She had to go with Boy on these roundabouts because of their deal. In the home camp sex was what Boy liked to call deuces wild—any man took any willing woman at any time, and they reveled in the debauchery. Any man included her husband.

Lei hadn't known what she was getting into when she ran away with Kanaka Boy. At first she'd been horrified. Then she'd spent a week weeping. Boy didn't ask what was wrong, didn't offer any consolation, but just let her work it out for herself. After she cried herself out, she demanded a deal. She would ignore what everyone else did on one condition—that Boy would protect her from the other men. She would belong to her husband and him only.

Boy had kept the bargain. But if she stayed behind on a roundabout, she knew what the men left to watch the camp would do.

She stood, stomped over to the bedroll she shared with Boy, and lay down. After a moment's thought she rose and pulled the blankets closer to where Boy sat, playing the odds.

Lei Palua hated her life and could barely believe she'd been drawn into it. Two summers ago, rebellious against her mother, she let Kanaka Boy romance her at Fort Walla Walla until she was giddy with love. Then she ran off with him. He was a big man with a powerful body and stone-strong Hawaiian face, and he was crazy about her. She thought she was homely—much too skinny, and with an odd hairline. At the roots of her hair, here and there, her black hair was spoiled by white streaks. Lei thought these streaks were awful, but Kanaka Boy said they were gorgeous. Because of them, when he was in a loving mood, he called her Magpie, after the beautiful black bird with white wingtips that they both loved. She liked being admired.

He also had big plans. Boy didn't see why the Kanakas should work for the white bosses anymore. The Kanakas could do just as well as the Brits trading with the Indians, or better—most of the Hawaiians were half Indian.

Lei was fed up with the Hudson's Bay Company bosses, too. She'd seen her father worked to death, and her mother would never escape the kitchen where she slaved over woodstoves for the Brit mucky-mucks. Anyone who wanted to stand up to them was all right with Lei. A fellow who wanted to stand up to them and was handsome and told her he loved her—that was irresistible.

The way to change things, Boy said, was to gather up a bunch of daring men like himself, set up a camp where they'd be hard to find, and make plenty of liquor. "You understand what the foundation of the Indian trade is?" he told Lei. He spoke a botched version of fancy English, which he'd patterned after the Brit bosses' way of talking. "Liquor. Liquor is the secret. And we will have plenty."

So she rode off with him, a new wife. When she saw the remote camp he'd chosen, it made her sick at her stomach. The spot was on the Owyhee River—named after the murder of three Hawaiians there by Indians—in a landscape Lei had never imagined. It was bleak, a parched desert in three directions. To the east the Owyhee Mountains cut them off from the Snake River, which was a normal world with timbered bottoms and two Hudson's Bay forts. South, west, and north stretched the desert, severe, forbidding, ominous. In those directions water was scarcer than virtue was in this camp. What little water you could find was alkali and ravaged your bowels. Only a few, widely scattered Digger Indians were able to survive in that country, and they were too poor even to afford clothing. This desert was death.

For the first week she thought obsessively of her home islands. Though she'd never seen them, her grandparents had told her they were the lushest islands in the world, green leaves and tall trees everywhere, flowers so abundant the air itself intoxicated you with its scent. She longed for the coastal country of Oregon, where she lived sometimes with her grandparents, not as sweetly warm as her country of origin but abundantly fertile. If you didn't plant a garden, the Hawaiians said, the grass and weeds would run you out of the country.

And she grieved because she found out about Boy. He made love her to every night, wild, wonderful, animal love. And he rutted, openly, with any other woman he pleased.

When Lei challenged him about it, he shrugged and answered simply, "A bull does not stop after he has one cow. He wants them all."

The barren desert around them was not as bleak as the landscape of her heart.

She wrapped herself tighter in the blankets and then took thought. She had to get through tonight, and she could think of just one stratagem. Lei was the only woman in camp, and in his cups Boy would want her. If she touched him, if she kissed him, he would keep her to himself, probably.

"Boy," she called softly.

Fifteen

"THIS RENDEZVOUS STINKS," said Esperanza.

Sam and Julia looked at each other, hiding their smiles. Esperanza had said the same thing almost every day since they left the village. Apparently everything stank.

"You've seen enough to know," Sam said lightly. She'd attended every rendezvous since she was a toddler.

Esperanza lipped the last of her deer meat off the tip of her knife, glared her misery at everyone, and walked off. Apparently she'd made a girlfriend in the Shoshone camp.

Julia thought how good it would be to teach her children to eat with table knife, fork, and spoon.

"Adolescent," said Sam.

"Not a bitch?" said Flat Dog. He didn't mean it.

"Adolescent," said Julia.

Not that Esperanza was alone in her moodiness. Sam himself

was edgy. *I've waited twelve years to get my family. Now I've got all but Tomás and I'm jumpy as a grasshopper.*

Julia was frazzled. Though she wanted to think about home—California, the ocean, even seeing her sisters and brothers again—she was kept on the run by the constant task of keeping everyone's life in order. During the two weeks' travel here the children were bored. They wanted to go off on little side trips, explore a creek, hunt a deer, and so on. When she wasn't watching them or the packhorses, she was cooking and cleaning. Comparatively, rendezvous was a rest.

Flat Dog was withdrawn and unreachable. He knew it was dumb. He knew California was right for one simple reason. He had loved Julia from the first moment he saw her. Still, his heart was pulled backward. His parents. His clan. His lifelong friends. His village. The Yellowstone country. So he was lousy company. *And you know what? I don't care.*

Every one of them walked around trying not to put their minds on one notion: Ten more weeks of travel to the Willamette. Then, maybe worse, a winter in Oregon, and then another month and a half or two months to California.

Andrew Drips strode up to the fire and waited for an invitation.

"Set," said Flat Dog.

Julia handed the captain a cup of coffee. He was a gray-hair and a big-belly, and this appearance added to his air of authority. He'd been the field leader for American Fur Company for a decade, once the competition, now the only game in town. Sam respected him, but since the man was all business, there was nothing to like.

"Not shining times," said Drips.

"Not hardly," said Sam.

"It gets worse," said Drips. "The company's not gonna send a supply train next year. Don't pay."

Sam, Hannibal, and Flat Dog looked at one another.

"Last for us, anyhow," said Sam. "We're headed to Oregon and then California."

Drips nodded. "You haven't traded yet."

"We'll keep our beaver," said Sam. "I've got a sizable credit with the company. Would you write me a letter of credit to Hudson's Bay?"

"Sure," said Drips. He grimaced. He knew these men would trade their furs at Fort Hall, where the price was better. He drained his coffee and left as abruptly as he'd come.

Sam felt a pang—last rendezvous. When he caroused at the first one, in 1825, he hadn't meant to attend the last one, just fifteen years later. Shining times? All gone.

Joe Meek and Doc Newell had already left. Doc hired on to guide a bunch of missionaries to Fort Hall on their way to Oregon. Since he and Meek were married to Nez Percé sisters, Doc got Joe to come along and help out. At Fort Hall, at least, supplies would cost less.

No one at rendezvous had liked the missionaries, and the soldiers of Christ disapproved of everything they saw. The Indians' dress, their customs, certainly their religion, their "barbarity"—these evoked no response of Christian love from the bearers of Christian light, but only a contempt they did not trouble to conceal. And they scorned the mountain men even more than the Indians, showing particular disdain for the half-breed children.

Several summers ago one of the first missionaries had told Hannibal a secret. When the missionary saw real Indians, he despaired completely of converting them. He'd written back to his mission board that the truth was, you'd couldn't make them Christians until you'd made them white men.

When Hannibal passed the story on, Sam said, "Give me a drunken Franciscan over a snotty Methodist any time."

"This preacher's plan," Hannibal said at the time, "is to switch careers, trade preaching for land development."

A week ago Pierre Jean De Smet, the first Catholic missionary to the mountains, had visited the rendezvous. He had conducted the first mass of the entire mountain country. Julia was disappointed. Had they arrived a little sooner, the priest could have baptized her children.

Altogether, rendezvous was a chance for Sam, Hannibal, Flat Dog, and Julia to rest after a couple of weeks of travel and to say good-bye to longtime friends they might never see again. A few drinks, some card games, some horse racing, a few shooting competitions, some singing and dancing in the evenings, and emotions they didn't talk about.

Drips found Sam and Flat Dog lingering at the morning fire. "Here's your credit."

Sam took the piece of paper, looked at the number, and tucked it away. He told Flat Dog, "Our plan is off to a good start."

Sam was more concerned about his family than religion or the state of the beaver trade. Everyone seemed more or less all right except Esperanza. If her moodiness and silence was the worst part of the trip, he'd count himself lucky.

Hannibal felt half-uneasy. He'd had a vagabond life, and his talk with Sam nettled him. At night in his blankets he started teasing himself with the faintest thought of getting married. A woman, children, a bond to life itself. As he watched his friends, he flip-flopped. *Is a wife the center that holds you? Or a weight that drags you down? Are children the people you love most? Or the ones you're most irritated by? Involvement? How does that fit with what I've always loved most, freedom?* Well, at least he could pretend to be the most cheerful adult in the party.

Sixteen

KANAKA BOY BURST into the tipi and said with a grin, "We're going to Coos Bay."

Lei Palua felt a geyser of joy. It was a beautiful harbor on the Pacific Coast. They would trade for lots of shells—dentalium, abalone, white clam, and olivella. The inland Indians loved these shells and paid exorbitant prices for them. They would also stop at the Hudson's Bay trading post Fort Umpqua to get useful objects. Shells excited Lei. The thought of smelling the ocean again, of playing in it, thrilled her.

"And to California."

The geyser turned to a dribble.

He sat down behind the fire. She poured his morning cup of coffee and sloshed the usual inch of rum into it. Boy had developed the habit of drinking from morning to night, and instead of the rotgut he and the men were brewing out here, he drank rum from jugs he buried in secret places. Sometimes he laced the rum with laudanum. His drunkenness didn't affect his hold on his men. They were loyal to him, would go anywhere with him. Of course, they stayed as drunk as Boy. This life was their idea of paradise, compared to being indentured servants of the Hudson's Bay Company, or even their hired men.

She got a sudden idea, sat down close to Boy, and put an arm around him.

"You're so beautiful," he said.

She knew he liked her brown Hawaiian face, as delicate as his was broad and strong. And her long black hair. She usually wore it pinned on top of her head during the day, for convenience. When they rolled up in the blankets at night, he liked to take the wooden pins out, let it down, and cover her breasts with it. Then he would stroke her hair from head to belly, murmur words of love, and tease his tongue through her hair to her nipples. He could be a tender lover or a wildly passionate one. That said enough.

Over time, though, she'd learned that he was wholly self-centered. So she learned to use his desires, as she was doing now.

"Can we go down the Columbia and up the Willamette?" She hardly dared hope. The Company would try to grab Boy and every other man and make them fulfill their contracts. And at Fort Boise, or Fort Walla Walla, or Fort Vancouver, she could slip away. . . .

"I want to visit my mother."

"No, no," said Boy. "The route is south to the Humboldt, along it to the mountains, and across to California. The trip will take all winter and will be very, very profitable."

She knew the Humboldt and dreaded it. A dicey crossing of dry country to an ugly stream, which gouged a line across a wretched country. *Then the ocean*, she reminded herself. And north to Coos Bay, and more ocean.

He looked at her for admiration. She often wondered what he

wanted from her, why he brought her to this awful place as his wife, when he was getting all the sex he wanted from the other women, the ones who were here because they liked raw liquor and rough men. She knew things, and she was smart. Maybe he wanted her to see how smart he was.

"It's a devil of a crossing, Delly says, from the Humboldt to the next water." Boy smiled savagely.

Her spirits sank again. Why did men preen about their ability to travel through country that did its best to snuff out life? Even now they were living on the Owyhee River, cut off completely from the main road to Oregon by the Owyhee Mountains, a place hard, dry, and barren, a place that did its best to burn all life to ashes. She hated this bleak spot, furnace-like in the summer, freezing in the winter, and utterly barren of everything graceful and beautiful, everything she loved.

She looked at Boy's face. His eyes were on the fire, his mind far away. She wondered if he ever thought of the homeland neither of them had ever seen, the islands of Hawaii.

Yet she was sure that Boy belonged here, not there. Raw desert was the landscape of his heart. And now they were going to ride across a desert that was worse.

"We'll leave in a couple of weeks, get across the mountains before the snows."

Boy professed to love challenges, loved to prove he could do what other men couldn't and thought he couldn't.

"I want very much to see my mother. We could come back from Coos Bay by the Fort Vancouver route."

Boy waved her off, didn't even bother to respond with words.

Lei told herself this would be good. It would make her heart dance to see an ocean. She'd seen the Pacific the first time when her grandfather took her downriver to Fort Astoria. She loved its vastness, its wildness, its grandeur. Back home at Fort Walla Walla, while other people complained about having to eat salmon every day, she reveled in it, for the smell of the sea was in its flesh.

Boy remembered that she was there and looked sideways at her. His eyes gleamed like a feral cat's. "This will be a great deal. You're going to love it. After this, I am a force to be reckoned with."

Seventeen

THE RIDERS OF the Morgan-missionary outfit looked across the bottomland at Fort Hall.

"The glories of civilization," said Hannibal MacKye.

Sam Morgan mimicked his friend. "Echoes of Greece and Rome." Education was not a high point among mountain men, but after listening to Hannibal for seventeen years, Sam had caught on to some things.

The fort squatted on the left bank of the Snake River. Twenty-five or thirty paces on a side, high walls built of wood, with a gate and a bastion—no threat to the Parthenon, and maybe not even stout enough to keep the Indians out.

"All this one wants is to wet his dry," said Joe Meek. Joe's slow, soft Virginia drawl made listeners wait a good while for even simple meanings.

"Is that all you think about?" Best friend or not, Doc Newell always took the contrary of whatever Joe said or did. Joe was loose and wild, Doc smart and carefully controlled. Sometimes Sam and Hannibal had discussed privately how close friendship could be based on opposition, but they hadn't figured it out.

"And," said Joe, "I put my mind on other things, too, like collecting my share of our fee so I can get drunk."

The outfits joined two days ago, Sam and his family catching Doc and Joe because the missionaries were so slow. They were also quarrelsome. Whiskey might help Joe forget.

This trip from rendezvous had been hard on Joe. P. J. Littlejohn, who considered himself the missionary leader, had found out what was in the kettle Joe kept sipping from all day long. The man snatched it out of Joe's hand and dumped the contents in the dust.

Joe gave the man only a small whupping before Doc persuaded him to let the poor bastard be. The missionaries might consider that the duties of the guides included leaving all scalps of holy men where God put them. However, Joe felt bereft when he had to drink water, and he'd turned into a grump.

"If we had twice the dollars," said Doc, "those wives of ours, Clap's as bad as Rain, would spend every cent on foofaraw."

Doc claimed that his wife's name, Clap, was the first syllable of a Nez Percé word, but Joe had always doubted that.

Now Joe turned in his saddle and looked back at the families belonging to him and Doc. Joe could see the mind of his wife, Rain, working away. Right now she was counting up the blankets, awls, kettles, beads, ribbon, calico, and other treasures she would buy tomorrow. Clap was worse. She would prove again that neither Doc nor any other man could control a woman.

Since Doc tried to be the boss of things, Clap was a thorn in his side. Even with this windfall in wages, he'd be lucky to end up with enough powder and lead to hunt buffalo and to fend off the Blackfeet. Joe's wages being smaller, he would have a less contented mate.

"We need a life we can afford," Doc said to Joe.

"Why don't you go to Oregon?" asked Sam.

"Hell, yes," he said, "let's go. It's the Willamette Valley for us. They say the grass grows so fast there, you have to hire a hand to walk from the door to the outhouse back and forth ever' minute or you won't be able to find the path."

Sam listened with satisfaction. Two more families with mixed-blood children going to settle on the western rim of America.

The outfit plodded down a long hill and through some cotton-woods until the fort came into view. Hannibal was the one who spotted it first. He grinned and said at large, "They're running up a welcome."

Up the flagpole slid a big declaration in red, white, and blue— the national flag of Great Britain. A political statement.

Sam thought, *Now this may kick up even more fun.*

"BARDOLF," ROLLER CALLED down, "there's visitors."

Frank Ermatinger climbed the stairs to the fort's bastion and pointed his field glass where Roller had been looking.

The nickname Bardolf was an irritant. When Ermatinger took the post's furs downriver to Fort Vancouver the last time, he took his one American employee, Roller, along for help, plus the two Owyhees—Hawaiians made first-rate laborers. On their arrival Dr. John McLoughlin welcomed them with a glass of rum. Though McLoughlin was the muckety-muck of all of Hudson's Bay Company's operations in Oregon Territory, and Ermatinger's supervisor, Ermatinger despised him. Knowing that, McLoughlin twitted Ermatinger whenever he had the chance. This time he had a little fun by calling Ermatinger Bardolf.

A backwoods American, Roller hadn't understood about Bardolf. McLoughlin explained that this was a drunken fool from some of Shakespeare's plays—"with a nose made red and bulbous by drink," added the doctor.

Ermatinger unconsciously covered his nose with one hand. It had been big and pink even when he was a child. "I am no drunk, Sir."

"We know you for a good and sober man, Bardolf."

Actually, Ermatinger did like his tot of rum.

Roller thought all this was a hoot and especially liked the idea of addressing his boss without the "Mr." Soon half the staff at Fort Vancouver called Ermatinger just plain Bardolf, and now all the staff at Fort Hall did. Luckily, the employees were only Walker, Roller, the Owyhees, and a German. The German, heir to a more formal culture, called him Herr Bardolf.

Now Ermatinger had the party riding toward the fort into focus. It was Morgan, with the other Americans and some Crows.

Ermatinger knew Sam Morgan, Joe Meek, Doc Newell, and the half-breed Hannibal MacKye well enough. Whatever beaver they took on the spring hunt was due to his generosity. Relying on their character, he supplied them on credit. The deal was, they would bring their furs to him and not take them to rendezvous, where the American Fur Company would be buying and selling. Ermatinger wanted to get a leg up on the Americans at every opportunity.

This time, from what he could see, it wasn't going to be much of a leg up. The packhorses bore only a meager number of furs.

Ermatinger snorted. He wondered if he'd ever get out of this country. He hated this post, the most remote in all of Oregon Territory. The supposed majesty of the Tetons meant nothing to him, and he had never seen the wonders his men described in the Yellowstone country. He hated the Snake River plains to the west. Somehow the plains had gotten the idea of growing lava rocks instead of grasses. Nor did he give a fig for the Indians he traded with, mostly Shoshones. He was not even deeply attached, if truth be told, to his attractive wife, Mary, and their daughter, a two-year-old everyone else found adorable.

In the center of his heart he held an ambition, hot as a dry leaf under a magnifying glass. He wanted a high position at Fort Vancouver. He believed he could get it, and to hell with however McLoughlin felt about him.

His performance here in the upper Snake River country was

critical to the Company. True, the beaver were getting trapped out. The advantage of that was, the American trappers were disappearing along with the beaver.

In a short time Ermatinger had increased the post's annual fur shipment by severalfold. He'd gotten more and more trade from the Shoshone Indians and the Blackfeet as well. They brought in buffalo hides and ermine and river otters, peltries now more profitable than beaver. They traded him dried buffalo meat to send down to Vancouver. And Ermatinger got the trade of whatever trappers had not yet given up working the streams.

It all added up to something important. This tough little man meant to keep the Indian tribes allied with Britain, not the United States. He intended to drive the American fur men out of the entire Oregon country. If Americans tried to emigrate to Oregon— so far only a handful of missionaries had made the attempt—he would welcome them, warn them of the dangers ahead, laugh mockingly at the idea of getting wagons across that rough trail, and turn them back.

Yes, Oregon now belonged by treaty to both America and Britain. But Francis Ermatinger intended to rule it all someday.

He took a last good look through the glass. *Damnably few furs*.

"Tell the cook to prepare sufficient food," the trader called down to Roller. "Then raise the colors."

He smiled to himself about that. The fort seldom flew the Union Jack, because the American trappers didn't like to be reminded. Once in a while, in his opinion, a gesture of empire was a good touch.

"IT'S AN INSULT," said Joe. "Let's tear the damn thing down. Goddamn Brits."

While the women put up the tipis, the men relaxed and took in the fine afternoon. Sam and Hannibal had decided that the chance of rain today on the Snake River plains was none. They would build their brush hut tomorrow, or perhaps never.

Hannibal watched the missionaries put their three tents up. He noted with amusement that they took care to arrange the tents in a straight line. What, a thousand miles from anywhere, was the point of a straight line?

"Hell," said Joe, "let's just shoot their damned Union Jack down."

Hannibal jumped up. "Hell, yes." He called to the tents, "Mr. Littlejohn, Mr. Clark, Mr. Smith, we need a confab." He always called the three preachers Mr. instead of Reverend, to keep the amount of ego in camp tamped down.

The three ministers pulled long faces and rumbled over to the mountain men.

"That flag," Hannibal said, "is an affront to American sensibilities." The Delaware was having fun.

Joe Meek sidled over to Sam and whispered, "What does 'affront to sensibilities' mean?"

"A slap in the face," said Sam.

"Let's get 'em," said Joe.

Hannibal went on about treaties and legalities. Doc echoed his words, both acting like they were in high dudgeon.

Littlejohn said, "What do you say, gentlemen?"

The missionaries tugged at their beards and muttered low. They'd called each other Reverend and gentlemen all the way across the plains and mountains. Joe Meek had said more than once that the West had never seen a Reverend or a gentleman, excepting Captain William Drummond Stewart, who was gone back to Scotland to play the part of a lord.

Now Joe piped up, "I don't care about nothing but that Union Jack flying in my face. Let's give 'em what for."

The missionaries nodded.

"Joe," Hannibal said at the end, "you will be our ambassador plenipotentiary."

"What do that mean?" said Joe.

"I say," said Littlejohn irritably. He was a British emigrant.

"It means you will approach the fort with a formal diplomatic statement."

Joe looked sideways at Sam and grinned.

"You must leave your rifle behind but carry a stick with a piece of white cloth tied to it.

"I am plenty of whatever you want," he said.

"Hannibal, I want to go with Joe."

This was Esperanza. Sam hadn't realized she'd walked up. She and Joe were buddies.

"Unseemly," said Littlejohn.

"Exactly," said Hannibal. "The presence of a woman will insult the Brits in a pointed way."

"I say," repeated Littlejohn.

"Now you've got to learn these words I'm going to give you to say," said Hannibal. "But Joe must do the talking," he told Esperanza. "He's an American."

In a few minutes the two strode the bottomland to the bastion. As Esperanza whispered to him, Joe called out the message to Ermatinger.

"We, being citizens of the United States of America, declare to you that this is American soil."

That was close enough. Everyone but Ermatinger knew that when the division was officially made, the Snake River would be part of the States.

"We are therefore . . ." Joe stopped and listened to Esperanza. He wanted to strike just the right tone. "We therefore demand that you lower the flag of Great Britain."

"Go to hell," yelled Ermatinger.

Joe was undaunted. He had a backup position.

"In case of your refusal we demand that the American flag be raised to fly beside it." Joe paused. "Indeed, above it." This was his own addition, and he was proud of the word "indeed."

"You and your strumpet both go to hell," said Ermatinger.

"Trumpet?" said Joe.

"Strumpet," shouted Ermatinger.

Joe and Esperanza looked at each other and shrugged. Neither of them knew what it meant.

Joe and Esperanza returned to his comrades and consulted with them. Then they marched back to the bastion. Joe weaved as he went. If he couldn't be drunk, he could at least pretend.

Joe announced, "We mountain men and this mountain woman, citizens of the United States, hereby formally give you notice. If you do not comply with our wishes within ten minutes, we will take the Union Jack down by force."

"I'll see you in hell first," said Ermatinger. "Walker," he called across the courtyard, "close and bar the gate."

Now, being forced into military mode, the trappers named Hannibal their general and Sam their captain.

"I say," protested Littlejohn. He brandished a smoothbore. "We of the cloth are able to fight." The others had gotten out rifles they didn't maintain or practice with.

"Oh, you men of God," said Hannibal, "on the battlefield God's representative is the general. He plans things out—he being me—and a captain leads the attacks."

"We do not appreciate your mocking tone, Sir," said Littlejohn.

"Having observed the battlefield," said Hannibal, "I declare that no planning is necessary. Captain Morgan, lead the attack."

Sam said, "Let's go." He, Flat Dog, Joe, and Esperanza straggled in a decidedly unmilitary formation toward the fort and the flagpole.

Easing alongside Hannibal, Julia said, "Is this all right?"

Hannibal said, "Azul and Rojo, follow Captain Morgan."

The boys sprinted forward, laughing and brandishing their bows.

The British staff of Fort Hall assembled on the ramparts, all six of them, and held their rifles at port arms, or whatever it was called.

"Reverend," Sam said to Littlejohn, "can you hit anything with that thing?"

"Decidedly, Sir."

"Ready, aim, fire!" said Sam merrily.

Littlejohn peppered the Union Jack with buckshot. It tattered nicely.

They glared at their opponents on the ramparts. These men had been friends for several years, drinking together, eating together, camping together. Everyone but Ermatinger was a good companion.

"Fire!" cried Ermatinger.

The British lifted their rifles to the sky and shot holes in the air.

"Azul, Rojo," cried Sam, "the flag." The boys aimed their arrows. "Ready, aim, fire."

After the arrows cut their holes, there wasn't enough of the Union Jack left to keep Ermatinger's wife decent. Joe knew her to favor indecency anyway.

"Men and woman," cried Sam, "it's time for the assault. Charge!" All the men rushed the gate. They laid their shoulders to it with a will, and the thing splintered. It had only been built for show anyway.

Ermatinger called a retreat, and the entire fort staff skedaddled to the trading room.

The mountain men charged up the ramparts, and Joe Meek shinnied up the pole. He had a little American flag he wore as a hatband, because he liked to make a show of being American when he went to Taos or up to the Hudson's Bay post at Flathead Lake.

At the top he stripped the Union Jack off its rope, spat on it, and hurled it to the ground. Then, with some reverence, he established Old Glory in its place. When the wind caught the Stars and Stripes, the attacking force fired their rifles into the air and shouted their triumph.

Joe leaped off the top of the pole, caught the ramparts with his feet, did a somersault, hit the floor of the plaza rolling, and stood up with a big grin.

"We're not finished," said Sam.

All the trapper soldiers, with Esperanza in the throng, marched to the trading room. "Bardolf," cried Sam, "come out!"

"Go to hell," said Ermatinger.

"Come out, or I'll shoot this lock and we'll come in."

"Bugger off."

"Bardolf, if we have to come in, we'll take everything in the trading room, down to the last coffee bean."

Silence.

"We'll make a nice profit, selling all your goods to the Shoshones."

Finally John Roller cracked the door open. "What do you want?"

"Come on out."

Roller was a friendly man, endowed with a goofy gap-toothed grin. The men knew him well and liked him.

"What do you want?"

"One keg of your finest rum," said Sam, "and all sins are forgotten."

"Stick a toothpick up your arse," yelled Ermatinger from inside.

"A keg," said Joe Meek, and cocked and aimed a threat bigger than a toothpick.

"Bardolf, give way, or we'll strip this place clean." Sam grinned at Meek. "I can't control Joe for long."

Roller stood in front of them and fidgeted. The poor man couldn't do a thing but gap-grin. Finally, the door cracked open again. Anonymous hands pushed a keg out. The mountain men seized it.

Roller said, "Mind if I join in?"

In less than an hour all ten mountain-man soldiers, plus eight wives, were sitting in front of a big campfire, pleasantly soused. Most of them hadn't tasted a proper rum before, for the traders usually kept that for themselves.

Sam noticed that Meek and Doc were dipping into one of their quarrels. Doc said, "I want to take wagons to Oregon, be the first to do it."

Joe gave him a queer look. "It can't be done."

"I've thought on it considerably," said Doc. "We can accomplish it."

"Doc," said Joe, "you got me to nursemaid the missionaries, but I'll be damned if I'll give suck to wagons."

"By God, Meek, listen." Doc, with his smidgeon of book learning, had developed the conviction that he could control life. Sam scooted out of that conversation as fast as he could.

He found a boulder and tootled on his Irish whistle. Esperanza, Azul, and Rojo did silly dances to his tunes. The twilight lingered long. It was a good evening.

"Esperanza," Sam called, "you were a good soldier. I'm going to play a march in your honor."

He piped it out, and Esperanza did a mock soldier step. Joe Meek even joined her.

Again, Sam thought, *Maybe it's all going to work out.*

Eighteen

Kanaka Boy took a score of men and left a handful behind to mind the camp and the stills. He liked to travel with an overpowering force. Anyone who saw the rifles, pistols, tomahawks, and belt knives these men carried would stand well off.

Lei wanted to stand well off herself, even though she lived with them. She wished—she'd wished over and over—that she could stay in camp, too, that . . .

This wasn't a roundabout, which worried her. They had brought whiskey only to drink, not to trade. And they didn't ride down the Owyhee, in their usual way, toward the Snake River and the villages of Nez Percé, Walla, and Cayuse that scattered beyond. They rode straight up into the Owyhee Mountains, which she disliked. These were not the pine-forested, snowcapped majesties she'd grown up around, just high, knuckly outcroppings too poor even to support much game. There were only a few springs where Digger Indians camped.

From what Lei had seen of Diggers she didn't want anything to do with them. They were the poorest Indians anyone knew of. They lived in brush huts, had no horses, and only the most primitive weapons. For most of the year the men went naked and the women wore only a kind of apron. People said they lived on rabbits, grasshoppers, and seeds.

When she asked where the devil they were going, Kanaka Boy gave her his sly smile and said, "You'll see."

THE NEXT MORNING the Sam Morgan–Flat Dog family, plus Uncle Hannibal, walked through the gate of Fort Hall, their children gawking.

"That's a cannon," said Sam.

The boys ran to it and started climbing all over it. Esperanza gave Sam a questioning look.

"It's a huge gun—it shoots these balls." He pointed to the pyramid of ammunition next to the cannon.

"What's it for?"

"Just to scare the Indians, really. In case of bad trouble, to shoot at them."

"Wonderful," said his daughter.

Julia looked at Sam, and the papa half-hid a smile. Sam wasn't used to fathering, and Julia was tickled at watching him learn to cope with a headstrong teenage girl in a pissy mood.

Julia didn't blame her. They'd jerked her out of the only life she had known, torn her away from the young man she fantasized about, made her leave her grandparents and all her friends. Not to mention the stinky rendezvous.

At the entrance to the trading room Julia reached out and showed Esperanza how to operate the door handle. It was a simple, blacksmithed latch, but she had never seen one before. In fact, she hadn't seen a wooden door until now. Only yesterday afternoon, when they made camp outside the fort and made a mock attack, had she first seen a building, much less a walled fort with a bastion.

Julia looked back at Azul and Rojo, running around the cannon and yelling, "Boom! Boom! Boom!"

Esperanza worked the latch twice and made an expression that said she wasn't impressed. They stepped in.

Sam smiled across the room at Bardolf and then reminded himself to call the trader Mr. Ermatinger. Ermatinger would be grumpy enough without Sam calling him Bardolf. Sometimes he acted jovial, but Sam knew him for a bitter and acerbic man.

"This place smells bad," Esperanza said.

Funny, the smells were what Sam liked about trading rooms, the aromas of big twists of tobacco, coffee beans, horehound candy, and pemmican, all swirled together. But strange to Esperanza, for sure.

She stood in the middle of the room, far from the displays of goods that she coveted—bolts of cotton and wool, ribbons, beads, everything to help a young girl look beautiful.

Hannibal said, "Look at this glass." She went to him—Hannibal was the one person in the party she was speaking to in a good spirit. He tapped it with a fingernail, and she did too, and then felt its smoothness with her forefinger. "Lets lots of light in, and lets you see out. But fragile. You can just push with your hand and it will break into sharp pieces. Cut your hand, too."

Azul and Rojo came bounding in.

Julia walked around and felt of the fabrics. Aside from trading their fur, they wouldn't do much trading here. They had Sam's letter of credit from American Fur for a good amount, profit from a herd of horses he'd brought from California, but they all knew prices would be better at the main Hudson's Bay place of business, Fort Vancouver. Julia could wait.

"Are you bound for Oregon, Morgan?" asked Ermatinger.

"Sure enough," Sam said. "The trapping life is done." Flat Dog and Hannibal came up next to Sam.

"The Oregon road will be well-worn this year," said Ermatinger. "More missionaries and their wives, I see. Joining their comrades among the Spokanes, I believe. You guiding them?"

"Not a chance," said Sam.

Like many men in the mountains, Ermatinger made no secret of his distaste for the preaching breed.

"Your friends Meek and Newell are giving up the life as well?" His lips lingered over the phrase, relishing the implication of failure.

"Yes," said Hannibal.

"Hard to picture Joe Meek giving up a beaver trap for a plow," said Flat Dog.

"There's a delicious bit there," Ermatinger went on. "Newell told me this morning he and Joe are taking two wagons."

"Wagons to Oregon?" said Hannibal. He didn't add, "And Joe Meek going along?"

"Indeed. He has in mind to prove it can be done." Now Ermatinger's tone was pure mockery.

Sam bought Esperanza a couple of doodads and got the family out of the range of Ermatinger's mood.

That evening the night sky was fully dark, the mountain air cool enough for them to use blankets, sitting around the fire. The season was changing, and the first frost wasn't far off. They chased the cold away with coffee they'd just bought from Ermatinger. The evening would have been perfect if Doc Newell wasn't trying to twist their arms.

"It's safer with a big party," said Doc. Joe Meek sat cross-legged next to Doc, but he was drinking more than talking.

Sam, Hannibal, and Flat Dog eyed each other. After they got the word from Ermatinger, they had talked it over and decided.

"Doc," said Sam, "you're a friend. And there's no man like Joe. But the Snake River plains? You're going to be sorry you ever heard a wheel squeak."

"You're just not thinking big," said Newell. "We could be first. Wagons to the Pacific Coast of Oregon!"

"No," said Hannibal.

"Hell, no," said Flat Dog.

"Joe," asked Sam, "you really all right with this?"

"I guess," said Joe. "But my wife, Rain, she has her doubts."

"A squaw's opinion," said Newell, "is of no value."

Joe swigged and looked sidelong at Doc.

"How long to the next post?" asked Julia.

"Fort Boise," said Hannibal. "About three weeks."

"Safer together," said Doc.

"We already told you no," said Flat Dog.

Nineteen

THE THREE OF them climbed up a low ridge, leaving the horses and men out of sight below. From this distance, though, Lei could see nothing. Dark bushes clustered at the foot of the slope, and the plants might mean a spring. Whatever Kanaka Boy was studying through his field glass, she couldn't make it out.

"I want to look," said Nell. She was one of the loose Kanaka-Indian women Boy kept around camp. Lei knew he had sex with her when he wanted to. Lei dealt with it by ignoring her.

Now Boy ignored Nell by handing Lei the field glass. He was proud of that piece of equipment—to him it represented leadership. He'd traded for it at Fort Boise, near the place where the Owyhee River flowed into the Snake.

Lei adjusted the focus a little for her eyes. "I only see bushes," she said.

Peering intently, she still saw nothing. Then a movement

caught her eye. A child, yes, a toddler, darting out of a bush—no, a low, domed hut woven from branches.

A woman stood up abruptly into the circle of Lei's vision, a Digger, naked to the waist.

Boy said, "This will be lovely."

"Let me see," said Nell.

Lei handed the glass to Boy and started back down the rise.

At the bottom Boy directed a half-dozen men to lead their horses off to the north and ascend the slope beyond the visible ridge and another half-dozen to do the same to the south. "Stay low," he said. "No riding. Get above the hut so you can charge down. Don't let them see you or they'll scatter."

"How we know when?" said Delly. He spoke a sort of Pidgin English that Lei didn't like.

"At sundown, when they're all back in camp. The signal will be my gunshot. When you hear that, ride."

Lei wanted to ask what on earth Boy wanted with the Diggers. They didn't possess anything of use to anyone. But Boy was being coy about this—he strode around like a man executing a fine plan—and she knew he wouldn't tell. She could only dread.

She lay down and took a nap on her saddle blanket. As she drifted off, her last thought was, *What has my life become?*

Kanaka Boy woke her with a shake. "We're heading in," he said. His eyes were alive with excitement. "You want to go?"

"No," said Lei.

"I do," said Nell.

"Good," Boy told her.

Nell flashed Lei a look of superiority.

Lei knew Nell, in fact all the women, scorned her because she refused to participate in dirty deeds. Or maybe they envied her because Boy treated her special. She didn't care which.

Boy handed Lei the field glass. "Watch if you want."

She climbed the rise again, and for a while she could see the action with the naked eye. Boy and his gang fanned out parallel to one another, their horses maybe ten yards apart. They rode openly and steadily toward the camp several hundred yards away. Lei suddenly thought that they were doing it in the style of a rabbit drive. They must not want to let anyone—

Shouts and screams came from the Digger camp. She could see figures stirring.

Boy spurred his horse to a gallop. He rode an enormous Appaloosa stallion he called Warrior, seventeen hands high, black with white spots like snowflakes—an easy horse to spot at a distance. From a long way out Boy fired, making the huge noise she would never get used to and sending up an eruption of white smoke.

Now Lei could see riders charging down the hill toward the camp from two sides.

As Boy rode into the camp, Lei raised the field glass and focused on him and Warrior. A Digger man ran straight at them, brandishing a club. Boy swung his tomahawk once, and the man crumpled.

Other riders charged across her field of vision. Some shot people with rifle or pistol, and some just trampled Diggers with their mounts.

Lei lowered the field glass. She shuddered. Why on earth did Boy want to kill these people?

Mesmerized, she couldn't turn her face away. Horses darted back and forth among the huts. White smoke formed a cloud above the camp. Indians scurried around, looking for a way out.

She turned her back to the scene and crumpled to her knees.

FOR SOME REASON Boy and the men didn't come back for a long time, maybe an hour. Lei sat wrapped in her saddle blanket, shivering, though not from the cold. When they came, they brought six women and ten children between the ages of about six and twelve. All had their heads down, their hands tied, and their feet hobbled.

Boy swung off Warrior and swaggered toward her. He was intoxicated with violence.

Lei knew the men's fate. She stared for a long while at the captives and finally asked, "What happened to the small children?" Like the toddler. "The old people?"

He gave a twisted smile and said, "They couldn't walk to California."

Lei started to speak, stopped, and told herself, *Don't stutter, you idiot.* Then she spoke one word: "Why?"

Kanaka Boy shrugged easily.

"Californios want slaves."

Twenty

TRAVEL, AFTER A long while, is not a matter of going somewhere. It is a way of life.

The whole Sam–Hannibal–Flat Dog–Julia crew hated the lava
plains of the Snake River. Even as summer wagon-spoked toward
fall, the days were blazing hot, beaten by a relentless sun. The
horses had to pick hoof placements through black lava rock where
there should have been soft earth and grass.

The family's days were simple. Get up at first light, make coffee, gnaw on pemmican, load the packhorses, and ride. Take a
long nooner somewhere with water and shade. Ride again until
the sun is mostly gone and you see a decent camping place. Un-
load. Eat. Drink coffee—Sam was glad he'd spend the rest of his
life where he could get coffee beans. And sleep, because you're
too tired to do anything else.

That anything else, fortunately, included Esperanza acting pissy.

Tonight, after three weeks on the trail and just an hour or two from Fort Boise, Hannibal wished someone would bicker. Supper was done. Flat Dog and Sam were leading the horses, one by each hand, over to the river for the last drink of the day. Esperanza sat off by herself braiding and unbraiding her hair. Though she still thought about how Prairie Chicken did her wrong, she was too tired to muster any hatred. Julia was playing cat's cradle with the boys, who were at least honest enough to grumble at each other. Baby Paloma hung from a cottonwood limb in her cradleboard, whimpering.

Sam and Flat Dog hobbled the last four horses and came back to the fire for one more cup of coffee. Sam glanced over at Esperanza unhappily, wishing for the hundredth time that she'd act like she was glad, finally, to be with her father. Flat Dog stared morosely into his cup, thinking how, halfway to his allotted three score and ten, he had abandoned an entire life.

Hannibal took his rifle and walked away from camp to the boulder he picked out for his watch. The last of the light was on the river now. The waters were dark where the trees cast shadows upon them, and silver-lavender where they rocked the last light in the sky. It was Hannibal's favorite time of day.

What none of the others knew was, Hannibal was half-jealous of them. True, right now they were mostly unhappy. Still, they formed a net of connection. They mattered to each other, for hurt or for joy. Even annoyance was connection.

Hannibal had led a vagabond life, and here he was vagabonding again. He'd been born without a decent world to live in, half white and half Indian in a society that didn't like breeds. He was vastly educated, in a country that was skeptical of book learning. He was alone—loneliness was the fate his parents gave him—in a culture where most people sought to bond to one another.

Because learning languages, getting along with different people, and making a buck by trading came naturally to him, he'd always survived, and he'd never been poor. He'd done a lot of thinking and had come to a personal motto that worked for him—*rideo, ergo sum,* I laugh, therefore I am. Somehow, though, wisdom didn't have the power of bonding.

Now, wonder of wonders, he was playing with the faintest thought of getting married. He shook his head. *Now that,* he thought, *is something to laugh about.*

Maybe California would be different. That idea had teased him since he first rode there with Sam in 1827. The races were mixing in the Golden Clime. A man could be accepted for who he was and what he could do, not for his family or race. Maybe he was letting hope get in the way of his mind, but Hannibal had hopes for California.

I probably have another thirty years to live. Why not?

Twenty-one

LEI KNEW SHE had to time it exactly right.

Right now it was hell—she had to block out of her mind what was going on with the slaves. On the first night the six women got topped over and over, the rapists led by Boy himself. In camp the scene turned from ugly to a nightmare of evil. Drunk, the men flaunted their power over these human beings they claimed to own. Not only did they force sex on the women at will, day and night, they took pleasure in making it public. They reveled in humiliating the poor creatures. The women had no defenders—Boy's ruffians had killed the men and the older boys.

The worst was when a boy of about twelve lost control and fought for his mother. Two of Boy's men beat him senseless. Boy refused to let Lei take care of him, and sometime during the second night he died.

She fled into the bushes and threw up. Then she came back composed, pretending it didn't really matter.

The men let the body lie where it fell, and ravens flocked to it. Lei couldn't let herself look at the mother.

Lei waited about a week, until the moon was full. Her plan was simple and terrible.

The first trick was to get Boy so drunk that he passed out. She turned herself into a Delilah of seduction and inebriation and got it done.

When she couldn't even shake Boy awake, she took what little she dared. She tucked his pistol under her dress and secured it with her belt. Though she didn't know how to reload it, she knew how to cock and fire it—in desperate circumstances she could shoot once. She took her own belt knife and the small belt bag where she kept beauty items. Under her blanket she carried a sack of jerky. These few possessions would have to do.

She slipped out of the tipi, bridled her mount and Boy's, pulled their stakes, and led them to the river. The guards would think she was watering the animals.

Her plan was to ride Warrior as much as she could and give him a break sometimes by riding her mare, Kauai. Her grandfather, who gave the mare to Lei when she became a woman, named her after his island of birth. She was a beauty, an Appaloosa with leopard spots and a rear end that promised speed.

Lei carried no saddles—that would raise alarms. Learning to ride as a child, she never used a saddle.

When she got into the cottonwoods that lined the river, she jumped on Warrior's back in a flash and guided him softly through the trees. Once they got out of hearing of the camp, she eased him onto the sagebrush flat and kicked him with her moccasined heels. The stallion bolted to a gallop. He was a magnificent beast—Boy always bragged about Warrior's speed and endurance. His strength plus Lei's determination equaled freedom.

Fort Boise was two long days' ride at a normal pace. She would make it in a lot less, depending on how much she had to sleep.

What would happen when she got there? She would throw herself on the mercy of the chief trader and . . . She couldn't think about that now.

Eight hours' head start. It would have to do.

She slapped Warrior's hindquarters and rode like hell.

LEI STOPPED AT first light.

The night had been crazy. The moon turned the landscape into a strange, phantasmagoric place she didn't recognize. She had to pick her way when she wanted the horses to run. While she was steering Kauai down an embankment to the river for a drink, the mare slipped and crashed down on her left side. Lei barely got her leg out from under the horse and ended up sitting on the poor animal's flank.

The result of it all was that Lei was exhausted. The horses needed grass and rest, and she had to sleep. If she didn't, she would pass out, fall off, and maybe lose the horses.

She didn't bother with a hidden camp. If Boy was somehow close enough to see her, she had no chance anyway. She tied the horses to limbs and rolled up in her blanket. *I'm going to sleep the sleep of the dead*, she thought. She smiled to herself. She tried to remember the story the missionaries had made her listen to, about the man-god who was raised from the dead. She couldn't bring the story back, but she told herself, *I will go down and then be resurrected by the sun.*

SHE WOKE WITH a start. The sun was maybe an hour above the horizon. The horses were grazing peacefully. No reason for alarm. Time to go.

She watered them, jumped back onto Warrior, and kicked him for speed.

She rode until midday and took a break in the shade of some cottonwoods. She felt like she could keep going, but she wanted to maintain the horses' strength—*they are bringing me back from the dead.*

She was making good time, she knew, and might even reach the fort tonight. But she was edgy and kept the break short.

LATE IN THE afternoon she left the Owyhee and crossed some low hills to the Snake River. Now she was on the last lap, about ten miles from the fort.

At the river she rode into the shallows, jumped off to drink upstream of the horses, and filled her belly. Then she splashed water on her face and dunked her long black hair into the stream. She had learned that her hair was a sponge for liquid that would keep her cool. Dropping the hair down inside the back of her dress, purely by chance, she saw it.

At first she didn't believe it. On the ridge behind her, about a half a mile back, the sun glinted off . . .

She knew damn well what it was—she'd seen it scores of times. Kanaka Boy's field glass, reflecting sunlight.

How?

I don't know and it doesn't matter.

She led the horses back out of the river fast.

What was left now was a horse race to the fort.

SHE SLAPPED WARRIOR, she hollered, and she kicked him. She did everything she knew to make that horse run.

She dropped Kauai's lead—Warrior would run easier and freer without Kauai. One big worry. Boy and his men loved to race their horses, and she knew from competing that she wasn't as fast. But she also had one great comfort. Boy wouldn't risk a long shot, for fear of injuring Warrior.

She ran, she ran, she ran.

She turned Warrior to shortcut a bend in the river. The best ford was downstream from the mouth of the Boise River. This was the time of low water, though, and beyond the bend was a place Warrior could get across and save some distance—one mile could mean survival or death.

At the bank she risked her first look back. Four riders, Boy the biggest, no more than two hundred paces behind her.

She blasted Warrior into the water at full speed. She wanted him to understand what they absolutely had to have—she wanted him to charge across this goddamn river.

Warrior's hoofs slipped on the slippery rocks. He didn't like the footing at all. He fought the reins, but she held his head down and kicked him straight. He staggered and went down on one hind leg.

"Up!" she shouted. "Go!"

He got up and went. The bottom turned to mud, slower but more secure. When she got to the other side, they faced a low-cut bank. Warrior stopped, looking at it wildly.

"Jump!" Lei shouted. At that moment her right leg erupted into fire.

Warrior reared, staggered on his hind legs, and toppled backward into the river and on top of Lei.

Twenty-two

HER EYES FLUTTERED open. She looked into Kanaka Boy's large brown eyes and sugary smile. He cooed sweetly, "I have saved your life, Magpie." His lips smacked open wide and his white teeth gleamed. "Now I can kill you in a more intimate way." His eyes laughed. "As a good wife deserves."

Lei shook with cold. She was lying in several inches of water.

Delly said, "Boy, let's get out of here. Someone might come."

Nell and an Indian named Turno stood and stared down at her.

"Maybe I would in my great mercy spare your life, but you forced me to hurt Warrior. My shot, it went through your lovely thigh and into his flank."

Yes, there was burn and cold just above her knee, from the bullet and from the river.

"He will live, but you caused him great pain, and this I cannot forgive."

"Boy!" said Delly.

"Yes, my friend is right." He scooped his arms under her and hoisted her out of the water.

Agony bolted from knee to toe to skull.

He threw her onto a saddle belly down. Pain thunderclapped her consciousness.

"Tie her on and take her back to where the cattails are. Keep her out of sight. Nell, stay with me."

DELLY LIFTED LEI off the horse, held her waist high, and dropped her.

The earth knocked her consciousness topsy-turvy.

After a few moments or eternities she swam through flights of quicksilver birds back to the world.

She felt her sopping-wet hide dress being jerked off her arms and shoulders.

A thought crossed her mind—*he's going to dress my wound*. Then she thought, *No, I'm tit side up*. Then she realized how stupid the whole idea was and started laughing. She couldn't help herself.

Delly realized he'd almost forgotten the laudanum. He stopped his hand just short of Lei's crotch. He'd thought about her privates for a long time, and now he meant to have some sport.

"You'll be a lot more fun with some of this," he said.

He screwed the top off Boy's flask. Opium, Boy said, mixed with alcohol. Delly knew Boy kept it around for bad pain. Now he said it also made people fly sky-high.

The bitch was cackling—she'd already lost it. He held the flask to her lips. "Swig on this," he said.

She shook her head wildly, left-right, left-right, and cackled louder.

Delly slapped her as hard as he could. That put an end to the shaking and laughing. He put the flask back to her lips. "Drink this," he said, "or I'll beat you so you'll never forget it."

She swallowed. He made her swallow again.

Then Delly put his hand on her privates and groped her roughly. He saw the fear and revulsion in her eyes and grinned. *No, sister, what I'm gonna do ain't love.*

He pulled her knees apart, knelt between them, and dropped his breechcloth.

He leaned forward and snarled, "Look at me."

She did, and he saw wild fear in her eyes.

That was what he wanted. Before she started flying, he wanted her to know she was being raped good and hard and he, Delly, was the bastard doing it.

Twenty-three

SAM AND FLAT Dog looked at each other and listened to the shot echo through the cottonwoods. They slipped to the edge of the trees. Beyond a curve in the river a wisp of white smoke jiggered on the breeze.

They saddled up, mounted, and gingerly walked their horses toward the smoke. Good to check things out, bad to ride toward a gunshot in a hurry. It was probably no business of theirs.

Sam saw two strangers, a man and a woman in their twenties. Holding his rifle casually, the man touched the woman's neck lightly with his other hand. She let both their horses water. As Sam and Flat Dog rode close, the man smiled broadly at the riders and led the woman and the horses out of the river.

Boy looked at the white-haired American and the stocky In-dian and wondered whether they'd seen Delly and Turno carry

Lei off. Probably not. Still, he said, "One of our hunters got lucky on a doe."

Sam thought the woman looked Indian, the man Owyhee, and their broad smiles spoke an intention of friendship. Sam introduced Flat Dog and himself. The Owyhee said his name was Kanaka Boy, the Indian woman's Nell. She was probably his wife.

"May we offer you a cup of coffee?" said Sam. "Our camp is around the next bend."

Boy breathed out his relief. They hadn't seen anything. He said, "Capital."

ESPERANZA AND JULIA sat by the fire stitching new pairs of moccasins for themselves. Just then Esperanza's two papas walked up with a strange man and woman. The man was huge, with a head and chest like a whale's, and he radiated masculine energy. The woman was small and ugly, not worth noticing.

Sam introduced the entire family, Julia first. Boy made a little bow and said to each woman, "Enchanted to meet you." She looked around for her two brothers and Uncle Hannibal, then remembered they'd gone hunting.

Flat Dog poured the coffee.

"What does 'Kanaka' mean?" asked Sam.

Boy spoke a word that sounded like burbling water. "The people of Hawaii, our name for ourselves in our own language."

Julia smiled with pleasure.

Esperanza thought irritably, *He's charming my mother*.

Boy's companion, Nell, seemed amused by the situation. Esperanza disliked her.

Their story came out quickly. From the big island called Hawaii Boy had signed on with Hudson's Bay to work in America, and he labored mostly at Fort Walla Walla. That place was several weeks downriver, Esperanza didn't know or care where.

Nell was a Nez Percé, one of the tribes that bred Appaloosa horses, which Papa Sam was interested in.

"I have graduated from the employ of Hudson's Bay," Boy said. He went on in an animated way—he was proud of his tale. "I am setting myself up as a trader, with some friends. We'll get goods from California and trade them to the Indians."

Esperanza loved listening to Boy's musical voice. His speech, directed mainly to Julia, had a touch of elegance. Esperanza had heard similar tones from Ermatinger, who was educated, unlike the common trappers.

"We Kanaka people have been on this continent for about fifty years," Boy said. "There are hundreds of us here. We've always been laborers, working for the British. I think it's time that we declared ourselves equal to the British, or anyone."

"Absolutely," said Sam.

"I agree with you," put in Esperanza.

Boy gave her a gleaming smile.

Now he spoke of an opportunity he was developing with the Californios. The British ignored California, said Boy, and that was a mistake. "Also, my men and I have an advantage," said Boy. "The British would have to bring horses over the Siskiyou Trail into Oregon and cross the Cascade Mountains with the herds somehow. But my Indian friends and I, we know the desert west of here. We know where the water is. We will be able to bring the horses to the Rockies, hundreds of horses. In California horses are common as . . . mosquitoes."

Suddenly he slapped a mosquito on his forearm. Then, with a look of fascination, he picked up the smashed creature delicately and rubbed it between his huge thumb and forefinger until it was nothing. Last, with a strange expression, he sucked the forefinger.

Papa Sam made some inquiries about where the great horse herds of the northern part of California were—always talking business. Kanaka Boy answered fully, with the names of rivers and valleys Esperanza hadn't heard of.

Too soon Boy and Nell stood up. Esperanza realized that Nell hadn't said a word, just watched as though everything was a tickle somehow. Esperanza was sure she didn't mean anything to Boy.

"We'd better get back to camp," Boy said. "Our friends will send someone looking for us." He met all their eyes warmly, and then gave Julia and Esperanza special smiles. "Aloha," he said. "That is how we Kanaka people say both hello and good-bye."

When they left, Hannibal, Azul, and Rojo materialized out of the last of the twilight. "Who were they?"

Julia spoke up. "Kanaka Boy, a Hawaiian who has lifted himself up to become something. Very admirable."

"And his wife," said Sam.

Flat Dog said, "I don't trust him."

Twenty-four

LEI FELT NICE, very nice. Kind of giddy, but she liked it. The hurt in her leg, yes, it was still there, but . . . where? It didn't seem to matter.

Something nagged at her mind. Yes, she needed to know something. Nice, so nice . . .

Oh, what was it?

Yes, she needed to know . . .

Where am I?

It didn't matter, she felt good. She felt a rocking motion, kind of like a boat on a gentle lagoon. Rocking, rocking . . . Her legs dangled down one side and her arms down the other side, bumping against something warm.

Boy was jabbering on about something, on and on. Man liked to hear himself talk. The words, she couldn't make them out now. They brushed by her like feathers—yes, the words were feathers. She liked that. Better than words being . . . meanings. Meanings?

The rocking, the words—she let herself float on the lake of consciousness.

LATER, MUCH LATER, she felt cold. Annoying. *I like the rocking—that rocking, endless rocking—don't like to be cold.*

She took some time and with great effort she formed words in her mind. *I'm cold, arms cold.*

She spoke, but only a sort of moan made its way out of her throat.

She decided to rest before she tried again. She turned her mind—*don't have much mind*—to where she was. She felt, she listened, she looked. No good to look—dark. Listen—*clumpety-clumpety-clump*. Feel—rocking motion, arms touching something warm. She felt with her hands—warm and hairy. Before long she put it together. She was belly down on the saddle of a horse. She rummaged around in her sensations for a moment and came up with something more. She was belly down and stark naked on the saddle of a horse.

She turned her mind back to the words, and this time she got it out. "I'm cold."

"Don't worry about it," said Boy. "Tomorrow morning you're going to be hot, as hot as any woman has ever been."

SHE CAME AWAKE gradually. She was warm now, wrapped in a blanket with Boy. Gray birds flicked around in pine trees, swimming through a gray light.

Her mind was a little woozy, but working. She was in trouble, shot by Boy, then raped by Delly and Turno. She remembered the rapes only hazily, but she knew what had happened. She even remembered Nell twisting her nipples hard while Turno was on top of her. She wondered if she'd been raped by Boy. Yes, rape—she wasn't his wife anymore, that was for sure. She was naked and felt sure Boy had probably done whatever he wanted to do.

Damn, I can't shake this fuzziness.

She lay still. Boy was asleep, the drunk-but-not-very-drunk sleep. He could wake up at any moment.

She couldn't quite remember what he'd said last night, something important, something huge. She listened to his breathing, very deep, very regular. Maybe she could risk it. Very carefully, she rolled onto one side.

It felt like a stab in the leg. Her mouth shot open to scream, but she clamped down and made the scream soundless. She'd been shot, she remembered now, above the right knee, a long-distance shot by Boy. The ball tore through her flesh and into Warrior's flank. She imagined the one red glob on his black coat, among so many white snowflakes.

That was the reason Boy was going to kill her. He said so. That was part of the huge thing.

She looked at the wound and felt behind it. There she fingered another hole, where the ball came out. Maybe she wasn't terribly hurt, if it didn't fester.

Feeling tender around the face, she fingered herself gingerly. Yes, it was swollen, very sore around the cheekbones, with dried blood on the outsides of her eye sockets, below her nostrils, and below one ear. She squeezed the ear lightly and got a jolt of pain for her reward.

What a sight I must be, brown skin blotched with purples and speckled with red.

She slipped out of the blankets—the pain was bad—and sat up. Now she recognized this place. Boy had brought her here on their honeymoon, as he called it. It was a grassy meadow, with several hot springs easing out at the base of the hill. The sulfur smell of the springs brought it all back to her. They lolled in the hot springs for those few days, and rolled in the luxuriant grass, too. She thought she loved him then.

She crawled over to a boulder. Before trying what she was

going to try, she looked around. Their horses were hobbled, the ashes of a fire smoldering, Boy's rifle and pistol under one of his arms. A few feet away lay his possible sack, with belongings he needed for traveling.

No more stalling, she told herself. She put her hands on the boulder, used the uninjured leg, tried to stand up, collapsed.

This time her scream wasn't quite soundless.

She watched Boy fearfully for a long moment. He flicked a fly off his nose with one hand but didn't wake up.

The opening of the possible sack caught her eye. Something silver . . . She felt a hot burn of frustration in her throat—she couldn't . . .

She knew what it was, Boy's flask of laudanum. He kept several flasks buried somewhere around the camp on the Owyhee, supposedly to help comrades with pain. Lei knew, though, he nipped on the stuff himself. He had invited her to join in. "Lotusland," he would say, "lotusland."

Now she knew why she felt fuzzy.

All right, do it this time. She made her left leg push her upright, leaning on the boulder. She looked around. They were camped so close to one of the hot springs, they could have rolled in. But this wasn't one they played in. This was—

Like a slap the memory came. This was the one that was much too hot—you couldn't even get a toe into it. Once Boy caught a ground squirrel and threw it in for amusement. The creature hit the water, spasmed violently, and went rigid. She supposed the bones must still be down there somewhere.

Boy's words came back: "Tomorrow morning you're going to be hot, as hot as any woman has ever been."

She whirled and stared at him. Did he just now speak those terrible words? No. No, but this was the huge something. This was what he'd said last night when she was out of her mind, when she complained about being cold. She knew exactly how he was going to kill her.

Twenty-five

THEIR FIRST LOOK at Fort Boise made them think they hadn't ridden several hundred miles downstream. It was Fort Hall on a smaller scale and in adobe, lying squatted in similar bottomlands along the Snake River. The big difference was the chief trader, who immediately came out to greet them.

"Francois Payette," he introduced himself in a Frenchy accent. "Enchanted to make your acquaintance." Where Ermatinger had been surly, Payette was all friendliness and charm, and his gray goatee gave everything a Gallic touch. "Will you join us for dinner, please, this evening at sunset? I promise you as fine a meal as the country will afford."

When the sun dropped behind the western hills and the bottomland dropped from cool to nippy, Sam and the whole family made their way from the river's edge into the small fort. Sam was tickled to see how Esperanza spruced herself up for the dinner.

She'd used the trinkets he bought her at Fort Hall to make herself as squaw-like as possible. She'd vermilioned the part in her auburn hair, rouged her cheeks, and tied small bells to the bottom of her hide dress. A statement.

"She's in for some surprises," Julia told Sam softly.

THE MOMENT BOY sat up in the blankets, Lei handed Boy his coffee, as she did every morning, complete with a fine dollop of alcohol. He started every day this way. He was still cobwebby from sleep, but he held the cup steady and got a good slug down.

Half of her wished she had killed him. She had a decent chance. His knife was in his belt. A quick grab, one hard thrust, it might have worked. And it might not. Boy was quick as a lizard, and far nastier.

But that was not the point. Lei had rummaged around in herself, and she didn't think she could kill a human being, especially not one she'd spent the days of her life with, shared so many meals with, laid next to, made love to, hoped with, feared with, joined her life to. She wished she could, but that wasn't in her.

"Taste good?" she said. She hoped her tone was meek, chastened. Everything she'd done was the role of the wife who had remembered her place. Crawling because of her bad leg, she had made a fire. She got his big mug and the small sack of beans out of his possible sack—Boy went nowhere without his coffee. She brewed his morning cup and kept it on the fire, taking not even a sip for herself, playing the obedient wife.

She'd made only one change. Instead of whiskey, the cup was half-full of laudanum. It tasted and smelled the way it always did, since the laudanum itself was mostly alcohol.

"Boy," she said, "I'm sorry."

He looked at something over the rim of his coffee cup, infinity maybe, but not her. He just took a big gulp.

She felt a jolt of hatred, like bile. If only she could have killed him. *How in hell am I ever going to get free of him now?*

"Boy, I'm sorry."

Still no response. "I went crazy. You surprised me with those . . . Diggers. I'd seen people die, yes, but . . . So many, all at once . . ."

She shook her head, as though trying to wake up from a bad dream.

"The little children . . ."

Boy stuck the cup out at her.

She took it, poured in black coffee, and added several glugs from his rum flask. The contents of the flask had been altered radically.

He took the cup and swigged deep.

"I apologize to you. I was insane to do what I did."

She forced herself to go to him, sit next to him, put an arm around him.

He drank.

"I'll do anything you say. I'm sorry I've acted . . . snooty, like some of the men stay. I'll do *whatever* you want."

He snickered. He knew what that word meant, "whatever." What Delly and Turno made her do yesterday.

She took his head in her hands, looked deep into his eyes, and saw the vagueness she was waiting for. "I am your wife."

Boy started to say something, one of his witticisms, no doubt, one that cut as much as it amused. But he couldn't put the words together.

She took his cup and filled it once more, with both liquids.

She had come up with a plan to survive. It was mad, it was dangerous, and it was the only path she could see.

KANAKA BOY DIDN'T pass out, exactly. When he had imbibed about three times as much laudanum as she'd ever seen him use, he drifted into another world, maybe what he called lotusland. His eyes were half-open, but he seemed to see nothing and hear nothing. He was utterly helpless. She went to work.

She stripped off his clothes, every stitch, moccasins, breech-cloth, legging, shirt, belt. She cut six inches of the leggings off to make them halfway fit and rolled up the sleeves of the shirt. She took all the gear he wore on his person, shot pouch, belt bag, knife, pistol. She got dressed, forcing the hurt leg to move. Actually, it hurt less as she used it. She crawled to Warrior, pulled herself onto her two feet, bent, and with one big effort lifted the saddle and plopped it onto the horse. Then she tied Boy's possible sack behind.

She walked unsteadily to a low boulder, belt knife in hand, and sat down. She looked around at the beautiful meadow, the perfect sky, the gorgeous morning. A tear ran down one cheek. With the knife she cut her hair off in huge hanks.

The task took longer than she'd imagined. She looked at the shiny black mass around her feet, then raised her eyes and refused to look back down.

Then she took Kanaka Boy's rifle and threw it in the hot, bubbling pot. She watched the handsome killing machine sink into the death intended for her. His knives, pistol, and shooting pouch she kept for herself.

One last job, another way to slow Boy down. She found a flat stone the size of her hand. She stood over her ex-husband's naked form, asking herself if she really wanted to do this. The answer was yes.

Could she get it done? Why not? She'd seen it done to colts.

She pulled his legs apart, knelt between them, put the stone under his scrotum, and pushed aside his penis. With one hand she pulled the balls toward herself. With his belt knife, she carefully cut off one testicle.

She looked into his face. He seemed to try to focus his eyes on her. The eyes swam and floated away again.

She cut off the other testicle. She held the two bloody lumps, like big peach seeds, and looked at them. For some reason, she didn't know why, she put them in her belt bag.

Twenty-six

PAYETTE SAT AT the head of the trestle table, surrounded by Sam, Flat Dog, Julia, Hannibal, and Esperanza. At the other end were the fort hands, including two Owyhees, plus Azul and Rojo. Esperanza looked nervously at the china plate, flatware, and napkin in front of her. Julia whispered to her, "Just watch what I do."

She looked nervously at her sons at the other end of the table. They were talking enthusiastically with the hired men. She hoped the boys' playfulness wouldn't include throwing food.

First Payette had a little fun. "Since we have no wine—rum later, gentlemen—it is our custom here to toast our guests with this drink almost unknown in the Rocky Mountains, none other than cow's milk." He lifted his glass. "To you and your journey— bon voyage!"

Now Esperanza had her first taste of milk since she was an infant. She made a sour face.

"Our guests from the United States," Payette told her, "are generally more delighted by our dairy products than anything else we can offer."

Esperanza looked at her mother and curled her lip.

More treats—plump loaves of warm bread and bowls of creamy butter. Esperanza watched carefully as the others used their table knives, not the big knives in their belts, to pick up and spread the butter. She did the same, took a small bite, then a big bite, then finished the slice and reached for another.

Sam thought, *At least there's something about civilization she likes.*

The next course was slabs of dried salmon.

"Thomas Aquinas gave us seven proofs of the existence of God," Hannibal told Esperanza. "I think salmon is the eighth proof."

Though his friend liked to say fancy things, Sam hadn't heard this one before.

"This tastes incredible," said Esperanza. These were the first words she'd spoken at dinner.

"On this river lower down and on the Columbia," Payette said, "are the Indians we call Salmon Eaters. They catch lots of salmon in weirs and dry it on racks to preserve it. Fort Hall trades with us and Fort Walla Walla, their pemmican for our salmon. Mr. Ermatinger says the fish represents a welcome change from the ubiquitous buffalo. We see it the other way."

Though Sam had learned to read a dozen years ago, he would never get used to hearing words like "ubiquitous" in conversation.

"The two basic groups of Natives in the Oregon country," Payette went on, "are Buffalo Eaters and Salmon Eaters."

Esperanza took a second piece of salmon and picked up some flesh with her fingers.

"Fork," said Julia quietly.

Esperanza took the hint.

The vegetables were green beans and boiled potatoes. Esperanza watched the others and used the potatoes as an excuse to consume more butter.

Sam thought that if they lived in civilization for a while, everyone in the family might not be so scrawny.

Payette crowned the meal with cups of coffee and pieces of fine Swiss chocolate. "The chocolate is a personal indulgence of mine," he told them.

From the look on her face, Esperanza's conversion to civilization got another boost from the candy.

When the table had been cleared and the company was waiting for glasses of rum, Hannibal said, "We met a man named Kanaka Boy, said he's a trader. What do you know about him?"

Payette gave them a look of amazement. Then he calmed himself. "I want to say you kept company with a right bastard—pardon me, ladies. But I confess I'm not sure." He looked around at each of them, uncertain. "He seems more a nuisance than an adversary. We shall keep an eye on him."

The rum arrived, and Esperanza asked for a glass.

"Just a sip," Julia told Payette.

Hannibal proposed a toast—"to the glory of salmon." Esperanza joined in the ceremony of clinking glasses.

Payette looked nervously at Julia and Esperanza, and Julia took his meaning. "I must put the children to bed," she said.

She took Paloma's cradleboard from where it hung, put it on her back, and put her hands on the boys' shoulders.

"Aw, Mom," said the boys. She pushed them along.

"Esperanza," she said, "come."

"I want to stay up," said Esperanza.

Julia looked at Sam.

"She's an adult," he said.

Esperanza threw a snitty look at her mother's retreating back.

"Let me show you a map," said the Frenchman—he said he'd been born in Montreal. He took a big scroll from a side table. "As it happens, I'm proud of this document. I myself trained the young man who made it in the use of surveying instruments." He spread the scroll on the table.

Sam, Flat Dog, and Hannibal rose and leaned over the huge drawing.

"The Company has put this together from the information of all their partisans," said Payette. It displayed the entire Oregon country, from far north into Canada to the border with California and from the crest of the Rocky Mountains to the sea.

Sam was impressed. The mountain men kept their maps of the West in their heads. None except his friend Jedediah Smith had ever written down the streams and mountains, plains and deserts, and Diah's were lost when Comanches killed him on the Cimarron.

"After you crossed the Snake River plains and followed the river north here," Payette said, pointing, "you saw the Owyhee Mountains off to the southwest. On their far side is the Owyhee River. It heads up in the mountains and flows through here—a terrible desert, terrible—and on north to where it joins the Snake." He fingered a spot near his own fort. "Kanaka Boy's camp is somewhere here, according to report. However, he might move the camp often. You can never tell about these types. We don't really know where they are.

"We have reliable reports that Kanaka Boy and his merry men distill whiskey to trade to the Indians. Villainous practice, harmful to the Indians and certainly contrary to the Company's interest. Now that we're aware of his activities, the factors of the three forts, Vancouver, Walla Walla, and here, are keeping a wary eye on Mr. Kanaka, or is it Mr. Boy?

"Unless you have a weakness for excessive inebriation," Payette said, "I'd say that pilgrims like yourselves are safe from him.

"Now I'd suggest one more glass of rum. What do you say?" He poured for the men and cocked an eye at Esperanza.

"Please," she said.

This time Julia wasn't around to say no, and Sam didn't.

Esperanza accepted a full serving, gulped it down, and smiled at both her papas. Sam saw only a slight flush of tears in her eyes.

A terrific crash came from the kitchen. The door banged open. A young Hawaiian propped himself in the doorway with a bent arm, head pulpy and bloody from a beating. One legging was stained with blood. He staggered a step forward, said, "Help me," and fell hard to the floor.

Twenty-seven

"WHO ARE YOU?" Payette asked several times, and then in a sharper tone, "Who the devil are you?" He gave the boy another sip of rum to bring him back.

"Jay," the boy finally said in a weak voice. "Call me Jay."

The boy's face was a bloody mess, and his nose looked broken. One ear was torn half-off, and blood was in his hair. His clothes looked like he'd been smashed into the mud several times. Underneath the blood, though, Julia could see that this was a Kanaka boy of about fifteen or sixteen, still beardless, a boy whose face had once been pretty in the Hawaiian way.

"Help me," he said.

"Let's have a closer look," said Payette.

Julia and Esperanza cleared the table, and the men lifted Jay onto it.

"I'll get hot water and clean cloths," said Julia. She and Esperanza disappeared into the kitchen.

Payette felt of the nose.

"Ow!" said Jay, and jerked his head away. That made him roar, "Ow!" a lot louder.

"It will heal," said Payette.

He pulled up the right legging and inspected the wound. "You've been shot," he said, "straight through, between bone and tendon."

Seeing blood on the shirt, Sam reached for the ribs. "Any injuries here?"

Jay covered up his chest with his arms. "They only beat me in the face."

"Who?" said Payette.

"Kanaka Boy and his men." Jay hesitated. "I wanted to leave . . . his outfit. Boy doesn't allow that."

Sam, Hannibal, and Flat Dog looked at each other, thinking there must be more to the story.

Jay tried to struggle up onto one elbow and fell back. He looked at Sam and Flat Dog. "You have to help me. Boy will kill me."

Julia put a pot of hot water near the boy's head, and Esperanza dropped clean cloths into it. "Be still," Julia said. "I'm going to sew that earlobe back in place. This is going to hurt."

She nodded to Sam and Flat Dog, and they held Jay's head hard, the injured ear turned up.

Julia produced a needle and thread from somewhere and sewed. Jay gritted his teeth, growled, and banged his feet, but he didn't cry out. The two men kept a vice grip on his head.

Then Julia washed the blood off his face and felt gingerly of the jaw, cheekbones, and forehead. "I don't think anything's broken except the nose."

Esperanza studied the face with an expression Sam couldn't read.

Jay was in a daze, maybe from the pain of the sewing.

"Those gashes are going to leave scars," Flat Dog said.

"I'm afraid you won't be pretty any longer," said Julia.

"Just as well in a lad," said Payette.

Jay muttered something.

"What did you say?" said Sam.

"Help. Please help me."

"So we are doing," said Payette.

"I mean you Americans," said Jay. "Please help me. Take me with you, down the river. If I stay here, Boy will find me and kill me."

"Shush," said Julia. "Get a good night's sleep and we'll talk about everything tomorrow."

"I'm scared."

"You'll be safe with us tonight," said Sam. "I promise."

Sam and Hannibal supported Jay under the shoulders, got him through the dining room, out into a night lit bright by the moon, and finally to their brush hut.

Jay looked at it, then at them, and seemed to recoil. He looked across at Flat Dog and Julia ducking into their lodge. Then back at the brush hut, where there would be barely room for the three of them.

"May I . . . ?" Jay couldn't get it out. He met Julia's eyes. "May I . . . ?"

Sam saw something happen in Julia's eyes. "Of course," she said. "Come into the tipi with us. You'll feel safer."

She came forward, wrapped her own blanket around Jay, and led him to the lodge.

"What do you think?" Sam asked.

Flat Dog and Hannibal spoke at the same time. "It's a risk."

Julia rematerialized in the darkness of the lodge door and came to them. "You will not," she said, "think for a moment that we can ride off and leave this poor boy."

Part Three

Twenty-eight

SAM, HANNIBAL, AND Flat Dog built a rope corral for the hobbled horses, from cottonwood to cottonwood in the bottom-land near the river. From her cradleboard Paloma watched Julia and Esperanza put up the tipi for the night. Azul and Rojo chased a sage chicken around and around a log. The bird didn't want to fly, and the boys wanted to whack it with a stick and turn it into supper. They tried this trick often and succeeded seldom.

"I'm still thirsty," said Flat Dog.

The three men walked back into the water calf deep and slurped out of both hands, cupped.

Hannibal said, "Don't you like Jay?"

Sam shrugged. "If I'm going to pick up more children, it would be nice to get laid along the way."

Hannibal and Flat Dog laughed. Their friend had one child the usual way, Esperanza, and then adopted Tomás. Now Jay, a

Hawaiian on the lam, seemed to be adopting Sam. And Sam hadn't had a mate in seven years.

He was now a determined bachelor. His first marriage lasted nine months, and Meadowlark died in childbirth. His long affair with Paloma Luna ended in cancer. He had made up his mind that, for him, matrimony was a blight.

They looked across at Jay, who was gathering the small limbs for the night's fire. Soon they would drag some bigger logs over.

"I don't get it, though," said Sam. "He always rides along with Julia and Esperanza. They don't need him to mind the packhorses."

"He's getting well," said Hannibal. "Getting well in the body and the head and the heart. He's had bad things happen. Worse, I expect, than he has let on."

Julia had implied the same. So while Sam, Hannibal, and Flat Dog rode ahead and on the flank every day, scouting for enemies, Jay walked his horse along with the women. Then, in the evenings, he hung around Sam like a kid or a dog.

Sam said, "If Kanaka Boy is after his ass, he ought to help us keep an eye out for him."

Hannibal said Jay could also help with a little of the other men's work, like taking care of the horses, sharing watch, and hunting.

"Not that he could do those without a rifle," said Sam. A boy of fifteen without a rifle, it was an odd thing.

Sam and Flat Dog both grabbed limbs of a downed trunk. "I'm thinking something," said Flat Dog. He said nothing more until they set the heavy log down for a moment's rest. He turned to Sam and said, "*Ba'te.*"

"Jay?"

"Yes."

"Didn't think of that."

"What is it?" asked Hannibal.

"Man-woman," said Sam.

Most tribes had them, men who dressed as women and lived as

women, often even married men. They weren't what people back in the States called queer, exactly. They were called by the spirits to live that way, just as others might be called to be a warrior or medicine man or even a contrary. Men-women were commonplace among the Crows and were honored as walking a sacred path.

Hannibal took a thoughtful look but said nothing.

Sam and Flat Dog dragged the log to the camp and dropped it. They looked around to make sure, and only Julia and Esperanza were nearby.

"Maybe we figured out why Jay seems odd," Flat Dog told his wife.

She looked at him.

"Ba'te."

"Man-woman?" said Julia.

Sam said, "Seems that way to me, too. Jay is *ba'te*."

Julia blinked at him several times in surprise.

Esperanza said, "That's dumb. He is no such thing."

But Julia, considering, said, "That may be it. In fact, I'm sure that's it."

"I think," said Sam, "that from now on we better call him he-she and him-her.

Flat Dog chuckled. "Let's not do that."

WHEN THEY WERE two days' ride from the Walla Walla River, Jay broke his habit of never looking Sam in the eyes. "I have a big request," Jay said in his melodic English. "Can we stay at the Methodist mission instead of the fort?"

They were sitting at the fire after supper, enjoying their plentiful coffee. Everyone waited for Jay to go on. The mission was two easy days' ride east of the fort.

"Boy worked at the fort. So did I. Everyone knows us. If I go there, word will get back to him fast."

"I want to stay at the mission anyway," said Julia. "Near

Narcissa Whitman." The two had met at rendezvous four years ago. Narcissa was definitely not the stereotype of a missionary wife. Instead of being appalled by the mountain men and Indians, she seemed delighted by them. They were delighted by her red-gold hair, full breasts, and merry laugh.

"I have to be honest with you. Me being there will make it dangerous for all of us."

Quickly, Sam said, "Us?"

Now Jay hung his head again. "I was hoping to go on to Fort Vancouver with you." He waited a moment and looked up. "The truth is, I'm terrified."

"Of course you may go with us," said Julia.

Sam took his time with what he had to say. "We're planning to spend the winter on the Walla Walla. We're going to trade for a lot of horses, break them to the saddle or the harness, and sell them to the Americans at the settlements on the Willamette."

"That's how we're going to make our money to get started in California," put in Hannibal.

Jay looked like a deer about to bolt.

"Of course you may go with us," Julia repeated. She spoke in a tone hinting that men are hopeless.

"You know there's no going over the mountains with the herd until spring," Sam said. "Too much snow."

"Then I can help," Jay said eagerly. "I know the trail over the mountains. It goes behind Mount Hood."

"But won't word get back to Boy?" asked Sam.

"The Whitman mission will be all right. No Kanakas work there. I'll be careful."

"Then we'll spend the winter with the Methodists," said Julia.

Sam looked at Jay. He seemed to be a member of the family now. Sam kind of liked him, a sweet kid with a good heart. But why didn't he just say he was *ba'te*?

Twenty-nine

NARCISSA WHITMAN BOUNDED down the steps of the mission house and swung Julia by the hands. "I can't believe it. I can't believe it. This is wonderful."

She insisted on hugging each of the boys, which made them pull sour faces, and she lifted little Paloma out of her cradleboard and kissed her face over and over.

Narcissa was thoroughly the vivacious woman Julia remembered from rendezvous. She looked up at her friend's husband, Marcus, the physician, standing at the top of the stairs. A shadow cut his face in half at a slant, and Julia thought he seemed more somber than he used to, much more.

Then she saw that he was holding the hand of a child about two years old. Narcissa followed her glance.

"This is our Alice Clarissa!" she exclaimed.

Alice jumped down the steps two at a time and into her

mother's arms. She immediately stuck her thumb into her mouth and peered round-eyed and wary at Julia and the kids.

"She's not used to strangers," Narcissa said. "Well, strangers that aren't Indians."

Julia thought, *But we are Indians*.

"I'm so glad to see you again," exclaimed Narcissa. This time it sounded like a question.

"I'm going home to California," Julia said. "We all are. The mountain life is changing."

"Oh, it is," said Narcissa enthusiastically. "We got six new missionaries right at the start, they came by sea, and five more families have joined us here at Wailatpu just this summer. We believe that tens of thousands of Americans will come to Oregon over the next decade."

Julia decided not to say that was the reason her husband and their friends were leaving the mountains for California.

"I'm sure you'll be so glad to live in a house again," said Narcissa.

"I will," said Julia. "Even more for the children's sake than mine."

"I should say so. Let's walk around the grounds," Narcissa bubbled on. "You must tell me everything, and I will show you all we've done.

"Wait." Her way was to make sudden movements with her head and hands, stop-start, the way a bird turns its gaze. "Where is your husband? Who is with you?"

When Julia pointed out the men unloading the packhorses and explained that Sam Morgan and Hannibal MacKye were along as well, and a Hawaiian boy named Jay, Narcissa got more excited. "We'll see them after our little tour."

The mission grounds were fine, set on a peninsula between two branches of the Walla Walla River, with the big house next to the main river. "We have more than two hundred acres under cultivation," Narcissa said, sweeping her arm to include it all. "Those little hills"—she pointed to the east—"feed our horses and cows, even in the winter."

She pointed out the Whitmans' large home, not of logs but sawn boards. Though they weren't yet whitewashed, she had a front door painted bright green. Clustered nearby stood a blacksmith shop, a mill, and a millpond. The new families were busy putting up basic shelter for the coming winter.

"Not only are we self-sufficient in growing our own food," she said, "we are teaching the Cayuses to be farmers. They borrow any plow we have and break the ground themselves. They are eager to own hogs, hens, and cattle, and several of them have obtained them already."

Julia thought there was something brittle in Narcissa's enthusiasm. Perhaps the four years of life in the wilds had aged her. The red-gold hair seemed not so lustrous, and Narcissa now wore thick glasses.

Flat Dog walked up, and Narcissa shook his hand eagerly. He waved at Dr. Whitman, still standing at the front door watching.

"My husband is telling me without saying so," said Julia, "that it's time for me and Esperanza to put up the lodge. Mind you, we've taught the men to help out."

"I'll come and say hello to everyone."

The adults were old friends except for Jay, introduced by Julia. Sam, Hannibal, and Flat Dog all knelt to say hello to Alice Clarissa, who wouldn't let go of her mother's hand.

"I have a great idea," said Narcissa. "You get your shelter up, and we'll have tea at the house late this afternoon. Just us ladies."

Which was just what Julia wanted.

ESPERANZA WAS SURPRISED when the time came and her mother asked Jay to come along. A man? At a ladies' event? She wondered what her mother had up her sleeve. *Mother is odd.*

When they came in, all three of them could see the surprise on

Narcissa's face. Everyone flushed with embarrassment. Perhaps their hostess was puzzled that they'd brought their Owyhee servant along, but she was gracious. "Welcome to our home. I get so little company. For this special occasion I've made shortbread, and a very good English tea with real cream from our cows."

Narcissa gestured at a low table actually set with a linen cloth, damasked napkins, and fine china. Julia smiled broadly. This was what she wanted Esperanza to experience. "So, the mission board has sent out your fine things."

"A gift from Mother, come all the way around Cape Horn, can you imagine?

"Alice, would you bring the cups and spoons? They're set out in the kitchen, one for each person.

"Speaking of fine things, here's a dazzler. "At our mission at Lapwai we have a printing press."

"A printing press?" said Julia, amazed. Lapwai was to the east, the Methodist post among the Nez Percés.

"We've printed the New Testament in the Nez Percé language," said Narcissa proudly, or at least she tried for pride.

Julia couldn't help thinking of what her husband would say. "Those people don't read Nez Percé, or some missionary's written version of Nez Percé, any better than they read English. It's not a written-down language."

Alice appeared at that moment trying to carry too many cups, and Esperanza rescued her.

Narcissa said, "While this tea steeps, may I show you around the house?" It was huge, and Julia was curious.

Beyond the parlor a dining hall. "We have so many people to feed. And this," Narcissa said as she passed into the next rooms, "is the Indian hall, a necessity. The greatest trial to a woman's feelings is to have her cooking and eating rooms always filled with dirty Indians, men, especially at mealtime. Now we devote this room to them especially, and don't let them go into the other part of the house at all."

She passed on to the kitchen and pantry.

"It sounds unkind, but they are so filthy, we must clean up after them. We have come here to elevate them and not to suffer ourselves to sink down to their standard."

That's what people will say about my husband and children, Julia thought. *Filthy. But their missions and towns, with their privies, smell worse than any Crow village.*

She saw Alice Clarissa with her hand in her mouth. The child had dipped the entire appendage into the cream and was sucking at one end while it dripped off her elbow at the other.

They swept into a large bedroom with a four-poster bed and—Narcissa showed this with an impish smile—a chamber pot. She went to the window. "The privy is outside. Tell them what a privy is, Alice Clarissa."

"It's where you poo. I'm learning, but the seat is too high."

Julia told Esperanza softly in Crow what "poo" meant.

On they went through the servants' bedroom to a room with a bookcase, a medicine case, and a desk where Dr. Whitman did his work, as he was doing now. It had a fine big window that let the morning sun in.

"We have seven large windows," said Narcissa, "some small ones, and oil-fueled lamps."

She showed them what Esperanza thought the greatest curiosity of all, a chest of drawers built into the wall.

"Our accommodations are fine," said Narcissa, "and that is deliberate. Part of what we do for the Natives is show them the refinements that civilization provides. To Christianize them we must first civilize them." Her voice quivered with hope.

Esperanza gave her mother a funny look, and Julia smiled back. *Yes, part of civilization, or at least the American version, is the fancy English some people speak.*

"Ha, he," said Alice Clarissa, "one day I try to hide from my mommy in the bottom drawer."

They found their way back to the parlor. The shortcakes and tea, Esperanza thought, were amazing. She watched her mother carefully for manners. Esperanza knew the Americans and British put a lot of stock in deportment, especially at the table. How odd, in her opinion, that they seemed to her not to know common courtesies. They didn't know how to listen to another person with full attention and how to avoid being intrusive, yet they made a big issue out of table manners. She noticed that Jay seemed to know what to do at table and was surprised.

When they were finished eating, Julia said, "You may have been surprised that I brought Jay along, but I wanted you to meet him. He's very interesting, and has quite a story to tell." She turned her chair a little toward Jay, raised her eyebrows, and said, "Jay, we are not taken in by your breechcloth and leggings. Why don't you tell us your real name? And why are you a woman living in disguise as a boy?"

Narcissa made a little squeak and put her hand over her mouth.

THE MAN-WOMAN SAID, "My name is Lei, Lei Palua. I'm sorry, for what I've done; I . . . I was so afraid."

"I know, Lei, but we must have answers." Julia was tolerating no evasions.

"How much do you want to know?"

"Everything."

Narcissa got up, saying, "I think we need another pot of tea."

Alice Clarissa held up two dolls Hannibal made for her from deerskin and dewclaws and banged them together, like a war.

They drank more tea, and the whole story came out. How Lei had thought Kanaka Boy was the most exciting man she'd ever met. She was enthusiastic about his plan for Hawaiians to be traders, not just laborers. Ran off with him to the camp he and the men had picked out, a horrible place in a horrible desert. How the men made whiskey and stayed drunk all the time. How they brought up other women and passed them around. How they sold whiskey to the Indians. How she began to think of escape. Then the terrible day when they killed all the Digger men and the small children and took the women and older children as slaves. Delicately, looking at Alice Clarissa, Lei told how the ruffians used the women.

Lei paused for breath. She looked into the eyes of her listeners nervously but saw only empathy. She gathered her courage and went on. She told how she escaped and fled down the Owyhee River, hoping to get to the fort. How Boy caught her. How his men raped her. And Boy took her to the hot springs to kill her.

"I, I overcame him the only way I could. He's fond of laudanum. I gave him triple the amount he's used to, and he passed out."

Julia looked to see that Alice Clarissa was paying no attention and asked, "Did you kill him?"

"No." Lei started to say one thing and said another. "No, I couldn't." She decided not to mention the castration.

"Well, you've got plenty of reason to be scared."

"Please." Lei hated the begging tone in her voice, but she couldn't help it. "If I stay anywhere in this country, all of Oregon, he will find me and kill me. There are Hawaiians working at every post. If anyone sees me, my mother, my sister, my friends, the news will fly to him. That's why I came up with the deception. Jay."

Now the shame left her face, and her voice took an edge. "Yes, true, Boy is a force of nature. But he is searching for his wife. His men will ask about a woman. So I cannot be Lei, only Jay."

All four women looked inside themselves at this reality and were stilled by it.

"We'll keep your secret," said Julia.

"From Sam and Hannibal and Flat Dog, too? I'm so scared."

Julia looked at Narcissa and answered, "From everyone who is not in this room." Narcissa nodded.

"I have to go to California," said Lei. "Lots of people at Fort Walla Walla know me. My mother is at Fort Vancouver. I'm not safe until I get out of Oregon."

Julia nodded, half to herself. "Yes."

For a long moment no one spoke. Then Lei said, "How did you spot me?"

Julia said, "A woman knows."

Thirty

JOE MEEK SHOWED up low in his soul. "Rain left me," he said. His Nez Percé wife, that is, the sister of Doc Newell's wife, Clap. "Back at Fort Hall she left me."

Julia handed him a coffee cup, full to the brim and steaming.

"But I see Helen Mar," said Esperanza. She nodded toward Joe's little daughter, playing with Doc's son at the Newell lodge nearby.

"That woman, she done left husband and child. If that ain't poor bull. I'm so lonesome I could snuggle up to a porcupine."

Esperanza laughed. She liked Joe Meek—he was a clown. Now a sad clown, which made her like him even more.

"Jay," said Julia, "would you grind us some more coffee?" Jay spent her time with Julia and Esperanza now, still dressed as Jay. She opened the leather pouch and began to use one rock to smash the beans on a big, flat rock Flat Dog had dragged to the front of the lodge for the purpose.

"Joe," Julia said, "have your wives left you before?"

Joe shrugged. Everyone knew the answer to that question.

She put an arm around his shoulders. "Two, at least?"

"Two," he said. Joe was only thirty, but he'd been in the mountains eleven years.

"So you've had three *wives*," Julia said, her arm still around him. She gave Esperanza a mischievous look. They both knew he'd had countless women.

Joe shrugged.

"You won't be lonely long." Julia took her arm away. "So how was the trip?"

"Sam and Flat Dog was right. Them three wagons? Trouble three times over."

Which everyone knew from the shape the wagons showed up in.

"On the Snake River plains we couldn't get the wagons through the sagebrushes, around the sagebrushes, in between the sagebrushes, or over the sagebrushes. Maybe we coulda cut down ever' one of the gnarly plants from Fort Hall to Fort Boise. When I think on it, maybe we coulda dug a tunnel from one fort to t'other and gone under them sagebrushes. What we done, though, we took the wagon boxes off and left 'em. Make somebody a nice fire one night. Brought just the running gear along."

Jay filled the pot with water and put it back on the fire to brew.

Joe grinned. "Dr. Marcus Whitman," he said, "he is making heroes of me and Doc—first men to get wagons to Oregon. We is the wave of the future, he says. On that case the women will have to be satisfied with getting their wagons here in the shape of skeletons and they'll have to go naked in Oregon. I mean, the living room will be naked, the kitchen will be naked, all their possessions will be naked, not the people. I'd druther it was the other way.

"I'd say, though, leaving them furnishings along the trail will be a service. Keep them as follows from getting lost."

Julia asked, "Are we few the wave of the future, Joe? Hundreds of Americans to come?"

"I don' know. Ever' one thinks so," said Joe. "But white women can't stand life so disorder-like. Ain't nobody out here follows their ideas of order, particular not the Indians."

"Don't talk like that, Joe," said Sam Morgan, walking up. "Julia's a white woman." Which was only more or less true.

Jay checked the pot and said, "Coffee's ready."

Sam sat down at the fire, and Doc Newell slipped in next to him. "Joe's just downhearted," Doc said. "Surely and truly, we are the future, right here as we stand. Oregon is the greatest country in the world for the agriculturalist." For a mountain man Doc Newell talked funny.

Sam watched Jay pour them coffee. He'd begun to have a different idea about this boy.

"No more of that talk that divides us into white and Indian," said Julia.

"White people are about to come in a tidal wave," said Doc, "because of the missionaries."

Sam hated this subject. Yes, red and white. Yes, waves of Americans. And the end of the Crow way of life, just as Owl Woman predicted. The whole Plains Indian way of life. Still, he was glad about his own outfit, and Doc and Joe's—more mixed-blood children going to settle on the western coast.

Joe said, "Some wagoneers we is. Them wagons is sure finished, and they near finished us."

Doc said to the party, "We're obliged to make a decision to leave the wagons here. Big mountains ahead, the Cascades. The route is the river gorge. If you go through with horses, it's narrow and rough. If you raft the river, there are big waterfalls, and you have to portage."

"What I hear is, it ain't no wagon road," said Joe. "Them

wagons cost me my wife," he said. "She wouldn't have no truck with wagon-driving fools."

"Maybe it was Oregon," said Doc. "She just wanted to stay near her people. Or maybe it was your drinking. Or your tomcatting around."

"Doc here," complained Joe, "he's got it all figgered out."

"I do. The way to work it is, float the wagons the rest of the way," said Doc. "From here the Hudson's Bay Company takes the fur down in bateaux. We'll use the river as our highway."

"Where I come from," said Joe, "we'd be honest and say the road stops more'n two hundred miles from where we mean to go."

Doc sighed. Finally he said, "Excuse me, please," and walked toward his lodge. He turned back and said, "The bateaux will be starting downriver in about two weeks, and the Newell party will be going." As he walked on, his spine was straighter and stiffer than it needed to be.

"Appears your brother-in-law doesn't see things the same as you," said Sam.

"Ex-brother-in-law," said Joe.

"And what about your daughter, and Doc's son?" asked Julia.

Joe twisted his mouth. "We're leaving 'em with the Whitmans for now. We've done wore 'em out."

The children did look wasted.

"The Whitmans are kind to take them in," said Julia.

"Good people," said Joe.

"More for Narcissa to do," said Julia.

"Joe," said Esperanza, "come with me. I want to show you my new trick." Esperanza had been learning trick riding from Uncle Hannibal and Papa Sam for years, and Joe was her favorite audience.

"Let's go, sweet pie," said Joe.

SAM UNHOBBLED PALADIN and led her toward the ring Esperanza would use. She would want the more experienced mare as well as her own pony. Hannibal and Flat Dog fell in with him and strolled to the ring she had laid out, using willow branches. Esperanza waited, her pony, Vermilion, standing free. Jay and Joe Meek sat cross-legged and watched eagerly.

Sam looked from his daughter to the man-woman, and inside himself he shrugged. Ever since they left her home village, Esperanza had been moody. Sometimes she was cheerful and like a kid again. Most of the time she was irritable. At those times she wouldn't talk to anyone but Jay the *ba'te,* and that helped, Sam didn't know how. So Jay was fine with Sam.

He took the lead off Paladin and looked at Esperanza and declared, "Let the good times roll."

Esperanza did a running vault onto her pony from behind. The difference was that she came to rest on her feet, not her bottom, and immediately stood up, hands held high. At a cluck Vermilion began to canter around the ring.

"Hot damn!" shouted Joe Meek. He whooped. He put two fingers in his mouth and whistled.

Esperanza glided by, balanced on the back of her loping horse. As she passed them, she made a curtsey to her small audience.

"I ain't seen nothin' like that afore," said Joe.

Sam said, "These Indians haven't, either."

Thirty-one

"THERE, SEE," JULIA said. The whole meadow was squishy with water and violet with flowers. "They're camas, a kind of lily, and you can eat the bulb." Mother, daughter, and Jay spread out, holding sacks to fill.

"Only the violet ones," said Julia. "The ones with the white flowers, that's the death camas."

As she picked, Esperanza felt drawn to the few lilies with the white flowers. Squatting, she pulled a white-petaled plant with her right hand and a lilac-petaled one with her left hand. The bulbs looked just alike. Life and death, just alike.

She looked around and saw that her mother and Jay were stooped and picking well away, too far to see what Esperanza was doing.

Esperanza felt the allure. The bulbs that you boil or roast? Or the ones that end all troubles?

She had known for half a moon now. One morning, when she was lying flat on her stomach and letting her mother do the breakfast work by herself, she felt a flip-flop in her belly. Then it came again, a sensation just like a fish was wiggling inside her.

She knew what it was. She had put her hand on the bellies of several other young women carrying babies. She even knew the word for it in English—the baby was said to quicken. The difference was, the other young women were glad to be filled with child.

Esperanza was . . . she didn't know what.

With child. One night with Prairie Chicken and now with child. But without husband.

Each morning, when the rising sun made the east side of the tipi glow, she felt the movement, lifted her blankets, and watched the skin of her belly make a wave.

With child, and with terror.

She let the death camas drop onto the mushy ground and put the other into her sack.

She looked long at the white one and then made herself look away.

I have to do something.

THE MEN WERE pitching in to help with the work, too. Sam and Hannibal helped build cabins—they felled logs, dragged them to the building sites, trimmed them with drawknives, and joined them at the corners.

Flat Dog found a piece of work he really liked. One of the missionaries, Barker, came up and said, "I had an indescribable accident on my mare." He showed them his saddle, which was split lengthwise down the middle. You could fold it like a book.

"We'll try to do som'p'n' on it," said Whitfield, a new comrade who was a practical man.

When Barker was out of hearing, Hannibal picked up the

smashed saddle and inspected it. "He must be an indescribable rider," Hannibal said.

None of them could guess exactly what had happened. "Some way that mare of his came down flat on her back," said Flat Dog.

"Coulda broke him instead of the saddle," said Whitfield with a sly smile. He didn't appear to be as sincere in his Methodism as the others.

They knew he'd worked a little for a saddle maker. "I can't carve a new saddle tree," he said, "but I can take this'n apart 'n' save the leathers. We take the rig over to the fort, it'll be a whole lot less money than startin' from scratch."

Flat Dog spoke loud and clear. "Let me help. I want to learn."

They found some tools and a worktable in a shed. Then Flat Dog learned more than he bargained for.

"There is more'n fifty pieces of leather in a saddle," said Whitfield. Carefully, together, they began to detach the stirrups, stirrup leathers and fenders, jockeys, cinches, skirts, and pieces Flat Dog hadn't even heard of. Sometimes stitching had to be cut, other times lacing undone. He realized what an ignoramus he was when Whitfield had to explain that the tree, the wooden frame everything depended on, was carved from a single piece of wood covered with wet rawhide, which shrank as it dried to make a tight surface.

"This tree is hardwood," said Whitfield. "Cain't get nothin' like that here. The saddler'll probably make it out'n fir."

The way the many pieces of leather fit together was damned clever—Flat Dog had never realized. Before the afternoon was gone, he was beginning to think how much he liked this work and how well it went with breeding horses.

He kept his discovery to himself.

JAY FOUND HIS own special work to do. He was comfortable being viewed as *ba'te*, and as everyone knew, one skill of *ba'te*s was art. So Jay got an idea to help beautify the main house.

At first he borrowed paper, pen, and ink from Dr. Whitman, and the Whitmans acted thrilled with the little sketches Jay did of mission life. Narcissa had several framed and hung on the parlor walls.

But Jay wasn't happy with the work—it wasn't his kind of thing. When he discovered that Dr. Whitman also had colored pencils, Jay struck out in a new direction. He filled pages with plants—a whole page of willow branches in leaf, for instance, and not just in the realistic colors of red-brown and green. He made the leaves every color in the rainbow. And his plants weren't separate, as they actually grew along the river, but all swirled together like one gigantic, growing thing, a world of limbs and leaves without earth or air.

Everyone loved them.

Jay proceeded to draw entire pages of blossoms of every color, an interconnected design that omitted stems and leaves. Once he made pages of horses' heads, except that the heads were tiny and the manes huge—the page seemed like a storm of hair.

Marcus and Narcissa started giving Jay coins for the drawings, and he was grateful. In a pinch, coins might mean freedom.

NARCISSA HEARD STEPS and then a knock. She could see out the window that it was Hannibal. He came to the main house toward the end of every day and spent an hour drinking coffee and talking to Dr. Whitman. She approved—they were the only two really educated men at Wailatpu. Narcissa thought Hannibal's education had made him too smart for his own good—or at least for his immortal soul—but she was glad her husband had this companionship.

Husband and wife put down their books, Marcus's a medical text and Narcissa's the New Testament. "I'll bring some coffee," she said, and stepped toward the kitchen.

"Hello, Alicia Clarisia," said Hannibal. This was his pet name for the girl.

"Hello, Hannibalee Smanabalee." She was playing on the floor with the two dolls he'd made her. He saw that her mother had stitched together a pair of dresses from scraps of cloth, probably to keep them decent.

Narcissa came back with two cups of steaming brew.

"I'll help finish up supper," she said.

"Ha, he," Alice Clarissa said, "supper 'most ready. Alice help Mama, go get some water," said the child, and trotted off behind her mother.

Marcus leaped into the subject of the mission's struggles with the Cayuse people. Not Hannibal's favorite topic, but these days Marcus could think of nothing else. "It's hard," said Marcus. "We told them it would be good for them to put several lodges together for a place to attend worship out of the open air."

Hannibal thought that the only place he ever felt an impulse to worship was in the open air, but he just smiled at his friend.

"They said they wouldn't do it—they wanted to worship in our new house. We said no. Having them in the house drives Narcissa crazy."

"I know it does." Hannibal had lived with Indian people for twenty years in perfect comfort. On the other hand, he'd grown up in the cabin his white father and Delaware mother kept next-to-godliness clean.

"They came up with a good one. They asked us if there aren't houses in heaven to worship in. That stumped me."

Since Hannibal thought Marcus's religion was castles in air, that is, metaphoric castles, he had nothing to say.

"We told them our house was to live in and we can't have them worship there for they would make it so dirty and fill it so full of lice that we could not live in it."

"I have an idea," said Hannibal. "You could start dwelling in a tipi and move it once a week a or so, leaving the lice behind."

"Your sense of humor is wicked, my friend. Anyway, when we couldn't agree, they started in again about us paying them for their land we live on. And they complained that we don't feed them more, and let them run all over the house, et cetera, et cetera."

"Tell them," Hannibal said, "that you are paying them with food, and by teaching them to grow food." He more or less believed this.

"I didn't know this would be such a hard life. More so, Narcissa didn't know it. These people, well, their Nez Percé cousins, sent a delegation all the way to St. Louis to ask to learn the Bible."

"I knew those Indians," Hannibal said. He had hinted at this but now decided to tell his friend the whole truth. "That was a big misunderstanding. The Indians thought that the white man's God had powerful medicine, to be able to give white people guns and pots and wheeled wagons and thousands of beads and mirrors and far-seeing telescopes and other wonders. They wanted to get such great medicine for themselves. What they were after was material, not spiritual."

Marcus considered these words. "I don't believe that. God works in mysterious ways his wonders to perform. He was simply using material goods to open their minds."

Hannibal said nothing.

"Not that their minds seem open. We thought they would welcome the Gospel—the good news!—with open hearts."

Hannibal nodded in a kindly way.

Through the closed kitchen door they heard the women who'd been gathering camas bring in their vegetables. Julia and Esperanza poked their heads in to say hello to the men.

Esperanza said, "Where's Alice Clarissa?"

"Helping her mother," said Marcus.

"She's not in the kitchen," said Julia.

A moment's conference showed that no one knew where Alice Clarissa could have gone. A cabinet door stood open. "I saw her climb up there," said a serving woman, "and take two cups."

"She said she was going to get water," said Narcissa.

"From the river?" Esperanza said, her throat tightening.

"No, she's afraid of the water. Probably from the barrels outside."

Esperanza stuck her head out the door and said, "I don't see her."

"She's really afraid of the water," said Narcissa. The words scratched her throat.

Esperanza ran toward the nearest spot on the riverbank. Why she ran she didn't know. The others walked along piecemeal, Marcus and Hannibal straggling behind.

Two cups floated in the eddy.

Esperanza jumped into the slow water. She swam back and forth. She sat on the bottom and peered around underwater.

The other women huddled on the bank and quailed.

When Hannibal and Marcus saw the cups, they dived in.

"Where would the eddy take her?" said Hannibal loudly.

Esperanza looked at the current, saw where, and waded straight toward a shadowed spot under the highest part of the bank.

When she got there, she dipped beneath the water and rose up with Alice Clarissa, limp in her arms.

They did what they knew to do. They pushed the water out of her lungs. They pressed on her chest to simulate breathing. Then they did those things over and over.

Narcissa wept quietly. Julia held her.

Esperanza sat and looked into the girl's eyes. The moment she saw the eyes, she knew Alice Clarissa was dead.

She put both her hands on her belly. She held life in her hands, death in her eyes.

Thirty-two

Narcissa wrote to her sister:

Your letter I received but a few days ago, or it would have been answered much sooner. You make some important inquiries concerning my treatment of my precious child, Alice Clarissa, now laying by me a lifeless lump of clay. Yes, of her I loved and watched so tenderly, I am bereaved. My Jesus in love to her and us has taken her to himself.

Last Sabbath, blooming in health, cheerful, and happy in herself and in the society of her much loved parents, yet in one moment she disappeared, went to the river with two cups to get some water for the table, fell in and was drowned. Mysterious event! We can in no way account for the circumstances connected with it, otherwise than that the Lord meant it should be so.

Here she recounted details of the realization and the search, then went on:

> *I had never known her to go to the river or to appear at all venturesome until within a week past. Previous to this she has been much afraid to go near the water anywhere, for her father had once put her in, which so effectually frightened her that we had lost that feeling of anxiety for her in a measure on its account. But she had gone; yes, and because my Saviour would have it so. He saw it necessary to afflict us, and has taken her away. Now we see how much we loved her, and you know the blessed Saviour will not have His children bestow an undue attachment upon creature objects without reminding us of His own superior claim upon affections. Take warning, dear sister, by our bereavement that you do not let your dear babe get between your heart and the Saviour, for you, like us, are solitary and alone and in almost the dangerous necessity of loving too ardently the precious gift, to the neglect of the giver.*

Thirty-three

"WHY WOULD I want to trade you horses, white man?" Amber Eyes smiled wickedly.

Sam looked at him and arranged his lips into a smile, more for himself than the Cayuse chief. This was a game, though Sam probably wouldn't enjoy it as much as Amber Eyes did. Sam wondered where the name came from. The eyes of the red-tailed hawk? Maybe that was his spirit animal. Sam would never know.

"I do not think you can afford our horses. The Cayuse people own the best horses in the world."

Actually, the Nez Percés had the biggest reputation for Appaloosas, but . . .

Sam said, "And you like to trade them for rifles, blankets, axes, cloth . . ."

"Sometimes," said Amber Eyes.

Sam did think Appaloosas were the best. They were perfectly

conformed, their markings beautiful. Most of them were short bodied and stocky, built for bursts of speed, which made them the ultimate buffalo runners. They had lots of bottom and could go at an easy pace all day. Sam had ridden his mare Paladin, an Appaloosa with the markings called medicine hat, for a decade and a half and would have no other mount.

Sipping, Amber Eyes looked across his coffee cup at Hannibal, who was silent. They'd agreed to let Sam start the negotiations.

It would take hours, perhaps days. But this was their chance. Several days ago the two rode over to Fort Walla Walla and used their letters of credit from American Fur to get all the trade goods they could, especially those favored by the Cayuses, the tribe that lived near the Whitman mission. This was the time to trade, and the stakes were high. These horses were the foundation of their new life in California.

"Perhaps you would like to walk out and see the herd," said Amber Eyes, setting his cup down.

They mingled with the beautiful animals. They talked with Amber Eyes about the conformation of this horse and that one. Hannibal lifted the front hoof of a limping pony and flicked a pebble out of the tender place. Soon Amber Eyes understood that he could not play the con artist with these men—they knew horses. When he said, "Good evening," he'd lost some of his cockiness.

As the two walked back to camp, Hannibal told Sam, "Lots of people have been eyeing our trade goods." During the day they kept the merchandise spread out under canvas near the tipi, minded by Flat Dog.

"Yeah," said Sam. "We're going to get a lot of horses."

"And train a lot of horses," said Hannibal, "sell them, and show up in California *flush*." They all dreamed of California more and more these days. It had become their word for hope.

"You know what else makes me feel good about California? Good, but strange?"

Hannibal watched his partner.

"For nearly twenty years we've been riding land that is free. The buffalo graze on it, everybody hunts on it, the water belongs to everyone same, your horses can get whatever grass they want. But in California we're going to have a piece of ground we own."

"You feel good about that?"

"Real good."

They took a few steps together while Sam thought. He said, "Let's invite Amber Eyes, his wife, and his children to dinner with our family."

Immediately Julia proposed to make something the Cayuses had probably never tasted, a creamed soup of carrots, potatoes, and onions, plus broiled deer meat, then a surprise to cap the evening—pudding.

"The wonders of civilization," said Sam.

It turned out that the Amber Eyes family thought the creamed soup strange. The pudding, on the other hand, was an even bigger hit than the sugary coffee—they scraped their bowls clean and looked disappointed that there wasn't more.

While they ate, Amber Eyes heard voices outside, jumped up, went out, and came back with three men. "My friend the leader of the Nez Percés is here. May he come in?"

"Sure," said Sam.

Three Nez Percés ducked in, and Amber Eyes introduced the leader, a tall, crane-like man named Ball, and two of his sons. Sam saw the look of immense intelligence in Ball's eyes and knew that he would be a leader of whatever people he was born among. "Join us for coffee," said Sam.

Ball told them that his small band was erecting lodges up the stream from the Cayuses. They had come for a visit with their friends.

"They often come to see us before the cold gets hard," said Amber Eyes, "and stay a couple of weeks."

Sam, Hannibal, and Flat Dog looked at each other with the

same thoughts in their minds. *What a stroke of luck. Trade, trade, trade.*

WHEN THE CAYUSES and Nez Percés had gone back to their camps and the children were asleep, the adults huddled around the inside fire against the crisp autumn night.

Hannibal made his case. "A week over to the Nez Percé village, a week back—we can't afford the time. We need to be working with the new horses."

"So the problem," said Jay, "is how to get them to make the ride back and forth and bring the ponies to us."

Sam looked at him. Jay was acting more like a real member of the outfit recently.

"People say the Nez Percé horses are better," said Esperanza.

Sometimes she spoke up just like a man. Sam wondered if that was his fault or to his credit.

"They are better," said Hannibal. "Better breeders." He was the only one of them who'd ever been to the Nez Percé home at Lapwai.

"How can we get this done?" repeated Flat Dog.

"Won't pay to give them enough trade goods to make it worth their while."

They stared into the fire, stumped.

"Easy," said Jay.

Everyone looked and waited.

"Have Esperanza give them a show. Demonstrate liberty training, just like she's been practicing. Here's my bet—they'll want to learn it."

Esperanza squealed with pleasure.

Sam jumped in. "They'll be so bamboozled they'll ask us to teach some of their young men the techniques."

"They'll stay for weeks," said Jay.

"We'll take payment in horses," said Hannibal.

"Damn right," said Flat Dog.

Thirty-four

ESPERANZA SAT TO the side of the lodge, half in shadow, dyeing the strands of rawhide on the hatband that was Papa Sam's annual present. She should have had it ready by rendezvous, but she just couldn't put her mind to it. The only good thing about it was that when she did a chore, any chore, her mother left her alone.

Julia was building up the fire in the center of the tipi. The autumn day was crisp enough to make the fire feel good. She started chopping carrots for dinner. Now that they were in civilization, or halfway in, she had a cutting board for this kind of work, which felt good.

She checked the water in the pot that hung over the fire and saw that it wasn't enough.

"Esperanza, will you go to the river and get us more water?" Two kettles sat by the door flap.

"Mom, I'm busy."

"Esperanza!"

The girl-woman threw down the strand she was working on, got up stomping, and huffed out of the lodge with the kettles.

While she was gone, Julia started chopping potatoes. They were a luxury—so many years with just wild onions and Jerusalem artichokes—and she relished every kind of vegetable.

Esperanza trudged back in, set one kettle by the door and the other next to her mother, and headed back to her private place.

"Esperanza, would you chunk that deer meat? I'm running late."

Esperanza just kept rubbing the blue dye, which she'd made by crushing berries, onto the strip of leather. The work calmed her hands.

"Esperanza?"

"Mother, I'm busy. Get Jay to do it."

"Jay already has a chore. You're a member of this family, too."

Esperanza sighed, came to the fire, and reached for one of the long strips of loin. Her mother handed her the cutting board.

"Why are you so moody?" asked Julia.

"You just don't understand." Esperanza's hands were trembling so much that she didn't dare start cutting.

"What don't I understand?"

Esperanza raised her butcher knife high and drove it hard into the board. She jumped up and headed for the door.

"You don't know anything about me!"

"I know," said Julia, in a tone that stopped Esperanza, "that when your baby is born, you'll have to start thinking about someone other than yourself."

Esperanza fled.

THE NEXT MORNING Esperanza got up before anyone stirred and slipped out of the lodge. She unstaked Vermilion and led him to the river for water. At least here no one would bother her.

The recollection of Alice Clarissa made her thoughts sink into the darkness at the bottom of the river. *No,* she told herself, *it's not that. Whenever I'm alone, whenever I have time to think, I get down. So why do I sit around with my chin in my hand and make things worse?* She let Vermilion splash into the shallows without a lead. He would come to her whistle.

These days she talked to no one, she avoided doing tasks, she didn't even play with Paloma. When Azul and Rojo suggested doing something together, she ignored them.

After Vermilion had some water but not too much, she led him to the practice ring. The ring was a sanctuary. The only time she wasn't down on herself was when she was practicing for her horse show. Joe helped her with that, and he made it even more fun. He would be along soon.

"REMINDER. IT'S THE first step you have to be ready for," Esperanza told him. "After that, it's just like riding. Get in the rhythm and stay there."

Joe started from the ground again, leaped to a sitting position on Vermilion, and stood up. Esperanza gave the hand signal, the horse went into a lope, and Joe kept his balance again.

"You've got it. You've really got it."

She'd started teaching him at rendezvous. Joe was a gifted athlete and learned fast. Now they were working up a surprise not only for the audience but for her teachers, Papa Sam and Uncle Hannibal.

"Now I'm going to add Paladin, so you can get used to her and the sound of her hoofs doesn't confuse you." She motioned Paladin into position behind Vermilion and gave both horses the signal to lope. They did, and Joe kept his balance. He even showed off by turning, facing backward, and sticking his tongue out at Esperanza.

"Great!" she shouted.

They did another dozen repetitions and quit.

They walked Vermilion and Paladin to the creek. The horses would drink and the riders would wash them down. The animals liked being rubbed with wet hides.

Esperanza felt herself slipping toward the blackness again.

Stop it! she told herself.

"You sure have been a pick-me-up," said Joe. "You brighten my day." He hadn't noticed her change of mood, hadn't even stopped chattering. "I'd be feeling low down if it wasn't for us doing this together."

Suddenly—didn't such things always come suddenly?—the truth hit Esperanza hard in the face. She didn't know why it hadn't come to her before.

She looked at Joe Meek in a new way, not a kid at an older friend but a woman at a man. She liked what she saw.

Time to do something.

ONE BY ONE Julia, Esperanza, and Jay ducked their heads and came out of the tipi. They ambled off toward the river, each carrying a bucket. "The moon is so bright," Esperanza said. "It's easy to see."

The nightly trip to the river made them uneasy, since Alice Clarissa's death.

Jay decided he couldn't wait any longer. "It's so bright I can see your baby on the way."

"What?"

"Soon even the men will notice," said Julia.

They squatted on the bank and dipped their buckets full.

"When is the baby due?" said Jay.

Esperanza didn't answer.

"Spring, from the look of you," said Julia. "That means Prairie Chicken is the father."

"Mother, mind your own business."

They stood up and started back toward the tipi.

Jay put an arm around Esperanza awkwardly. "She's trying to help you."

Esperanza pulled away and looked at her mother in the moonlight. "And what's your help?"

"Talk to Papa Flat Dog and Papa Sam. Tell them."

"Oh, sure." Esperanza had no idea what either of them would say.

"Tell them the truth," said Jay.

"I can take care of myself," said Esperanza. She set her bucket by the tipi door and strode off in another direction.

Thirty-five

"Showmanship," said Hannibal. He knew something about that—circus work will teach you to please a crowd. That was where he got the skill of trick riding and learned to train liberty horses. Audiences were always amazed by it—you freed the horses of saddle and rein and directed them with hand signals. Hannibal had added a refinement, whistling to get them to come to the bridle. That would be impressive enough, and Hannibal was making it showier. He and Esperanza tied ribbons and bells in the manes and tails of the two liberty horses, Sam's Paladin and her pony, Vermilion.

Sam and Flat Dog circulated among the Nez Percés and Cayuses and tipped everyone off about the big show down near the river. Soon a score of each were gathered around the ring, waiting.

Amber Eyes said to Sam, "No telling what you crazy white people will do." Sam considered it a weird comment, considering that Hannibal the ringmaster was half white and half Delaware and Esperanza, the star performer, was half white and half Crow.

Hannibal cried out in the Nez Percé language, "Ladies and gentlemen, here come the medicine horses."

Esperanza looked at the cluster of horses grazing fifty paces away. She put her fingers to her mouth and screeched out two ear-splitting whistles, each entirely different. Two horses, Paladin and Vermilion, immediately pranced toward her. People gasped at how beautiful they looked in their regalia. The two horses loped into the ring at the east entrance, as was proper, and at her hand signal began to canter around the ring.

Sam watched the crowd instead of the show. "Notice," called Hannibal, "that she can call the mounts to her from a distance. Think how useful that would be if you got knocked off your pony in a buffalo hunt. Or if your enemy was stealing your horse." Everyone laughed, and Sam could see that the men were really impressed with this idea.

Esperanza lowered her hand and drew a circle in the air next to her feet. Paladin and Vermilion came to the center and bowed to her. She jumped onto Vermilion and began to circle the ring bareback. Then she stood up. Even such expert horsemen as the Cayuses and Nez Percés had never seen such a stunt. The men gaped, and the women trilled.

Hannibal called out, "You can even go to war with a horse like this."

Joe Meek stepped into the ring, carrying a stone-headed club. Sam knew Esperanza and Joe had been working on something, but he didn't know what. Joe raised his club fiercely. Still standing, Esperanza rode Vermilion hard at Joe and brushed his shoulder. He faked falling down. Everyone laughed. Esperanza made a tight circle, jumped off the horse, and landed astride Joe, her fists in his face. The crowd hooted.

Like a flash Joe slipped out of his deerskin shirt and dashed to one side.

"The horse will even fight for you."

At Esperanza's hand signal Vermilion reared and then attacked Joe's shirt with his hoofs. He beat it into the dirt convincingly.

"One more amazing trick," called Hannibal.

Though Sam could hardly believe it, Joe jumped onto Vermilion. At Esperanza's signal the pony began to circle the ring. Paladin fell in close behind.

"I give you," boomed Hannibal, "the master clown Joe Meek! There's no man like Joe!"

As Vermilion kept cantering, Joe stood up on him. Sam didn't know Joe had learned this skill. They passed under a big cottonwood limb. Joe grabbed it, vaulted completely over it, and as he headed for the earth dropped toward Paladin's back. Except that he missed and banged his rump onto the ground.

People roared with laughter. Joe used his forefingers to make pretend tears coming down his cheeks.

They laughed harder.

Esperanza beamed at Sam, and he gave her a thumbs-up.

"Here's the best news," Hannibal shouted. "We can teach you this trick of calling your horses to come to you from a distance. We can even teach you to ride them standing up. We'll be here all winter, ready to give you this medicine. In exchange for horses."

They spent the rest of the day making promises and bargains.

That evening Sam wrote briefly to Grumble, informing his friend that the entire family was on the way, the horse-gathering enterprise was going very well, and they would all arrive in Monterey some time next summer. "I don't know that we will be new men, in your words Adam and Eve on a new continent," Sam wrote, "but we are ready to be Californios."

Thirty-six

AT FIRST LIGHT someone scratched on the flap of the lodge.

Sam and Julia jumped up together. It wouldn't be Esperanza—she wouldn't scratch—but at this time of morning it must be news. She'd been missing for two nights.

Sam opened the door and saw the mousy face of one of the Frenchies from Fort Walla Walla, Remoulet. "I am sorry to come so early," he said in his reedy voice and Frenchy accent, "but . . . You must be anxious." He held an envelope in his hand.

"Come in, please," said Julia.

"They made me promise to wait until today. Zis may be early, but it ees today."

He handed Julia the envelope. "I t'ink they ask Madame Whitman and she write ze words for them."

"Jay, would you make some coffee for our guest?" said Julia.

Sam watched Julia slip a finger under the flap and open the container slowly. He had a terrible sense of dread.

"Dear Mother, Papa Flat Dog, and Papa Sam—," Julia read in Spanish.

I am gone to Oregon City to be Joe Meek's wife.

"I'll kill the son of a bitch," said Sam.

"Sam," said Julia.

"They could have told me!"

"Sam! Listen to the rest."

He hung his head.

The bateaux carrying the Hudson's Bay men from the up-river forts and the Newell party had sailed from Fort Walla Walla yesterday. By now the boats would already be past the great rapids, and in three more days at Fort Vancouver. And every night Esperanza and Joe would be rolled up in the blankets together.

I love Joe, and he loves me. We would have told you, but you all want to keep me under your thumb. Please understand. Joe and I will be glad to see all of you in the spring.

"It's signed 'Esperanza.'"

Sam and Flat Dog traded disgruntled looks.

"There's another letter."

Dear Sam—
I love your daughter and will take good of her. I will also be a good father to her child.

"Child?!" exclaimed Sam.

Sam, we have been friends for a long time, and I ask you to trust me. Do not follow us to Oregon City now. I warn you, do not. Next spring will be the right time.

Then we'll hand you your first grandchild.

—your friend, Joe Meek

"It's a damned outrage," said Sam. He stood up and paced.

"Let me know when you want me to speak," said Julia.

"California, we were going to make a home in California."

"Are you ready?"

"It was all working out!" He whirled on Julia. "Did you know she was with child?"

"Yes."

"I am betrayed!" shouted Sam.

"Here's your coffee," said Jay, and thrust a cup into Sam's hand.

"Listen to me!" Julia grabbed his hand. "Grow up."

"Grow up? She's the one needs to—"

"Sam," Julia said, pulling him toward her. "She is grown-up. She's about to be a mother. She's going to make the home she wants. Whatever home she wants. Not yours, not Flat Dog's, and not mine."

"I ain't easy with this," said Flat Dog. He stared into his own cup and then sipped the steaming brew.

Julia gave both of them a stern eye.

"Then she has two fathers who need to grow up."

Silence held them together and pushed them apart.

"Monsieur Remoulet," said Julia, "would you like some more sugar?"

The Frenchy held out his cup. "I be sorry I bring such news," he said.

"It was very kind of you," Julia answered.

Sam and Flat Dog held each other's eyes hard. Stymied.

Julia studied her husband's face and worried more.

Thirty-seven

IT WAS A bleak winter at the mission at Wailatpu. Narcissa Whitman kept Alice's bed made perfectly and her clothes untouched in the closet and the drawers. Her two dolls rested against her small pillow. The grieving mother seldom stirred out of the house. Julia spent only an occasional moment with her.

Narcissa also withdrew from contact with the Indian people she had come to save. Instead she threw herself into her correspondence with her fellow missionaries in Oregon and her family back in the States. Her words about her charges were impatient. She wrote her mother:

> They are an exceedingly proud, haughty and insolent people, and keep us constantly upon the stretch after patience and forbearance. We feed them far more than any of our associates do their people, yet they will not be satisfied.

Marcus Whitman kept to himself and his medical books. Though Hannibal visited him from time to time, for the moment the pleasure was gone from the friendship. Which was too bad, because Hannibal thought Whitman was a good man.

Sam, Hannibal, and Esperanza worked hard at trading for horses, training them, and teaching both Cayuses and Nez Percés how to train their best mounts to respond to hand signals and voice commands. Flat Dog rode several times over to Fort Walla Walla and helped the saddle maker there, learning all he could. But everyone watched the lower slopes of Mount Hood for the day when the snows would be melted enough and they could get started for the American settlement at Oregon City.

On a bright spring morning Sam had had enough. *Sometimes,* he thought, *what's needed is action.* "Time's a-wasting," he said. "Life is waiting for us in California. We start tomorrow morning."

Everyone was relieved.

That evening Hannibal wrote a letter to his friend.

Dear Marcus—

Tomorrow we leave, and I don't know when I'll be back to this good place, or when we'll get to share coffee and conversation again.

I am leaving with words clanking around in my head unspoken, words I have been too shy to utter to you directly. I mean them as kind, helpful to you. Certainly they are intended in the spirit of friendship, so I give them to you in this letter.

I believe that the religion of the Cayuses and the Nez Percés is as good for them as yours is for you. In fact, I might say better.

You worship the Lord of all Creation. They worship creation itself. Your Lord is an angry God, full of demands and threats of retribution if obedience is not forthcoming. Their Mother Earth is the essence of nurturing. She brings forth each spring

*the bountiful life upon this planet. She provides sunlight and
the water that living things need, indeed the very air we breathe.
She is truly the most loving of all possible mothers.*

*My fear at this moment is that you will think I am saying
that your mission is a vain one. Not at all. I believe it to be thoroughly worthy. In my opinion, what you have to give to the
Native people is not Jehovah or his divine son. It is the vast
knowledge of Western civilization. Medicine, agriculture, science, mechanics—all these and much more you can give them,
and they will love you for it. You will be delighted with yourself
for your good deeds.*

*I do not believe they will love you for your preaching of Je-
hovah. Indeed, I fear that they may come to hate you for it.*

*I write these words hesitantly. Please believe that they bear a
message from a true friend.*

> *Yours truly,*
> *Hannibal MacKye*

In the morning Hannibal reread his letter and tore it up.

REMOULET LED SAM, Hannibal, and Flat Dog to a good spot to
see The Dalles. They made such a nasty froth and roar that the
horses pulled back against the hands that held their reins. The
walls of the Columbia River narrowed and plunged over a falls.
Beyond the falls the water turned from a current to a torrent.
Waves stood taller than a man and curled back upstream, like las-
civious tongues. "Man-eaters," said Flat Dog.

"No place for the herd," said Sam.

"Jay was right," put in Hannibal.

"The Company, it take ze men and furs through in those
bateaux," said Remoulet. Sam and Hannibal had hired him to
help take the herd around the mountain. "And they have sometimes to portage."

"Oh my God!" said Sam.

What made him cuss right then was a salmon hurtling up the falls right next to them.

"I bet that fish goes forty or fifty pounds," said Hannibal. "I've seen plenty that do."

"Every time it make my bones go willy," said Remoulet.

"The Indians like them fine," said Hannibal.

The Indian men were fishing on the other side of the river now. They lived on the salmon that came up the Columbia during this spring run. They caught the fish any way they could and dried the meat on racks over a low fire, just as the Indians of the plains dried buffalo meat. Salmon were the buffalo of the Northwest.

Sam turned backward and looked up at Mount Hood. "One hell of a mountain to go around." The volcano blotted out the entire southern sky.

"Bigger zan a thousand grizzly bear," said Remoulet. "Also, must I say to you, ten times so mean."

"A bitch," said Hannibal.

"I'll be . . . ," said Sam.

The others saw the same gaped-mouth expression.

All of them saw another one fling itself straight up the falls.

"Oh my God!"

"Save that prayer for Mount Hood," said Hannibal.

They took a last look at the Indians dotting the north side of the river. They used nets. They had traps. Where they had built small fences to coop up the fish, they prowled with cocked spears. They showed no interest in the strangers. Their focus was the fish and food enough to last until the next salmon run.

There were Indians, people said, who would build a raft and float you through the mighty waters. But you could never float a herd of seventy-seven horses through.

"We're leaving the river tomorrow morning?" asked Hannibal.

"Yeah," said Sam, mesmerized by something in the stream.

He dived into the torrent and immediately stood halfway up with a mammoth salmon in his arms.

The huge fish wriggled and flicked Sam away like a fly. He fell backward over a boulder. Then the salmon circled in the pool and made the upward leap.

Hannibal, Flat Dog, and Remoulet were so astonished by the fish that they lost track of Sam for a moment. His holler caught their attention.

Sam's tumble had taken him from the pool into the current. Now he was bouncing downstream like flotsam. They saw him rise up one of the tall waves and get flipped backward. On the second try he swam hard and kicked his way through it. He fended off a boulder with one stiff leg and swept around it. For a moment he was caught in the eddy on the back side, but he got both feet on the rock, gave a mighty shove, and splashed back into the current.

They were dashing alongside the river now, keeping Sam in sight.

He washed straight over a big rock headfirst—no, he didn't wash over, he beached!

Sam waved his hat at them and dived as far as he could downstream. The rapid turned from a rock garden into big waves alone, waves that lifted Sam like a dinghy of human bark, dropped him into the troughs behind, and flung him into the sky again.

Hannibal tried to figure out what else he was seeing and realized it was that foolish hat, zigzagging in the air.

The rapid turned to duck feathers and then pooled out in a big eddy. By the time Hannibal, Flat Dog, and Remoulet arrived, Sam was standing in the shallows.

"Still got my hat," he yelled over the roar of the rapids, grinning. He clambered onto the bank.

"How come you do such a crazy t'ing?" said Remoulet.

Sam looked at him funny and answered, "To catch the fish!"

"We Frenchmen of the canoes," said Remoulet, "we do not swim." His tone added, "nor want to."

"Let's go see if we've still got horses," said Sam.

They trotted back upstream. The way was so rough that Hannibal was surprised they'd been able to run it without thought.

All four mounts stood calmly where they'd left them, no Indian nearby. With Sam's mare Paladin and Hannibal's gelding Brownie this was no surprise. That pair was trained to ground tie—you could just drop the reins and the horse would stand still as if it was staked.

The others apparently liked equine company.

"We leave the river tomorrow," repeated Hannibal, "if we're all still alive."

"LET'S EAT THE horseflesh," said Flat Dog.

Everybody laughed, and laughter was a good thing, a healing and relief.

They had labored their way across the southeastern slopes of Mount Hood for several days. The old Indian trail was good for a few hunters or warriors but not for a herd of loose horses, plus pack animals, two horses dragging travois, and ten riders. It was narrow, steep, and blocked by thick stands of evergreens. In places you had to pick your way through downed timber. All too often the slope angled up forever and a day. The horses kept trying to turn back, and the people felt like doing the same.

Then they came into a pleasant valley called Tygh where some Chinook Indians lived. They spent two days resting the horses on good grass and doing a little trading.

After they turned west from the Tygh Valley the southern slopes of Mount Hood got steeper, and they learned to believe what the Chinooks had signed to them—snow ahead.

The horses sank above their knees. The riders climbed off and led their mounts. The people had to stovepipe it, pick up each leg, one at a time, slide it forward on the snow, and plunk it straight down into the cold, white stuff one meager step ahead. The horses had almost as much trouble. It was slow going, and the steepness made it much worse. The animals were on the edge of turning surly. Some of the human animals were beyond that edge.

"I was in too much of a rush," said Sam. "It's too early in the season."

"That's why we should stop and eat them," said Flat Dog again.

"They look tastier with every step," Remoulet agreed.

Sam and everyone else had been wrapped inside the same rush. This herd was their stake, their start to a new life. Everybody wanted to get to the American settlements on the Willamette River, sell these horses, and get headed south. Also, the mares would be foaling in another month. Best to travel now and foal on better ground.

"This is not worth it," said Julia.

"The filly's down again," Sam told her.

Julia led her mount twenty yards or so down the slope and helped the year-old filly to her feet. She was undersized and having a hard time in the snow. Julia had appointed herself the filly's caretaker.

"Julia's irritable," said Sam.

"Me, too," said Hannibal.

"Horses gonna be cranky tonight," said Sam.

The men didn't see any hope of getting beyond these snow-fields today, and the poor animals would have to spend the night in knee-deep snow without anything to eat.

"We've been on the road for ten months," said Hannibal. He didn't mention that they had several more months to go. "More than enough to make anyone cranky."

THE NEXT DAY they got out of the snow just in time for the herd and all the people to slip and slide down a ridiculously long, steep hill lined with laurels. Beyond the hill, though, they came on good grass.

"Let's call a halt for a day," said Sam.

People would have cheered, but they were too tired.

Flat Dog squeezed out, "The horses need the rest."

Julia and Jay put up the tipi. "I'll have a fire and a big, extra-strong pot of coffee in a few minutes," said Julia.

"We'd best set a guard," said Sam.

"Just one," put in Hannibal.

"Ain't gonna be no Indians fool enough to come up into these snows and glaciers," said Remoulet.

"I'll take watch," said Flat Dog.

"I'll go find us some meat," said Remoulet.

In half an hour all but the hunter and the guard were toasty. In two hours they were broiling strips of backstraps on skewers. Julia took coffee and meat to her husband, perched on a boulder above the herd. She sat with him awhile, looking south across vast reaches of evergreen trees and chatting softly. Neither of them had ever seen such timber, big and rolling as the ocean.

When Julia got back to the tipi, she saw that Sam was dozing behind the fire. She shook him gently. "Almost dark, your watch."

Sam sat up alert. "Sure," he said,

As he raised the tipi flap, they all heard the gunshots.

First off Sam ran his eyes to Flat Dog on the boulder. Sam saw a blast of white smoke and heard a boom and knew his friend was alive.

Four or five thieves drove hard down the far ridge toward the herd, shouting and waving their blankets. From their dress they were half-breeds.

Sam pulled Paladin's stake and jumped on her bareback. As he kicked his horse toward the trouble, he heard and felt his friends close behind him. A glance showed Hannibal, Remoulet, Jay, and Azul.

"Azul," screamed Julia, "come back here."

The youth ignored her.

The herd was stirring, starting to skitter down the little valley, just as the thieves wanted.

Shots! Some of the damned horse thieves had reloaded and were making a racket to . . .

The herd bolted. They charged downhill the way the Columbia River charged through The Dalles.

Sam spurred Paladin. His mind screamed, THAT . . . IS . . . OUR . . .

He felt Jay pull alongside on his mare, Kauai. The kid didn't know how to use his pistol but was willing to fight. Sam let out a war whoop.

Quickly he saw that running at the herd was only making things worse. His horses just ran off faster.

Sam looked at Jay and motioned left. When Sam turned his head back, Hannibal had already led Remoulet and Azul off toward the right-hand ridge. They had to get ahead of the horses and turn them. First they probably had to shoot the damned breeds who were driving the horses off.

Paladin had speed and nimble feet—Jay's mare struggled to keep up. The ridge timber was thin, and the herd now began to slow the thieves. It was weary beyond weary and did not want to run.

We have a chance, thought Sam.

Sam and Jay gained ground. Sam could see the thieves at the back of the herd, parallel to him. He reined Paladin up, jumped off her while she was skidding to a stop, and sprinted up a rocky outcropping to get a clear field of vision. He leveled his rifle, the Celt, and as he began to squeeze the trigger—

BOOM!

The shot came from nearby.

Kauai screamed, reared, and went down.

Sam could see the white smoke no more than fifty yards ahead, behind some rocks.

KABOOM!

"AMBUSH!" he hollered.

White smoke fizzed into the air on the opposite ridge. Sam saw Azul fly off his mount.

"AMBUSH!" Sam hollered again. "AMBUSH!"

He ran behind a big rock, Jay diving in beside him. "Kauai is dead," said Jay. Sam saw the mare's head covered with blood.

Sam held his rifle on the rocks beneath the smoke.

A barrel slipped upward and came level. A head rose behind it. Sam fired.

The head went down.

From the way the rifle jumped, Sam thought he'd hit it, not the head.

He left the Celt, jumped on Paladin, and galloped straight at the rocks, yelling like a madman. To hell with whether he'd hit only the rifle. He rode with his knees and waved his tomahawk in one hand, his pistol in the other.

A big breed stood up with a pistol gripped.

Sam fired to make the bastard duck. Then he used a lesson he'd learned long ago. He ran Paladin right over his foe, trampling him.

Christ! Sam pulled Paladin up and made her rear just before she galloped onto some low outcroppings.

Sam spun Paladin and reined her down, front hoofs directly on the bushwhacker. Getting the idea, Paladin reared and thumped the bastard again.

Instantly, Sam saw the fight was over. The man's head was bloody, and he was unconscious.

"Tie him!" Sam shouted at Jay, and slapped Paladin's hindquarters to send her after the herd.

After a dozen strides he reined up and looked back. Flat Dog was running from his sentry rock across the valley toward the other ridge, toward Azul. They were down to a few minutes of fading light.

This ambush could be a sign of another one waiting. Sam looked after his fleeing herd. *Not much I can do alone in the dark.*

He noticed a last thief running out of the trees on the opposite ridge and chasing the herd. Out of range for a shot, unfortunately. But something niggled at Sam about that horse.

He lifted his field glass and brought horse and rider into twilight focus. He tracked them carefully for several seconds, unable to believe what he saw. He wouldn't have been able to identify the rider from behind, except that he knew that big black Appaloosa with the snowflake markings. It was the stallion Warrior, ridden by Kanaka Boy.

Sam rode hard toward the other ridge. He was scared about Azul.

Thirty-eight

"I TOLD YOU you weren't ready yet," Flat Dog barked at Azul.

The boy was writhing on the ground, moaning, shot through the calf. Hannibal and Remoulet stood above him, looking helpless.

"Remoulet," said Sam, "go to the other ridge and help Jay out. He needs you."

The Frenchy mounted and galloped off.

Flat Dog took the leg in both hands gingerly and tried to move the bone.

"O-o-o-w!" shouted Azul.

The bone held.

Sam felt for the kid. While Rojo was a boy clown at eleven, at fourteen Azul was struggling to play the man.

"I don't think it's broken," said Flat Dog. "Bone may be nicked."

"Let's get back to the lodge," said Sam.

"And off this goddamn mountain," said Flat Dog.

The two men lifted Azul onto his saddle belly down. The kid hollered again. Flat Dog lashed the boy on.

"You should have stayed back," said Flat Dog. The anguish was gravel in his voice.

WHILE THE FATHER muttered disapproval, the mother oozed sympathy. Which didn't change the fact that the job had to be done. Mother and father laid their son on a buffalo robe next to the fire, inspected the wound, and agreed with their eyes.

Flat Dog still owned the older kind of rifle that used powder in the pan. Now he poured a little onto the wound and dabbed it around. Sam saw the gentleness in the father's finger and the pain in his face.

Rojo knelt close and watched, awed.

Flat Dog lifted an ember with the tip of his knife and slid it onto the powder.

Flame popped and sizzled.

Azul screamed. Both parents held him down by his shoulders.

When the boy's legs stilled, Sam looked and thought the flesh was properly cauterized.

Julia lay down beside her son and held him.

Sam heard hoof plops. He stuck his head out the flap.

"Come on out," said Remoulet. "You better see this."

He and Jay lifted the breed off the saddle of his horse and dumped him on the ground. Flat Dog and Sam slipped outside, held the flap open for light, and looked at the dead face. The skull was split open. The corpse was Hawaiian.

"Everybody," said Jay, "meet Delly."

"I SAW KANAKA Boy in my field glass," said Sam. "I think you better tell us whatever you know."

Jay looked at the faces around the fire. A thin, icy wire of fear coiled around his heart and squeezed. *If they find out, will these people kick me out?*

"It was Kanaka Boy. He let this man beat me up," Jay said. He swallowed hard, because he'd almost said "rape." He looked into Julia's eyes and took comfort in their warmth. "Boy told him to beat me up.

"Delly was one of his henchmen. They came after us because of me. Stealing the horses was just a handy way to deliver the insult."

He saw that his right hand was shaking and put it on the ground to stop the trembling.

"The shot that killed Kauai wasn't meant for her. It was me. Her head just got in the way, and saved my life.

"Kanaka Boy was in the ambush on the other side. I saw Warrior, too."

All the adults looked into Jay's face. *Will they guess now?* Jay wondered. *Will Julia tell them?*

"I'm lucky Kanaka Boy wasn't on my ridge," he said. "He's harder to stop."

"How did they know?" asked Sam. His look was severe.

"Someone of the Cayuses or Nez Percés must have spotted me. Or one of the Hawaiians from Fort Walla Walla. I was scared that would happen. Boy has spies everywhere."

"Anything else?" said Sam.

Jay thought. He breathed in once and out once and decided. "Yeah, now he's got the herd, he may come back after me."

"I don't think so," said Sam. "I think we're going after him."

Thirty-nine

"HANNIBAL AND I will track the herd and get it back," Sam said.

"I'm coming," said Remoulet.

"On what horse?" said Sam.

"The small boy's."

"That's my horse," said Rojo.

"Son," said Remoulet, "I'll give you my pistol for it."

"You will not," said Julia.

"I'll give you my tomahawk and knife," said Remoulet.

Rojo bit his lower lip.

"Look, me son, your brother can no walk. He must be dragged on a litter. You must walk an' lead his horse. No way around zese things."

Rojo teared up a little.

"And me, I must go," said Remoulet. He extended the tomahawk and knife, and the eleven-year-old took them. His parents held their tongues.

"Soon as Azul can be moved, probably tomorrow," said Flat Dog, "we're getting off this mountain."

"Go on all the way to Oregon City," said Sam. "It's just a few days."

"Jay, you go with them," said Sam.

"Thank you," he said. Jay could feel his legs trembling.

"No thanks to it. They need your help. Flat Dog, teach him to use that pistol he carries." Sam looked Jay hard in the eyes. "You can do that, can't you? Learn to shoot?"

He hesitated.

"You better," said Flat Dog.

Sam finished up. "We'll be along. If we're not in Oregon City in three weeks, we're not coming."

Everyone avoided one another's eyes.

"Find Esperanza for me," Sam said.

Jay said, "The horses, are they so very important?"

"The horses?" said Sam. "To hell with them. They shot my nephew. They tried to kill you. Nobody attacks my family and walks away."

THE TRAIL OF the herd was high, wide, and handsome.

Sam, Hannibal, and Remoulet dared not follow it.

"Kanaka Boy will set up ambushes along the trail, for sure," Hannibal said.

Luckily, Mount Hood was big and steep and the canyons ran like spokes off the peak. Sam and Hannibal backtracked two canyons to the east of the herd trail and rode like hell.

If Jay was right, Boy would head back to his outpost on the Owyhee. First off, he would get the hell off this mountain. The terrain to the south turned quickly to high desert, easy traveling if you knew where to find water. Jay had drawn a map for them, how Boy would run south to the upper Warm Springs River first, two days away, and follow it for three more days to the Deschutes River. One of the main tribes that bought whiskey from him lived at the mouth of the Warm Springs, Wascos. If Boy didn't rest the herd on the upper Warm Springs, he certainly would at the village. He also might trade some of the horses there.

Sam, Hannibal, and Remoulet didn't intend to let them get that far.

"HE'S GOT A lot of men," Hannibal said. He was using his field glass.

"I make out nine," said Sam, also glassing. Remoulet had nothing to say. He was just waiting to fight.

The three were stretched out flat on a ridge north of the river, looking east, the setting sun behind them.

"Three on guard, six lounging around that fire."

"And boozing," added Sam.

The herd was scattered over a wide bottomland along the Warm Springs River. Kanaka Boy had stopped at the first good grass and water. Probably he'd had trouble getting the weary herd even that far. Sam and Hannibal wondered whether he'd killed some horses from exhaustion, especially mares in foal, pushing them too hard.

Beyond the fire, against the river, Boy's men had rope-corralled their mounts. Nine—it checked out.

Sam, Hannibal, and Remoulet had beaten Kanaka Boy here and watched him ride in.

"Tonight, you think?" said Sam.

"Tomorrow night," said Hannibal. "Tonight the horses will barely be able to walk. We wouldn't have a chance against pursuit."

"You figuring he'll rest the herd tomorrow?"

"If he doesn't, we'll still have the same chance tomorrow night."

Remoulet said, "Me, I am hot to go now."

"And maybe I got a good idea for that," said Sam.

They waited while Sam double-checked it in his mind.

"What about when Boy's bushwhackers came back? When they told Kanaka Boy we weren't coming after them?"

"If it was me," Hannibal said, "I would think we were too worn down to chase him."

"If I am Boy," said Remoulet, "I t'ink we no have ze sand to try. We being so few. And zat would make zis child careless," said Remoulet.

"I suspect he is careless," said Hannibal, "but 'maybe' gets people killed."

"Well, if he guards against anything," said Sam, "it will be someone trying to run off the herd."

"Or maybe just part of it," said Hannibal.

"That's where my idea comes in," Sam said.

They talked the notion out. It was daring.

"It must be a buffalo bull's balls you joined with," said Hannibal.

Sam grinned. "The whole buffalo," he said. "And a buffalo bull protects his relatives."

THE NIGHTTIME ARRANGEMENT was the same as the day, three guards on watch at any one time, the others resting, sleeping, or drinking.

"Swig that jug," whispered Sam. Not that he needed to whisper, two hundred yards out. They'd left the horses in some firs to the north. Azul's pony was tied hard, Paladin and Brownie only ground tied. This was an on-foot attack.

They'd waited for the three-quarter moon to rise. They'd also stashed their rifles. If they needed the rifles, they'd probably be dead.

Sam started the crawl forward. Inching up palm by palm and knee by knee was the hardest part. He liked *doing*, not skulking.

They spent an hour getting within fifty paces, hidden behind the sagebrush. Now they were dependent on hand signals, Sam in the middle, Hannibal and Remoulet on either side.

After a long time three drinkers got up and walked out to change the guard. One of the men departing was Kanaka Boy.

Sam motioned forward. This was the time to be silent and quick.

The attackers stood upright and padded forward slowly, every sense turned up. They had to hope the guards didn't see their relief and start back. They had to hope the three men left were groggy with sleep or half-drunk. This part had to go absolutely right.

Sam stopped behind a bush about ten paces away. Hannibal and Remoulet did the same. From the look of it, one of the three men remaining had rolled up in his blankets and fallen asleep or passed out. The other two, a big one and a shrimp, were sitting and staring into the fire, passing a jug back and forth.

Sam wished he had some sound for cover. He wished he spoke Hawaiian. He wished a lot of things.

He pointed at Remoulet with his hand, meaning, take the man on the far left, the sleeper. He signaled to Hannibal with his right hand—take the one on the right, the shrimp.

Both comrades nodded.

Very quick and very quiet—the three guards would be returning soon.

Sam took off like a herd bull, stock-still one moment, a blaze of speed the next.

The giant Hawaiian cocked his head and then turned it backward. Sam slammed his pistol barrel hard into the man's forehead.

Sam heard sounds of scraping and panting from Hannibal's direction but had no time to look. He dropped the pistol and drove his butcher knife deep into the man's chest.

He looked at Hannibal. His friend had his man in a bear hug from behind. Hannibal dropped him, and the shrimp fell like a loose blanket.

Remoulet stood up, grinned, and held his knife up in the moonlight, gleaming and dripping.

Sam despised fighting people. When he killed someone, his dreams were haunted. *Price to pay,* he knew.

They slipped back into the darkness to wait. The three sentries would be coming back.

THE FIRST MAN straggled in alone. Hannibal cocked his arm and sank his throwing knife hilt deep into the man's belly. He crumpled, one arm flung across the fire.

The three comrades smiled grimly at one another. That burning arm might mess things up.

The other two came back talking low. In the dark, behind their bushes, the assassins couldn't hear their words.

Cocked pistols raised, the assassins waited until firelight lit the figures. They wanted noise now, and a lot of it. The moment one of the guards began to look queerly at the dead man, Sam shot him in the chest.

Hannibal fired within a split second.

In a flash they grabbed the fallen men's rifles and checked that they were capped or primed. Grim smiles showed that they were.

Sam and Hannibal whistled—first a long, ululating call from Sam, then a short, low-high shriek from Hannibal.

They couldn't hear their mounts over the shouting of the returning guards.

They crouched back behind some bushes, reloading their pistols in a fury. Hannibal and Sam had the luxury of loaded rifles.

Sam prayed, *Give me Kanaka Boy.*

The first man dashed into the light bellowing. He must have thought his war cry would stop a lead ball. Hannibal showed him otherwise.

Where in hell are the other two guards? The minds of all three attackers were screaming to know.

Paladin galloped into the circle of firelight and hesitated. Just as she smelled Sam and started toward him, a dark figure leaped out of the bushes and grabbed her reins.

The mare shook her head violently, and the man fell to his knees. Sam shot him for his arrogance.

Sam jumped onto Paladin, Hannibal onto Brownie. They looked around wildly for Kanaka Boy. *Where is the son of a bitch?*

Then they heard hoofbeats.

"The rope corral," Hannibal shouted. They kicked Paladin and Brownie in that direction.

They couldn't get any better fix on the location than the drumming hoofs until they heard the splash.

"The river!" Sam yelled.

By the half-moon they saw the dark shadows of horse and rider against the meandering water.

Only Sam had a loaded weapon. He reined Paladin still and took the only shot he had.

Horse and rider didn't even flinch as they disappeared into the darkness.

Sam and Hannibal rode back to the fire. "They're all dead," said Remoulet. "You boys are wild ones."

They looked over the herd. "They would have run off—," said Hannibal.

Sam finished his sentence, "If they had any energy to run on."

"We'll rest them tomorrow."

"Tonight we can sleep any place but here," said Sam.

They bivouacked in a rocky gully.

The next morning Sam tracked the man who got away for a short distance, but it was a fool's errand. Kanaka Boy could bushwhack him from a hundred places. And the tracks headed straight away at a run.

All day they watched the eastern hills for a sign of Kanaka Boy.

"You think he's gone?" said Hannibal at sunset.

"I guess so," said Sam.

"My bones, they feel more easier," said Remoulet, "when we get a hundred miles away."

"Mine will feel easier," said Hannibal, "when this herd is sold."

Remoulet said, "Sam, that was no a bad idea. Forget the herd and go for the guards."

Sam grinned.

Forty

SAM DISCOVERED, DURING the week he spent driving the herd to Oregon City, that the struggles of fighting Mount Hood and then Kanaka Boy and his crew had one great advantage. They kept Sam from thinking about Esperanza.

His first grandchild was born by now, and he had missed it. He had left his daughter alone. He was at the age when the fruit drops off the tree and now was the propagator of a grandson or a grand-daughter. He was amazed at what a grand-height age thirty-six could be.

As he dawdled along behind the herd, gentling the animals down the easy route of the Clackamas River, pictures fuzzed into his mind. Esperanza giving birth. A child, which in his mind was nothing but an obscure object swaddled in a blanket. Joe Meek holding the blanket, rocking the baby. Himself holding the blanket and rocking the baby.

"More than half a lifetime," Sam said to Hannibal. "Middle-aged. I wonder if I've learned anything." The day's ride was done, coffee perking, meat broiling, and Remoulet on guard.

"Supposing you have," said Hannibal, "what is it?"

"There's a lot of earthquakes," said Sam.

Hannibal looked at him quizzically.

"You get a wife, you lose her. You get a tribe to live with, they kick you out. You get a son and a daughter, you lose them."

"Feels like quakes," said Hannibal, "but change is what it's about. Changes are sure as water runs downhill. You wake up in the morning and the lay of the land is different."

Sam said, "No satisfaction in those words."

" 'Nothing endures but change,' " quoted Hannibal. "Heraclitus."

"Philosophy isn't good for much, is it?"

"Another word for it is 'the human condition,' " said Hannibal.

"A man can't ride under a flag with those words. You got anything better?"

"Sure. *Vita Luna!*"

"What does it mean?"

"Crazy life!"

"Now you're talking. I'll take that as my motto. Let's see, in Spanish *Vita Loca?*"

"Or *Vita Lunatica.*"

"That's the flag I ride under from now on. Not as much fun as *rideo, ergo sum*, but more home truth."

"A man who goes the route of family ends up mixed around, and tumbled up and down besides."

Sam eyed his friend and decided to ask. "Say it. You're tempted."

"Yes, I am. Then I'll be just like you." He smiled and shook his head.

"Prairie Chicken will never know he has a son."

"He got what his contribution was worth. And he probably has others he doesn't know about, right there in the village."

"I was going to California to make a home for a son and daughter who were going to get married and go off somewhere else."

Hannibal grimaced and looked across the rumps of the horses. Sam wondered exactly what was on his mind. "The bread always lands butter side down," Hannibal said.

THEY DROVE THE herd upstream of Willamette Falls and made a crossing that was harder than they expected. Sam couldn't get used to these coastal rivers. Mountain rivers were long, stringy, and crooked, like fly-fishing lines. Coastal rivers were short and thick, like thumbs. Also deep.

Two old-time French-Canadian trappers came out from their cabins on French Prairie to help with the crossing. Remoulet knew them both and greeted them heartily.

Now Sam started to get the lay of the land around here. The country upriver for ten or twenty miles or more was settled by retired Hudson's Bay Frenchies, even named after them. The little community by the falls, Oregon City, and the country west of it was settled by Americans, mostly Methodist colonists. One language on your left, another on your right.

The Frenchies knew about Doc Newell and Joe Meek and gave Sam directions to their cabins, well west of the river in a region known as the Tualatin Plains.

"A Crow named Flat Dog?"

"And his beautiful wife who is Spanish?" said the Frenchy built like a bear. "Ever' *personne* know her. They live in their tipi on the Tualatin River two, maybe three miles above ze mouth."

"The husband," put in the one slinky as a weasel. "Flat Dog? Fonny name. Zere is empty cabin he could use, but he want last time to live in a circle instead of a square, so he say."

"Zere be good grass zere by the Tualatin," said the bear.

"We and me," said the weasel, "ze both us, we would like to trade for horses."

"Come see us at Flat Dog's lodge," said Sam. "We'll give you a good price. Thanks for your help."

Remoulet said, "I stay here now, you *comprenez*? Ze job, it is *fini*. You pay me now, zis my home."

Sam counted out some gold coins. "Something extra for risking your hair. Thanks for good work."

The Frenchies nodded and rode off.

Sam's mind was eased. The first people he saw wanted to buy horses. He thought the Methodists would, too, and he would sell the rest to John McLoughlin, head of Hudson's Bay for the entire Oregon country. The White-Headed Eagle was said to be some man to deal with.

So Sam was in a good frame of mind when he saw Flat Dog and Julia riding out to meet the herd. The grass was as good as the bear had promised, and the herd was going to be happy.

Sam and Hannibal jumped down and clapped Flat Dog's shoulders. Julia kissed Sam on the cheek and said, "We haven't seen Esperanza in a month. She told us to stay away."

"Where are they?"

"The cabin is maybe fifteen miles on further west."

No ANSWER. SAM and Flat Dog took turns banging on the door of Meek's cabin with the heels of their hands—they'd been told Joe was there. When Sam hammered on it with the butt of his pistol, he heard stirring sounds within.

Joe Meek opened the door and used its handle to keep from falling down. He was drunk and more than drunk. From the look of him he'd been drunk for days. Nothing they hadn't seen before.

"Hi, Joe," said Sam.

"You come to shoot me?"

Fear shot through Sam like when he hit his elbow wrong. *Meadowlark died in childbirth.*

"Not today," said Flat Dog. "We want to see Esperanza."

"That." Joe's head waggled. "That. For that you best go to Fort Vancouver."

He started to close the door.

Sam kicked it open, knocking Joe on his ass.

Sprawled, he wrenched his head around toward them. "I don't mean you no harm," he said, "never did, nor your daughter, either. But she done flown to the nest of the damned White-Headed Eagle. Go find her there." He got to his knees.

"What about the baby, Joe?"

"You can ask her." He asserted his dignity by standing up. "And you can leave me alone. Tomorrow I'm going hunting and I'm gonna stay gone."

Forty-one

ESPERANZA TOOK A buffalo robe outside and curled up on the grass in a sunny spot. Sun seemed so rare in Oregon—she wondered if winter was always like this. Winters in the Yellowstone country were cold, but they were also brilliantly sunny. She liked that. Whenever she felt the sun on her skin, she felt good. Here the days were barely cool enough to require a buffalo robe, but they were drearily gray. She felt gray herself.

Well, that was some of the time. Lots of times she felt content and peaceful, and that was everything to do with the baby. In the mornings, before getting up, she would lie on the pallet she and Joe used for a bed and stroke her own belly.

A human being was forming.

She stroked the person and got to know it. This was her person and no one else's. She was growing it every day, growing, growing,

growing, and her life curled up around a feeling whose warmth was hers alone.

When she got out of the robes each morning, she would brew coffee with cream—she loved the cream some of her neighbors made—and ask the baby if he wanted cream. She was sure it was a he. The baby always wanted cream. Then she'd fry some bacon on the iron stove Joe had gotten for them and say to the baby in her mind, *Here's some bacon. Isn't this good?*

Though she was fond of bacon, deer meat was a more typical breakfast. She'd sit at the little table, pat her belly, and simply be. It felt lazy just to be, but it also felt good.

Sometimes, right while she was patting the baby, he would move. The thrill was a jolt, a lightning bolt from inside to outside bearing a message. *I am here. I will come forth.*

She tightened the robe against a freshening wind.

I will come forth.

She took a nap there in the sun, while her child did his growing, and then she went into the cabin to cook dinner. She didn't like the darkness of the cabin. Joe and Doc had built it fast, and they only put in two small windows, covered with thin-scraped deer hide instead of glass. The cabin was far darker than any lodge, which let the sun in all the time. It was also colder in the corners. She didn't see any advantage in a cabin over a tipi.

On the other hand, some houses were nice. She remembered perfectly the day last autumn the bateaux unloaded their passengers, furs, and gear at Fort Vancouver. She got to see the homes of the officers, though only from the outside—they looked like grand places. Her mother had lived in a grand place once, her father's hacienda. Esperanza wondered if she and Joe would ever have a fine house.

She cut up potatoes and put them on the stove to fry, then did the same to the deer meat. She was used to a monotonous diet in the winter.

She was cooking only for two, and one of those was in her belly. She didn't know where Joe was and didn't expect him for supper.

He spent his days somewhere else, it seemed, hunting or trapping or drinking with his friends, just as he'd done for all his years in the Rocky Mountains. He spent his nights somewhere else, too, much of the time, especially since she'd told him that he mustn't touch her anymore until after the baby was born. Her mother had taught her that.

She lay down on the pallet and listened to the sizzle. She felt tired a lot and spent a lot of time resting. She held the bulge of the baby with both hands. This was one person she loved, and she was glad he was inside her. But she needed Joe, too.

THE RAINS CAME and came, relentlessly for several days. This day was dark, like the ones before it. And where the hell was Joe? Esperanza was sick of wondering where he was. This time he'd ridden up to Fort Vancouver to trade his furs for provisions, and it was true that they needed things. It was also true that she needed him.

Esperanza had never seen such a rain. Doc and his wife and the families of some other ex-trappers lived nearby, but not close enough to walk to. Esperanza was afraid to ride Vermilion, not with the child due so soon. Because he was about to come—she could feel it. She knew.

The cabin was cold. She hadn't restarted the fire this morning. Though the thought of food repelled her, she wanted warmth and she wanted coffee.

She got up, threw chunks of wood into the stove, and got the fire going. Then she reached for the coffeepot, already full of water. Coffee, the thought was so good, something warm and sweet for her. . . .

Just as she lifted the pot onto the stove, she felt the first pain. The muscles in her belly squeezed like a fist, and after a moment they let go.

She added new grounds to the old ones and went back to her pallet. So today was going to be the day. Her feelings flipped side to side, excited and scared, excited and scared.

Another pain came and made it hard to think.

Where the hell is Joe?

ESPERANZA WAS FURIOUS. She was squatting, the way Crow women always gave birth. She held on to the cold stove, for lack of anything better. She couldn't light a fire because she needed something to hold on to. She was cold. She didn't have a woman to help her, and she didn't even have a husband.

The pains were huge now, earthquakes she would never survive. Between pains she was mad as hell at Joe. Or mad at Papa Sam for taking her away from her tribe, where she would have had some help. Or mad at Papa Flat Dog for the same thing. Or mad at Prairie Chicken for putting this baby inside her, this baby that was never going to come out, that was going to kill her. She was mad at all of malekind. She was *mad*.

Then the pain quaked her, and pain snuffed out all other consciousness.

SHE WANTED MORE than anything in the world to see the baby's face. She knew by feel that it was a boy, but she felt a huge urgency to see the face. She picked up the tiny creature, crawled to the door, and shoved it open with her bare foot. Through the drizzle and the last of the day's gray light, she saw a face crinkled like a dried berry and a dusting of auburn hair.

She also saw the cord extending from her and wrapping around his neck. She saw how blue his face was.

Cradling him in one arm, she crawled back to the stove, reached up, and grabbed the knife. Though she could see the cord only dimly, she grabbed a thong and bound the cord tight near the baby. Then held it against the floor and whacked it in half. Instantly, she unwound it from her son's neck.

She cradled him in both arms and rocked him.

A thrust of panic hit her. She crawled with her son to the door, which was still swinging back and forth. She jutted him and herself out into the rain, which was getting harder. Though she wasn't sure, it didn't look like he was breathing.

She turned and sheltered him from the pelting drops. She put a finger to his nose and felt nothing. She dried the finger on her skirt, licked it, put it back to his nostrils, and still felt nothing.

Frantically, she squeezed his back and chest, in, out, in, out. She had no idea what to do. She blew breath into his nose and into his mouth. She screamed. She squeezed and screamed.

After several minutes she knew he was dead. She had failed her son. He was dead. She'd never even seen his eyes. She swiveled back across the threshold and stood up in the driving rain. She thumbed his right eye open and looked. The brown eye was flat, without depth, lifeless.

Tenderly, she fingered the eyelid shut.

TWO DAYS LATER Joe Meek found his wife curled up in a corner of the cabin like a feral creature, clutching a dead baby.

He tried to hold her, but she wouldn't let him. He sat beside her and murmured every word of apology he could think of. He wept for the child, for his wife, and for himself. Weeping was easy when he was soused.

After a long time she let him lead her outside. He dug a small grave on the rise behind the cabin, placed the little form in it gingerly, and shoveled dirt onto her son.

Esperanza watched, wordless and blank faced.

Part Four

Forty-two

"MY LORD!" SAID Sam. Most of the family were sitting their horses on the rise on the south side of the Columbia, Flat Dog, Julia with Paloma on her back, Hannibal, and Jay. Azul, barely able to get on his pony, was back home watching the herd with Rojo.

From here everyone could see that Fort Vancouver was much more than a fort. It looked bigger than St. Louis, Los Angeles, or Monterey, reaching from the north bank back for maybe ten miles to heavy timber, and more miles both upstream and downstream.

"They've got as much pasture as a mission," said Hannibal.

"Growing thousands of acres of crops," said Sam.

"A whole town where workers live," said Julia.

"That's Kanaka Village," said Jay.

"Look at the fort," said Hannibal.

That palisaded building, the hub of all this economic bustle, was built to make an impression.

"A hundred paces on a side, probably," said Sam.

"Plus a section that's been added recently at the top," said Hannibal.

Sam lifted his field glass and brought that part into focus. "At the top of the top," he said, "there's a kind of . . . mansion. It has three cannons in front, pointed straight into the middle of the fort."

Hannibal laughed. "The Brits are big on show."

"You gotta be able to shoot your own people," said Sam.

"That's what they call the governor's house," said Hannibal.

"Mr. McLoughlin means to make an impression," said Sam.

"Dr. McLoughlin," said Hannibal.

"A doctor of science or medicine," said Sam, "is a critter that would die of thirst knee-deep in a lake."

"The question," Julia said, "is whether he can take care of a young mother with a baby, or wants to."

WHEN THEY RODE their horses out of the river and into what was called Kanaka Village, Sam's democratic and anti-Brit feelings were inflamed further. It was shacks of every kind, miserable dwellings compared to the fine buildings inside the fort. As they passed through, no one seemed to notice them. They heard a babble of Canadian French and two languages Sam didn't know.

"Chinook," said Hannibal, "a mixture of real Chinook, French, English, and whatever else."

"And Hawaiian," said Jay. He drew a lot of stares, with his Hawaiian face and rough-cut hair.

"Is your mother here somewhere?" said Julia.

"In the fort."

"Do these people know you?" asked Sam.

"No. I was raised at Fort Walla Walla," Jay answered.

"Eyes straight ahead and make for the fort," said Hannibal.

As they rode, Sam watched the hubbub. The place bristled with strong, rough men, busy as sailors in port. In fact, this was, among other things, a port for great seagoing vessels.

At the gate Hannibal said, "Mr. Hannibal MacKye to see Dr. McLoughlin."

The guard eyed the men, who were obviously rough trappers, the woman who looked like a half-breed, and the Hawaiian. Fort Vancouver was the strictest of caste societies.

"The doctor is not available," said the guard, "nor will he be."

Now Hannibal spoke French in a Parisian accent, far from the métis patois heard in those parts. "The doctor and I are old friends. Announce my presence immediately, unless you want to feel his displeasure, and mine."

The guard twitched with alarm, surveyed the common-looking crew in front of him again, swung the gate open, and led them toward the mansion at the top of the slope.

"Oh, aren't the staircases beautiful!" said Julia.

"I guess," said Sam. Two arcs of stairways led up to the mansion's front door, each a semicircle, like a French dandy's mustaches. Half of him hated the staircases because they were a sign of class superiority, and the other half resonated to them because they were lovely.

Another functionary greeted the party at the door. "Good morning, Mr. MacKye," he said. "Is the doctor expecting you?"

"No."

The functionary disappeared, and in a moment the White-Headed Eagle himself strode forth. He was a tall man with extraordinary intensity of eye and visage. He bore a great shock of white hair, said to have turned that color overnight when he nearly drowned in Lake Superior as a young man.

"*Rideo, ergo sum,*" he declared, and braced Hannibal by the shoulders.

"You came, my friend, you saw, and you have truly conquered." Hannibal hadn't seen the fort in half a dozen years.

"I have great responsibilities," said McLoughlin. "Join me in the sitting room."

It was a warm-looking room, luxuriously furnished and smelling of leather books and waxed floors. The doctor invited Julia to sit beside him on a sofa. At another time her heart would have been touched. She hadn't seen a sofa in a dozen years.

The doctor addressed Hannibal. "How may I be of service to you?"

Julia spoke up. "Dr. McLoughlin," she said, "we come to you on a matter of great urgency. Our daughter Esperanza left her husband, fled here for help, probably carrying a newborn child. Is she here?"

McLoughlin's imperial manner evaporated. He put his arm around this woman he'd never met before. "Oh, my poor dear," he said.

Julia burst into tears.

He lifted her by the hand and led her away. "Come to my office," he said to everyone. "It's more private."

ESPERANZA RAN INTO the room calling in the Crow language, "Mother, Mother!"

She hurled herself into her mother's arms and broke in huge, breath-sucking sobs.

Dr. McLoughlin left discreetly.

When she recovered slightly, Esperanza said to Flat Dog over Julia's shoulder, "Papa." And to Sam, "Papa." She reached out her hands to both of them.

Hannibal decided he should follow Dr. McLoughlin. Jay sat on the floor close to Esperanza.

The story tumbled out like water over falls, all full of turbulence. The day of the birth, alone and afraid. The effort of the delivery, followed by the bliss of holding the baby. The sense that something was wrong, but inability to see in the half darkness. The sight of the cord, the fierce cutting, the unwinding—all too late.

"It's all my fault," Esperanza said. "I was too slow to understand. I couldn't see well."

"If Joe had been there," said Flat Dog, "he would have seen."

"I've thought so much about it since I left him," Esperanza said. "He was gone most of the time. Hunting, trapping, drinking, all the things he likes to do with his friends. Sometimes I've hated him. Sometimes I've told myself he was only being Joe, just like always. 'No man like Joe.'"

Sam just held her hands, looked into her eyes, and felt how much he loved her.

"How did you get here?" said Flat Dog.

"I rode Vermilion. Left when Joe was over at Doc's."

"Have you been treated well here?" asked Jay.

"Dr. McLoughlin has been so nice. He gave me a job in the kitchen right here in the governor's house, and they gave me a bed here with the servants. The doctor didn't want me out in Kanaka Village in case Joe came and was mad." She snuffled. "I've eaten better here than in my entire life."

They had a lot more emotional conversation. Sam savored every word. He savored even more his daughter's hand in his own.

Finally Sam put it to her. "Do you want to go on to California with us?"

Esperanza said, "I want to be with my mother and my two fathers."

AFTER MAYBE HALF an hour, Dr. McLoughlin rapped lightly on the door.

"Come in."

He and Hannibal entered, an aroma of cigar smoke and an aura of camaraderie wafting in their wake.

"May we offer you a place to stay tonight?" Dr. McLoughlin said to the group. "We have accommodations for visitors."

"That would be very kind," said Julia.

"And I would appreciate your being my guests at dinner. We like to feed our guests well."

Jay spoke up. "Dr. McLoughlin, I have a special request. My mother is your cook."

"What's her name?" said McLoughlin.

"Maylea Palua."

"She's our chief cook!" cried McLoughlin. "She's excellent."

"May I see her now?"

"Certainly."

"She's in the kitchen," cried Esperanza. "I was just working with her." The girl was excitable.

"Also, Dr. McLoughlin, would you invite her to dinner with the rest of us?"

Hannibal saw conflict tighten the doctor's face. He was bound by strict ideas about the superiority of Englishmen. But his eyes softened. This was a special occasion in what was truly a New World.

"I can do better than that. We shall free her from her duties," he declared, "invite her to spend the afternoon with us touring the premises, and ask her to join us at dinner."

HOW ON EARTH, thought Julia, *is Jay going to keep his secret with his mother around everybody?*

The solution turned out to be simple. Maylea spoke only Hawaiian and Chinook. As a matter of fact, Jay and his mother had most of the fun on the tour. They rode Jay's gelding together, because Maylea had never been on a horse before.

The doctor was as kind to Maylea as to anyone, deliberately including her in the conversation and waiting for Jay to tell his mother what was said.

At the back of the riding party Sam noticed something. "He's kind," Sam murmured to Hannibal, "but he's kind like he's God and we're his children."

"British imperialism," said Hannibal. "We fought a war to give that the boot."

"I don't think I like God," said Sam.

Hannibal grinned. "Here's a truth about the four winds, Mother Earth, and Father Sky. They're real, and they're the same for everyone."

Dr. McLoughlin showed off the crops, orchards, and dairies. "We have met the Company's goal of being independent for our comestibles," he said. Only Hannibal knew what he meant, but the others could guess. He also had established shops for all the everyday work of a town, blacksmithing, wheel making, barrel making, sewing, and the like. His eyes gleamed with proprietorship. "I regret that this is too vast an estate to see in a single day."

Sam and Hannibal smiled at this sideways brag.

"The missions in California have accomplished nothing so fine," said Hannibal.

"And nothing at all anymore," the doctor said with a tight smile.

Esperanza showed them the room she had shared for nearly one moon with other kitchen workers. In it were the few belongings she'd brought from Joe's cabin, her clothes, two blankets, and a cradleboard.

"I made the cradleboard myself," she said. The pride showed even through her wan voice.

The front piece was fully beaded in Crow blue, Cheyenne pink, and white.

"Beautiful," said Julia.

Esperanza grimaced.

They had a sumptuous meal with everyone in good spirits. Esperanza seemed giddy with happiness and drank a little too much wine.

Three parents, the grown-up daughter who was not quite a parent, and three children shared a room. When the oil lamps were wicked out, Sam, Flat Dog, and Julia lay in the dark thinking of the boy who had died, their first grandchild. Death corraled each one in his own mind, lonely and afraid.

FROM THERE OREGON was easy business for the Morgan–Flat Dog family. The White-Headed Eagle himself rode upriver with the family to the Willamette Falls, to show them how he had laid out a town plat on his land claim there and was offering lots for sale. He was also about to get his mill running.

"The Methodists have recently claimed the same land," he declared, "that I filed on in 1829. My claim should take precedence, and I trust it will. Over-patriotic, those *missionaries*."

He put a little twist on "missionaries" that tickled Hannibal. Though the doctor was a Catholic, he had strictly forbidden any attempt to interfere with the religions of Indians of his territory. The Methodists took the opposite attitude. And while the Methodists were quick with criticism of McLoughlin, they had to admit he'd invariably been kind to them. If he hadn't advanced them provisions on credit to get through their first winters here, they would have starved.

"Everyone knows this will be American Territory, south of the Columbia," said McLoughlin. "I plan to live here myself, when I retire." He looked at the immense power of the Falls. "What energy for a mill," he murmured.

He rode up the Tualatin River with the family to see the horses and was delighted. Hannibal insisted that he get on several of the saddle mounts and ride in the hackamore style they'd been trained in.

"Capital!" he said. "First class!" He followed that with a bid for the entire herd. "Or if you will accept a letter of credit," he said, "I will give you one to the Hudson's Bay in Yerba Buena, on San Francisco Bay. My daughter and son-in-law have just started our new post there."

Yerba Buena. The name made Sam think how soon he would see Grumble and at Monterey Tomás, Abby, and others.

He talked the offer over quietly with Hannibal and Flat Dog.

"We could probably get more if we took our time and sold them a few at a time," said Hannibal.

"He's offering a lot of money," said Flat Dog. A dozen years' wages for an ordinary worker, in fact.

"I'd like to get on the trail to California," said Sam.

"And we're indebted to the doctor," said Hannibal.

They accepted.

"In gold," Flat Dog told McLoughlin.

IN THEIR TIPI, back on the Tualatin Plains. Warm evening air cozied up to them like a blanket. They sat outside and ate and talked quietly. They discussed teaching Joe Meek a lesson for abandoning Esperanza, but they didn't have the heart for it. Julia said, "Being gone, being drunk—just Joe being Joe."

Esperanza said, "I don't want to go anywhere near him again, ever." She added, "No man like Joe."

Otherwise they were lost in their own thoughts. Jay wanted nothing but to get out of Oregon and into California, where he would be safe. Esperanza huddled close to Julia and pecked at her food. Azul and Rojo played quietly. Flat Dog and Julia sat close to each other, somber. All the great labors were behind them and the dream of California on the near horizon.

Sam shared the feelings, but he also felt empty. Hanging from a lodge pole behind Esperanza was the cradleboard, the one she'd spent countless hours beading. A work of art. But it was empty. One place at his family table would always be empty.

THE NEXT MORNING a Frenchy messenger arrived in a lather from Dr. McLoughlin. First he handed them a good map. A glance showed that it was even better than they needed. Up the Willamette River to Salem, three days, the Frenchy said, pointing. The Methodists had a mission there. Farther up the Willamette several days and over a divide at its head to the Umpqua River. "Indians *dangereux*," the Frenchy said, "very treacherous. Maybe ten year ago zey wipe out party of your Captain Jedediah Smith completely, but for three men."

Over another divide to the Rogue River and up that to its head. When you cross Siskiyou Pass, you're in California. South straight past Mount Shasta, a volcano, to the head of the Sacramento River, and down it all the way to San Francisco Bay. Probably more than seven hundred miles altogether, about two months' travel. Rugged country, those mountains at the border of Oregon and Alta California.

Then, like an afterthought, the Frenchy handed Sam a letter. "It come on big ship *de la mer* only late yezzerday. Ze doctor, he t'ink maybe you want."

Sam opened the letter, saw it was in Spanish, and recognized the handwriting of Tomás.

At Santa Fe
November 2, 1840

Dear Uncle Grumble—
I write this news to you and Aunt Abby and trust that you will forward it to Sam.

Sam winced a little at the word. "Sam" instead of "Dad." That was one of the ways Tomás used to put distance between himself and his adopted father. Funny, when Tomás was just twelve, it was he who had the idea of adopting Sam as his father.

I have been offered a great opportunity by de Vrain, one of the great traders of this city. On condition of raising my own capital, I am permitted to join in the enormous de Vrain trading caravan bound to Chihuahua, the mining district, below, and on to Mexico City. Our old friend Sumner has put up the capital, as he often did for my father, and we will share the profits equally.

I look forward to a journey rich in experience and earnings. As you know, I have not been in my native mountains, the Sierra Madre Occidental, in a dozen years, nor have I ever seen the land beyond them, the principal cities and industries of my native land, and the capital. You can imagine my excitement!

Sam hoped Tomás wasn't planning a side trip to his birth village. When the Apaches made the raid that enslaved Tomás, they killed the men of the village, including Tomás's father, and the small children.

You and Sam will understand that this is too great a chance to pass up. Though it delays my arrival in California for about a year, I will arrive as a man better prepared to start a prosperous life.

Please give my affection to Abby, and when my father arrives, tell him I shall make him proud of me.

Your devoted
Tomás

Sam folded the letter and put it away. *I'd rather he was just here. Just here with us.*

Forty-three

AT FIRST LIGHT of the day of departure Sam daydreamed of Monterey. The sunlight on the bay, like no other light in the world. He saw the mission and its fine buildings, and the cemetery where Meadowlark was buried.

His mind played back good times with the best friends of his first days as an adult on his own, Grumble and Abby. Also his longtime partner, Gideon Poorboy. After Sam had to cut Gideon's gangrenous leg off, the peg-legged man became Monterey's expert silversmith and goldsmith. Sam remembered the two women he had loved, both gone over. He brought back to mind the day he bought Tomás out of slavery. Tomás was an ache in Sam's chest.

Just as he reminded himself that today was an important day to live, Julia said, "Coffee's ready."

Two hours later, under a bright summer sun, the tipi was

packed onto lodge poles, the packhorses were laden with other gear, the riders mounted, and their horses prancing nervously.

Sam said, "Let's move out."

THE TRAVEL WAS pleasantly boring, and time spread softly across the days like soft butter. Sam couldn't remember feeling mellower. As captain he kept up the usual precautions. He himself rode lookout ahead. On the left and the right flanks Hannibal and Flat Dog. Beside Julia and the kids, on the gelding that had replaced her dead mare, Jay always carried his pistol. Sam smiled and wondered if the Hawaiian would ever learn to use it. The first few days they were passing the farms of the retired Hudson's Bay Frenchies and then the farms of the Methodists. When Esperanza or Azul, who was now fully healed, wanted to ride along with one of the lookouts, that was permitted.

In the evenings Sam encouraged Jay, Esperanza, and Azul to practice shooting the pistol. Hannibal, an exceptional shot, instructed them. In real Indian country, they wouldn't have dared make that kind of racket or waste the gunpowder.

When they crossed over to the valley of the Umpqua, the country got rougher, and Sam cut out the pistol practice. He couldn't help thinking about Jedediah and the brigade and the massacre here by Umpqua Indians. Sam had ridden all the way from the Great Salt Lake with those men, and nineteen of twenty-two died here. Sam missed being one of them because he left the outfit at Monterey to find his daughter, over Jedediah's objections.

Jedediah, the best of captains. He might have been the best of friends, but his God kept him righteous and solitary.

On the Rogue River Sam's mind turned away from the past and toward the future. He looked every day for the way through the mountains to the south, Siskiyou Pass. That marked California.

About noon one day he saw it. Esperanza was riding with him at that moment. "Go tell everyone that notch in the mountains is it, why don't you?"

His eyes and his thoughts were on California all that afternoon. Maybe that's why, when he stopped the outfit for the night's camp, he hadn't missed . . .

"Where's Esperanza?"

"Must be riding with Flat Dog or Hannibal," said Julia.

"I'll go see," said Azul. He sounded uneasy.

Sam nodded to him.

No point in riding out to Hannibal on the western flank, though—here came the Delaware at a lope on Brownie.

Azul headed for Flat Dog.

"I haven't seen her since midafternoon," said Flat Dog. "We walked along awhile and talked and then she rode off into the bushes to pee. I supposed she'd gone back to the main outfit."

Sam, Julia, Flat Dog. Hannibal and Jay. The boys. Shadows of suspicion swam in everyone's eyes.

"Let's go," said Sam to Flat Dog.

"I'm coming," said Jay.

"You?" said Sam. "Why?"

He hardly knew himself, or hardly admitted it. He just said, "I'm coming."

Esperanza's two papas and a Hawaiian woman they thought was a man rode back fast along Flat Dog's trail on the northern flank. The summer sun poured light onto the world late into the evening. Having a warrior's memory for terrain, Flat Dog was able to point out the exact spot where Esperanza had dropped behind.

They followed Vermilion's tracks easily. Saw where the girl-woman had dismounted and where she had relieved herself.

A strange pair of moccasin prints treaded to that spot. Sam could almost hear the silence of the foot pads. He felt like he was falling into the bottom of a well.

Where Esperanza had fallen, the lush grass was still crushed, and anyone could see how her feet dragged over to where Vermilion had been tied. The strange moc prints—no need for silence now—led Vermilion away. Soon the tracks led to the top of a little rise. Beyond that a foot-wide stream flowed. A hole was visible where a horse had been staked. And from there two sets of hoofprints led up the creek away from the river, to . . .

Where?

Two men shared the identical thought.

Where has my daughter been taken?

Jay provided the answer to a different question, a more important one. "See this break in the left edge of the hoof? Kind of a quarter-moon shape? That hoof is Warrior's. Left front."

He looked hard into the eyes of one father and then the other.

"Kanaka Boy has her."

Part Five

Forty-four

"YOU'RE STAYING HERE," Sam rasped out. He could barely keep from shouting. Rojo slid behind his mother.

"I'm going. She's my daughter," barked Flat Dog.

"Dammit!" Sam spun all the way around on his heels. "Dammit! You've got to stay here! You have a family to take of. A whole outfit."

"You're captain here. You take care of it, you and Hannibal."

Sam turned away and looked up at the North Star. The distant light had no guidance for him now.

"This is your wife. These are your other children. Three of them."

Julia reached up and pulled Flat Dog's hand. He sat down beside her.

"I'll be ready at first light," he declared.

Sam whirled on him. "I'm ordering you to stay here."

"You don't give me no goddamn orders."

"I have to take care of her."

"I did when you didn't."

"God awmighty."

Sam strode to the edge of the light from the dwindling fire. He stared into the darkness. Somewhere out there things were happening to his daughter. He refused to imagine them.

He turned to the whole crew around the fire. Calmly, he said, "I'm going alone. End of—"

"My husband," said Julia, "I am going to ask you something. Stay with us."

Husband looked into wife's eyes, searching.

"Take us to California. Your wife and these children beside me. I ask you. We need you."

Flat Dog couldn't speak.

"Sam will do everything that can be done."

Flat Dog dropped his head. "Goddamn," he whispered. He squeezed Julia's hand. "Yes," he said.

Sam had never felt so relieved. He wished he could leave right now.

"But *I'm* going."

Sam couldn't believe the voice. He jerked his head toward Jay. "No way on earth," he said.

"Yes, I will. The reason is simple. I know where Kanaka Boy is going. You don't."

"Jay is right," said Hannibal.

Sam looked at his friend like he was a traitor.

"A *ba'te* on a war mission. If that doesn't beat all." Sam walked off. Time to give Paladin some water and cool himself off.

"You need to learn something," called Jay.

He turned toward the man-woman in utter disgust.

Jay crossed his arms, grabbed the bottom edges of his deer hide shirt, and lifted it up to his neck. She held the shirt there for a long moment. Everyone saw, and her small breasts were worth showing off.

Sam took a long moment to recover speech. "A woman and a liar. Even worse."

Lei played her trump card again. "I know where he's going."

"She's right," Hannibal said.

It took Sam a moment, staring at Lei, to wrap his mind around the word "she."

"Something else. It isn't Esperanza he wants. It's me. He'll never stop until he gets me."

Lei let that sit and then added in a simple tone, "So this time I'm going to kill him."

Forty-five

AT DAWN THE outfit rode out toward that notch in the mountains. "We'll meet you in Monterey," Sam told Flat Dog. "All three of us."

When they were gone, Lei unhobbled her gelding and lifted her saddle onto his back.

"We better stay here," Sam told her.

She gawked at him.

"The son of a bitch will be waiting for us."

Lei put the horse back on some grass and wondered what to do. She sat cross-legged near the dead fire and started drawing flowers in the dust with a stick. She drew an elaborate pattern of stems, leaves, and blossoms.

Sam looked toward the low mountains in the east. "I got no question he's set an ambush for us."

"Don't talk about it," she said. "It makes my bowels crawl."

She devoted herself to her drawing. She had brushed a circle clear several feet across. The flowers grew almost like living things.

Sam stood and stared off to the east. "This is gonna drive me crazy."

"I know where he's going," Lei said again, her eyes on her moving hand. "It won't be hard to find him. Could be hard to do something about him."

"He's clever."

"He likes to hurt people."

Sam grabbed the Celt and started toward Paladin. "I better get us some fresh meat," he said.

Lei looked directly at him. "Don't leave me alone," she said.

"Don't . . . ?"

"How do you know he's not watching us right now?"

Sam fidgeted and sat down at her side. "He must have been watching us right along."

"He knew where we were going. His buddies told him we were taking the herd to Oregon City. We made no secret that we were going straight on to California. There's only one trail."

Sam got the willies. *Watching us right along*. Watching Esperanza. Seeing when she rode along with her mother or rode ahead with Papa Sam or on either flank. Watching when she led her pony to the river to drink, morning and evening. Watching when she peed. Watching very closely when she was alone. Figuring out when she would be alone. Waiting for the right place and the right time.

Boy could have killed her easily. Could have killed any of them. But that wasn't his point. He wanted to inflict pain, lots of pain. Torture, then kill.

"Clever bastard."

Lei looked at Sam like, "What's up with you?"

"He's smart," she said. "He's strong. He's wild as can be. Plus all the way crazy and all the way mean. Don't underestimate him."

Sam took it in and then shut his mind off that track. He made himself watch Lei draw. He needed some time to get used to Lei instead of Jay. He needed some time to get used to the idea that she was not a man, boy, or *ba'te* but a woman.

"Listen," she said. "I don't want you to treat me any different, now you know what I am."

"I was just thinking about that."

"We have a way we are around each other, you and me. You've pissed right in front of me. Carry on with that. You cuss, that's fine. Treat me like your sister."

Sam got it. She was worried about sleeping next to a man who might want to touch her.

"You're an attractive woman," he said in a kind tone. "I wish I'd known all along that you are a woman. But the way we are together is set. No trouble."

"You sure about that?"

"Maybe not," Sam said. "I'm uneasy about chasing a killer with a woman, any woman."

"Watch me," she joked. She pulled the pistol Hannibal had loaned her out of her belt. "I managed to hit a big, fat cottonwood from three paces the other day."

Sam chuckled.

"That was using Hannibal's shoulder to rest my hand."

She mock-aimed the pistol and said, "Bang!"

He squatted beside her and studied the drawing. It was beautiful, really, the way she made a stem open into a leaf, a leaf give birth to a blossom. The whole pattern looked like an opening up of itself, an emerging.

"I like to do these," she said. "One of the few things about the desert where the camp is—the only thing, really—is that there are a lot of different-colored sands and soils. I gathered them. I would spend a whole day making a drawing like this and then fill it in with lots of colors."

Like a Navajo sand painting, Sam thought. He said, "Where is he headed, exactly?"

Without looking up, she said, "To his main camp on the Owyhee River near the mouth of the Little Owyhee."

"What's the route?"

"We came across to trade whiskey at Coos Bay. Give me a minute to remember."

She thought it out by sketching it very roughly in the dirt. "From here over to Tule Lake, about four days. Beyond the divide it's dry, but there's an old trail. Then around the south end of a big mountain range, drier. Can't make it without carrying water.

"Then the hard part—you cross the Black Rock Desert. You have to know the springs. That brings you to the Humboldt, another week. Up the river about three days, then straight north to the Owyhee. About three weeks altogether, traveling steady the way men travel, not families. Most of it is old trails. Just on the Black Rock Desert you have to know the springs."

"Do you?"

"No way to forget. It's the driest place on earth. My tongue remembers."

"You sure he's going to the main camp."

"Yeah."

"Why?"

"He wants to give Esperanza to the men." She looked directly into his eyes. "To use."

Neither of them spoke.

"I saw a Digger woman die from being used that way, all those men in a row."

Sam huffed a hot wind out of his gullet. He twisted the words as they came out. "He's using her himself every night."

"No, he's not."

"He's not?"

"No."

"Why not?"

She took a moment to put the last touches on her drawing.

"Now I'm going to tell you why he hates me. I'm his wife. I

was." She waited a moment for Sam to get that and be ready for the next. "He raped me, and he gave me to his men to rape."

Sam looked into her eyes for a long while. They were steady. He understood some things about Lei but not why she was willing to go up against Kanaka Boy again. And not whether, when the moment came, she would cave in.

"The way I got even was, I cut his nuts off."

"You what?!"

"I got him out of his mind on laudanum—he loves that stuff—and cut his nuts off. I have them with me, right here." She touched her belt bag. "In this pouch."

Sam went for a short walk. When he got back, Lei was halfway finished with another completely different drawing. This one was all swirling stems and tiny leaves. Instead of peace it was rage.

"He's headed for the Humboldt?"

"No water any other way."

"Then we don't need to track him."

Lei looked up and took his meaning. "Actually, we don't."

"He can't hurt her."

"He can hurt her. He just can't engage in sex with her."

Sam parsed his breath in and out. "He has to cross the Black Rock Desert."

"For sure."

"Using springs."

"That or die, most especially this time of year."

Sam ran it through his mind again, to be sure. For Esperanza, he had to be very sure.

"Then let's get there first and wait for him."

Forty-six

THE WAY THEY treated each other in fact didn't change. Sam and Lei made good traveling companions.

During the day they were all business, finding a good route. They didn't dare use the Indian trail. Maybe Boy was waiting behind them in ambush, but maybe he wasn't. They stayed a couple of divides south of the trail and traveled rougher country.

They made camp without fires—a high level of caution—and munched on dried meat. The packhorse carried plenty of meat and four kegs of water.

The first night out Lei got Sam to tell her his story. How he ran away from home because of Hannibal's advice. Sam could still quote it exactly: "Everything worthwhile is crazy, and everyone on the planet who's not following his wild-hair, middle-of-the-night notions should lay down his burden, right now, in the middle of the row he's hoeing, and follow the direction his wild hair points."

Sam told how he made his way to St. Louis and went west with the Ashley beaver brigade. Spent the winter with the Crows. Got caught in a prairie fire and would have died if he hadn't crawled inside a buffalo carcass. Which earned him his Crow name.

The second night she told how she got infatuated with Kanaka Boy, a Hawaiian who had the sand to stand up to the Brits and outdo them at their own game. How the new bride had been disappointed by the camp, made nervous by the loose women, fearful of the rough men, and then shocked to see how the men and women got drunk and fornicated every night.

Over several days Sam and Lei became friends. And part of what friends did, the way Sam saw things, was steer clear of questions that made the other one uncomfortable.

Lei brought up one tender subject herself. She told him how she'd been horrified at the attack on the Diggers, killing all the men and the elderly and the very young, capturing all the others as slaves. How she ran away, Kanaka Boy caught her and administered the lesson of multiple rape. How she tricked him and got away. "I didn't want to pretend to be a man. However, I wanted no one, absolutely no one, to be able to report seeing a woman to Boy."

"You're tough."

"No, I'm not. I'm soft inside. I just have to act tough, for now."

Another night she spoke of something else that was hard for her. "At first it was good to be a man. Horrible to be a woman. So . . . vulnerable. I became a man so no man would touch me. I never wanted to be touched again. But during the winter at Walla Walla . . . It was a such long winter, so much training of horses, so much trading, so much ordinary life. . . .

"When we got to Walla Walla, Julia told me she and Esperanza knew my secret and promised to keep it. Before the winter months passed, though, I lost most of my fear of discovery, and got very tired of my disguise. Especially, I chafed against it—that is the word, no, 'chafed'?—because one man especially appealed to me."

"Appealed to you?" Sam was flabbergasted. He hadn't caught one sign of this.

"Your friend Hannibal. He is very kind and very intelligent." Sam could see her smile at the darkness. "With his coloring, half white and half Indian, he might even be Hawaiian.

"It was . . . tricky. I couldn't look at him in, you know, that way. Think of his reaction. Poor fellow, put off, very put off. If I did look at him, though, I knew he would see it in my eyes. . . . So I spent the winter working alongside him with my gaze downcast."

Sam couldn't believe he hadn't noticed any of this byplay.

"Do not be deceived, though. I do not dream of Hannibal, nor of anyone who might be the so-called right man. I no longer dream of family and children. I feel . . . ruined for that.

"What I dream of is home. I want to go back to Kauai. I've never even seen Hawaii—so much a beautiful name compared to 'the Sandwich Islands'—but my father used to tell me about them. They are the most beautiful . . . Everything verdant, trees always leafed out, flowers always blossoming. I dream of home. I will put flowers in my hair every morning. . . .

"The English brought my grandparents here, however, half as slaves. I will never have the money to pay one of their ships to take me home." It was the first time he'd heard bitterness in her voice. "You go to your dream, California. No matter where I go, I am a stranger."

THE BLACK ROCK Desert looked as far from verdant as anything Sam had ever seen. He knew deserts, from greasewood country like the Mojave to redrock and cedar landscape like Navajo country to the high, sagebrush alternations of basin and mountain between the Sierra Nevada and the Rockies. He had walked with Jedediah across a stretch of desert west of the Salt Lake so dry that he'd persuaded Jedediah to bury him to the neck in sand and leave him to die. But the Black Rock Desert was something from the human race's nightmares.

Around it were high, barren mountain ranges. The foothills grew the usual desert foliage, sagebrush, saltbush, rabbitbrush, greasewood, and even a few grasses. No doubt if he scouted around, he would find a little animal life in the hills, some deer, and coyotes, and plenty of reptiles.

Yet Sam had never imagined a desert like this. A dry lake bed, black as tar, flat as a slab of polished marble, and absolutely devoid of any sign of life.

He lifted his field glass and studied it. Black and flat, black and flat. "How far across?"

"You start at sunset, carry water, and get to the hot springs over there by sunrise. They're right below that notch in the hills." Sam couldn't make out any foliage from this distance. "Maybe twenty miles. Hardpan all the way, plenty hard, there's a blessing."

They had three and a half kegs of water from the last stream they'd seen.

Sam glassed to the north and the south. Twice as long as it was wide, he estimated.

"He could be ahead of us." The route they'd taken had been longer and rougher than the trail. On the other hand, they'd pushed like hell. "Is there a way to check?"

"The Indian trail comes over the ridge about there." She pointed. "If we go back up this wash to the rise, we can see the spring. There he will fill up, and that's where the trail goes onto the hardpan. From there you couldn't miss tracks."

They rode back. Sam glassed the dry lake bed to the northeast carefully, microscopically. The trail came to the lake about two miles north. No tracks. He made sure, no tracks.

The picture of Esperanza's face flickered into his mind again, and he shoved it away. All week he'd been hard with himself. *Don't think about her. Don't imagine what she may . . .*

Then he saw it, off to the southwest, black, ugly, and way too close.

"Let's go!" he said, and put the spurs to Paladin.

* * *

THE SANDSTORM SLAMMED them quick and hard. Sam figured they were less than halfway to where the packhorse was hobbled. They absolutely had to get back. That horse bore what they would need to survive, blankets and water.

They fought their mounts down the wash. If the route hadn't been a wash, they would have gotten hopelessly lost. Only the two sides of the gully and the downward slope told them which direction to go.

Lei's gelding stumbled and refused to get up. Coughing, hacking, and eyes stinging from grit, Sam could hardly see to wrestle the animal onto his feet. When Sam got it done, he decided they'd have to lead the horses. After a dozen steps the gelding lay down on the downwind side of a boulder and refused to budge.

Sam fought him, heaved on the bridle, screamed at him, and kicked his hind end. When Sam finally got the horse on his feet, he couldn't find Paladin. Then he saw her lying flat in the lee of the next boulder, bigger.

All right. No choice.

He grabbed Lei's arm, pulled her to Paladin, and sat her on the prone horse. In one motion he snatched Lei's hide shirt off. Automatically, she covered her breasts with her hands. He wrapped the shirt around her head and used the arms as ties. Then he pushed her down between Paladin's back and the boulder.

He wrapped his own head in his shirt, snorting to get the damned sand out of his nostrils, rubbing it out of his eyes but only making things worse. Then he wedged himself next to Lei, kicking and squeezing his way down. He'd never been closer to another creature. Sometimes he couldn't tell what was himself, what was Lei, and what was horseflesh.

He tried not to breathe. If he breathed, he would suffocate.

Slowly, bit by bit, he sipped in little bits of air. He found that if he pulled air in very shallowly and pushed the gritty breath out hard, he might not suffocate. He did this a hundred times. A thousand times. More times than the sky had specks of light. Almost as many as the damned wind had flecks of sand.

He did nothing but breathe and tell himself to do this same damn thing over and over and stay alive.

An hour later, a day later, a week later—who knew?—the wind eased. It didn't stop blowing completely, but it eased.

Sam muttered to Lei, "Give it a few minutes."

In about half an hour they got to their feet, and so did their horses.

Sam had never felt worse in his life. He had a bad cold in his nose, but the mucus was sand. His ears were clogged with the stuff, and he couldn't hear. He had entire dunes behind his ears. His white hair could be combed and the yield used for potting soil. There was sand under his belt and in every fold of his privates. It was in the wrinkles behind his knees and between his toes and was threatening to pry all twenty nails right off his fingers and toes. His butt crack felt like someone had caulked it, and his next shit would probably be sand.

Without thought or self-consciousness they both stripped off every stitch of clothing and gear, brushed themselves off, and shook their clothes out. Then they dressed, which was painful, and rode to the edge of the lake bed.

By a miracle the packhorse was alive—flat on the ground but alive. Without hesitation Sam and Lei dipped water out of one of the kegs, swilled it around their mouths, and spat it out. They sniffed it up their noses and snorted it onto the ground. After about five minutes of repeating this wastefulness, they grabbed blankets, shook them out, dunked them in the keg, and gave themselves sponge baths. They used water extravagantly, indecently, absurdly. Not a drop of booze, but they got drunk on water.

When dark fell, they soaked clean blankets, wrapped up in them, and slept like the dead.

Sam was pleasantly surprised to wake up alive.

Lei seemed to be alive as well, and all three horses.

"We've got to go back to the last spring," he said.

She nodded.

Neither of them wanted to waste words, because the sand in their throats still scratched.

At the spring they played in the water like tadpoles. Two human beings were dunked like doughnuts most of the day. The innocence of yesterday's nakedness, though, was gone. Sam wore a breechcloth, Lei a long shirt. They would have been sexless anyway—that was just their way. Sam wondered whether, after Lei's rotten experiences, she had just turned that part of herself off. He wouldn't blame her.

When their bodies were watered, and the horses, and the kegs, they started back toward the lake bed.

They stopped and glassed the black lake surface for tracks. "Still none," Sam said.

They had lost a day, exactly one, but they were still ahead of Kanaka Boy and Esperanza. Sam wondered how those two came through the sandstorm. He thought, *When they get to the spring on the other side, I will be the storm Kanaka Boy doesn't survive.*

THE MOMENT THE sun dropped behind the western ridges, they started across the black desert floor. Sam could see the notch that marked the spring. He put a hard control on his mind. It was going to be a dry, grueling night.

When the last light seeped out of the sky, he navigated by the light of the half-moon. The Black Rock Desert, though, turned spooky. The surrounding mountains turned into smudges, perhaps smoke, perhaps nothing. To the south the black lake bed shone with a single line of light running straight toward the moon. To the west, the north, the east, and the point north of east where they were headed, it was a dark and fathomless sea.

They stopped every couple of hours, opened a keg, drank, and watered the horses from their hats. Sam believed they had plenty of water. Plenty of confidence? He didn't know.

About halfway through the night—and halfway across?—the moon set.

Sam had never seen a darkness like this. It was absolute. He couldn't see what Paladin was putting her feet on, if anything.

He called a halt, dismounted, watered the riders and the horses. He and Lei sat and rested a few minutes, but they spent no words. Finally, Sam said, "Let's lead the horses. Easier on them."

In truth, he felt they were walking on the dark spaces between stars. He wanted to put his own moccasins on whatever surface it was, so he knew it was real.

Now he steered by the North Star. He knew, though, that this was an inexact way to navigate. He began to worry that he might veer off as much as thirty degrees in either direction and end up several miles away from the spring. Finally he said, "We're not short of water. It's two hours, maybe, to first light. I can't tell whether the spring is this way or that way." He held his arms out at right angles. "Let's take a nap and head in then, when we can see."

"He might spot us out here."

Sam shook his head. "He hasn't made it to that side yet."

They stretched out on the surface Sam couldn't see, but they couldn't sleep. They talked quietly. Lei told Sam about her years with her grandfather, who was good with his hands and could make anything out of wood. He also was full of stories about his own childhood in Kauai, which sounded like a fairyland to her. When he died, she was ten, and after that she spent her time as a servant in the fort, cleaning and serving meals. The only good part about that was learning English.

Sam talked about his own dad, Lewis, who showed him the ways of the woods, how everything relates to everything else. After Lewis's death, Sam's older brother leaned on him until Sam ran away from home.

At one point Sam realized that they were both telling stories and neither was hearing the other. Then they fell into silence, and in the darkness Sam's only hint of any other living being was an occasional chuff from the horses or a clomp of hoof.

At first light they rode toward the notch. In half an hour Sam could see the greenery that marked the spring. In an hour they were holding the horses back to keep them from galloping ahead. Shortly, Sam and Lei rode up to the little haven of grass and shade made by the miracle of water.

There, unarmed, with his feet in the spring, sat Kanaka Boy.

"Good morning, my friends," he said. "I have been waiting for you."

Forty-seven

SAM LEVELED THE Celt.

"You don't want to kill me," said Kanaka Boy in a sweet, melodious voice. "At least not yet."

"Why not?" said Sam.

"Because then you don't know where your precious daughter is." He chuckled.

Sam waiting, hating.

"Oh, I assure you, she stays where she is until I loose her bonds. She be well tied. She be without food, without water, without shade. Did you enjoy the sandstorm? So did she. Right out in it, unprotected. Last night I gave her the mercy of a good drink of water—I mean for her to live—but her body, it must feel like someone filed it with a rasp. Very bad, hmmm?"

He grinned and spread his arms wide. "What a very big desert, is it not? Magnificent, I believe. And a magnificent day, it is upon it, with a sun of power like a god.

"So, all desert creatures know how to outsmart this sun. They drink plenty water. They stay in shade. They move about only at dusk and dawn, or, like you, during the night. The beautiful Esperanza, she knows as well as any to behave in these ways. But, alas, she cannot, being tied up and in the sun."

If Kanaka Boy was expecting the satisfaction of a response, Sam gave him none.

"Such a grand, big desert, too. How many gullies you think slink down those mountain ranges with so many gullies each? Five or six ranges, no? She is maybe deposited in any one, and any gully of that. How many sagebrushes grow upon those hills, you think? She is maybe next to any one."

He paused in his prepared speech.

"Oh, you find her, I'm sure of that. And Lei is sure, too, aren't you, my dear? The buzzards will lead you to her.

"Why no get down and join me? Have a drink, and let your horses rest from their long night's work. We maybe talk, do you not agree?"

They did.

SAM BRUSHED AWAY Kanaka Boy's flask, stepped upstream of the horses, lay flat, and drank deep. Then he dunked his face and hair. Last he filled his own flask and sat down cross-legged facing the Hawaiian. Keeping his face blank, he studied how big the Kanaka Boy really was, a grizzly bear of a man.

Lei drank and sat next to Sam. Though she tried to hide it, he could see the quake in every movement. Kanaka Boy saw, too, and smiled at Sam and shrugged. A woman, what do you expect?

"I have set my rifle and pistol several paces away," said Kanaka Boy, "and my knife." He gestured to them. "Maybe good that you do the same?"

Sam did.

"Your hunting pouch, too. Your patch knife, it is there."

Sam put it down.

"Since I don' know you, I can no trust you not to act foolish. So I ask you, permit me to search your person for weapons."

Sam stared at him.

"Maybe you like to search me first."

Sam did. He thought of grabbing the bastard's balls and twisting, then enjoyed the memory that Lei had done away with them.

Boy searched Sam and found nothing. No one would be able to find the two weapons he kept hidden.

"Now you, my dear, put down that silly pistol."

Lei took it out of her belt and set it on a boulder.

Boy held his flask to them again, and both shook their heads no.

"I sense that you are no in a mood for pleasantries."

"Damn right."

"A shame. Then we go straight to the deal. I speak it in plain terms, which no are negotiable. You give me your weapons and your horses. You must, I am sorry, have no chance to follow me. You give me my wife."

"I am no such thing," growled Lei.

Kanaka Boy inclined his head politely. "Then I treat you as a slave. I prefer that."

Lei started to retort, but Kanaka Boy stopped her with a hand and looked into Sam's eyes. "In return I give you your life. You may take all the flasks you can carry, even my own, for I am a generous man. You set out on foot, back across the hardpan. Wait until this evening, if you like, we spend the day in a pleasant chat." He looked across the black desert floor, beginning to simmer under the morning sun. "It's a long way to California, but you have maybe decent chance to survive, I think. In any case, is only chance I can afford to give you."

Sam just glared at him.

Kanaka Boy looked back at Sam, a slight, twisty smile on his face, until Sam finally spoke.

"My daughter?"

"She is mine. I possess her. I have been think . . . I have been think I give her to my fine set of ruffians. They know how to enjoy her. But now I think I give this ex-wife to them. They hate her for her high-and-mighty airs, and right off they fork her until she dies.

"Your daughter I keep for my own blankets. She is good in the blankets. I have train her well to delight me."

So Kanaka Boy was at least part bluff. Sam didn't let his inside smile show.

"Bring me Esperanza or we have nothing to talk about."

Kanaka Boy laughed. "Tell me exact how you intend to force on me this ultimatum? What you offer in return?"

"I came for one purpose, to get her. Dying doesn't scare me."

"Made friends with death already, so you claim? Could be. I t'ink you American trappers, you are brave. Stupid, but brave."

Sam sprang, and he saw the flick of surprise in Boy's eyes. Sam shoulder-blocked him onto his back. With the first elbow Sam broke Boy's nose, and blood gushed everywhere. The second elbow went straight onto Boy's throat. Sam leaned his weight on it. One hard shove and he would break whatever part in there allowed Boy to . . .

Sam saw laughter in Boy's eyes. He eased up. Speak. He needed Boy to speak.

Sam eased up very slightly. Kanaka Boy wheezed air in and out, barely able to breathe. He might have to whisper the words like a man hanged by a noose, but he could get them out.

"Lei," said Sam in a tone of command. "Take my wooden hair piece out."

Lei slipped out the finger-sized rod that tied Sam's white hair back.

"Twist the two ends in opposite directions. It comes apart."

She did, revealing a short, stiff blade. It looked sharp as a splinter of glass.

Sam leaned a little on the elbow to remind Kanaka Boy.

"Pick a nice, tender spot on his inner thigh," Sam said. "Slide the knife just under the skin and cut a strip off."

Lei reached for the place she was told.

Kanaka Boy pointed at his mouth.

Sam eased up ever so slightly.

"Kill me," Boy rasped, "and Esperanza is dead."

"I don't mean to kill you," said Sam. "We're going to skin you. We're going to slice off little piece by little piece until you decide there's things worse than being dead."

Lei made the first cut.

Kanaka Boy rolled so swift and strong, it felt like trying to wrestle a mountain lion.

Instantly on his feet, Boy swung a boning knife at Sam's chest.

It ripped his hide shirt all the way across his chest, and a lot of skin.

Lei shrieked.

Sam took one step and bounded on top of the nearest boulder, waist high.

Boy lunged at Sam's legs with the knife and he had to jump down backward.

Boy circled the rock at top speed, and Sam sprinted around it in the other direction, tugging at his belt buckle. When the buckle knife popped out, he did a full spin and swiped at Boy's arm. He felt flesh tear. He let his momentum take him two steps beyond Kanaka Boy and whirled to face him.

Boy charged. Lei dived and tripped him with one hand. He hit the ground hard. Sam dived at him, buckle knife arcing down.

Boy rolled. *Damn, he's quick.*

The moment Sam took to think gave Boy an opening. He kicked Sam's wrist and the knife flew.

Boy head-butted Sam in the chest. They both hit the ground, Boy on top.

Boy sat up, his weight crushing Sam's belly. He raised the knife, and Sam fixed on the gleaming blade. Already he could feel the plunge into his chest.

BOOM!

Boy's knife arm exploded in blood.

The knife skittered into the bushes.

"That's enough!" shouted Esperanza.

Hannibal MacKye set his rifle down, raised his pistol, and said, "Next shot takes your head off."

Kanaka Boy stood up, hands high, one gripping the bloody forearm.

"All right! All right!" he said. "Enough for now. We talk."

BOOM!

Kanaka Boy grabbed his gut with both hands.

White smoke drifted on the air above Lei's hand, and she stared down the barrel of her pistol at her fallen husband.

They all stood, unbelieving.

After a long moment Esperanza threw herself into Sam's arms.

Then Lei moved. She reached into her belt bag, took out the pouch, fished two small lumps of flesh, and dropped them into Kanaka Boy's open mouth.

His eyes understood for a moment and then glazed.

Part Six

Forty-eight

LEI INSISTED THAT they leave his body out for the buzzards. Even though the heat of the day was bearing down, they filled the kegs from the spring, mounted, and got out of there. "This trail leads to the Humboldt," she said, "two days." That was the last sentence anyone spoke for a long time.

At midmorning they came to a dry wash with a big cotton-wood, which meant there was probably water in the winter. They took a nooner. When Sam woke up, he started to dig in the wash. An hour's work produced nothing. Lei said, "We have enough anyway."

Sam sat down. Hannibal sat up and blinked.

Sam looked for a long moment at Esperanza, sleeping. Her eye-lids quivered like she was having dreams. He wondered if they were nightmares. He hoped to make the long ride to California a trip back to normalcy for her, maybe with lots of talking. He hoped so.

He turned to Hannibal and noticed that Lei had stretched out near his head. Now she was looking at him from behind.

"All right," Sam asked his partner, "how did you do it?"

"I followed you. You should have guessed I would. When I saw you weren't going to track Kanaka Boy, I did, a day behind. Had to go real easy at first, couldn't take a chance he'd see me, wanted him to swallow your idea no one was following him.

"On the second morning he decided you weren't coming, or more likely he figured out what you were up to. Probably just asked what a smart fellow like himself would do in the same situation. Anyway, he rode like hell. That man was a traveling maniac—he could cover ground. I had trouble keeping up, and I thought he was going to wear Esperanza to death. He didn't check his back trail at all. He was beelining, with a purpose.

"When we got to the Black Rock Desert, he went up to the spring on the near side real cautious. Looked around for tracks and didn't find any. Filled up on water and circled around the north end of the lake. Long way, an extra day compared to going across, but he knew where a spring was. He moved at night, and I lagged back. On the way around he got hit by the same sandstorm.

"I thought he must be playing a trick. When he got to the spring where you found him and made camp, I knew. Trouble was, Esperanza wasn't with him. That's when I understood the trap.

"I went back. Had a good idea where she might be. He didn't give a damn whether he killed her, but he wanted Vermilion, always eager to have another horse. On the northeast side of the hardpan there was one rocky gully I'd seen, looked like a grove of trees about a mile up.

"Sure enough, there she was, tied up tight and right out in the sun.

"I had to give her a lot of water and let her rest in the shade before she could ride. Not a bit too soon. We no more than rode up and I saw Kanaka Boy sitting on top—"

"I was a dead man," said Sam. "Truth is, I'm still too rattled to thank you properly. But thank you."

Hannibal beamed. Hannibal had one of the finest, most generous smiles on the planet. "You're welcome," he said.

"You know that's the third time you saved my life?" said Sam.

"At the Mojave villages and where else?"

"When you gave your speech about the wild hair."

"That's not the same."

"And look where it's got me."

Hannibal held an arm out to the wide desert. "You got plenty o' nothing."

"You got us, in a way," said Lei, indicating Esperanza, too. "And you got Warrior, too."

"Warrior is yours," Sam said. "You inherited him."

"I will touch nothing to do with that man. Nothing."

Sam looked at Hannibal, who looked at Esperanza.

"Want one of the best horses you'll ever see?" asked her papa. "Fine breeding stallion—got size on him."

She managed to nod yes.

ESPERANZA KNEW PAPA Sam wanted to help her, wanted her to talk about what had happened and set down some of the burden of it. But she couldn't. She couldn't face any of it. Being ripped out of her home, losing the man she loved and got pregnant by, that seemed small and distant now. Taking Joe as a husband, being left alone, losing the baby—she could barely cope with that.

Being Kanaka Boy's plaything, though, that was beyond . . .

He tortured her. All day he rode like a madman with Vermilion on a lead. When they stopped at night, he started his talk. He couldn't be bothered with her, he said, a contemptible creature barely old enough to bleed between her legs. He had a couple of dozen men would enjoy her, though. He would give her to them right off, and they would do her. Every man of them would do her right in a row, and then they would do her again. Every one would stick it between her legs and go on to places she didn't know men stuck it. They would do her everywhere hard and mean, so it hurt. He would tell them to use her up all the way. Last time he did that, there was a Digger woman who slapped one of them who came up to her with his cock sticking out. So they did her and he did her and over and over until she gave up and died. No accident, either, that's what they wanted. That's what they would do to Esperanza.

Every evening, that's all he talked about. He acted like the kind of boy who builds a little grass fire and throws bugs and lizards on it. They were going to do her until she died, and he was going to urge them on and, when she was dead, piss on her face.

He didn't rape her, which seemed bizarre. He said he was waiting for the orgy.

That whole week she never stopped shaking.

Now she'd heard from Lei that Kanaka Boy couldn't do it—that explained one thing. But at the time Esperanza believed every other word Kanaka Boy said. She knew that for the rest of her life she would be looking over one shoulder, scared of seeing the mocking face of a new version of the mad Hawaiian.

She sneaked a look at Sam. What was she to do with this man who was her papa, sort of? She realized he loved her. He had ridden across the worst deserts anyone knew about to save her. He had nearly thrown his life away to help her—she'd seen what a hair's-breadth call that was. Even now he didn't seem to want anything for her, just to help her.

She wanted her mother. But Esperanza understood that Papa Sam was a good man. Sometimes she wanted to crawl into his arms and bawl. Maybe she would.

ESPERANZA LAUGHED FOR the first time as they approached the Humboldt sink. "I'm sorry to say good-bye to the river," said Hannibal.

They looked at the pitiful stream and waited.

"It's so convenient. I can walk down it with a foot on each side, and when I'm thirsty bend down and drink it dry."

She said more than one syllable for the first time that evening they got to the Humboldt. As they stopped the horses for the night, a sandhill crane lifted up a few paces out in the marsh. Esperanza exclaimed several words of amazement and then looked at Sam sheepishly, realizing.

The sink was a huge mishmash of lake, dry lake bed, and marsh. Sam and Hannibal knew it from when they brought a herd of horses from California to the mountains in 1836. "Last water for about forty miles to the Truckee River," the men told the women.

"Does the river really disappear here?" said Esperanza.

"Sinks into the sands, end of river," said Sam.

"Then?"

"We walk dry to the next river, the Truckee, about forty miles."

"Can we rest a day?"

They rested three. Esperanza was still listless, but she began to talk to Sam. She said nothing about Kanaka Boy but only spoke of small matters of these first dozen years of her life, when she was still a child. She talked about happy memories, many of them about Vermilion and some of them, Sam was glad to hear, about rendezvous.

Lei was thrilled by the plentiful birdlife of marsh. She led Hannibal on hours and hours of treks around its ledge, spying every kind of bird in his field glass. "In the desert," she said over and over. "Incredible."

In the evenings she drew mosaics of birds, or sometimes just wings, in the sand.

After they got over to the Truckee River—dry crossings seemed hardly to matter anymore—they followed it up to the crest of the Sierra Nevada and looked out on the huge valley of the Sacramento.

Sam looked out at what he could see, the foothills of these great mountains, and what his mind's eye pictured beyond. The huge, sluggish river, which watered one of the continent's great tall-grass prairies. San Francisco Bay, where the river came to the sea. The road along the east side of the Bay, running south to the most beautiful land he'd ever seen and the capital of California, Monterey.

Since he thought the word, he said it. "Home." He hadn't used it in that meaning in two decades.

"Do you suppose they'll make us become Catholics?" he asked.

"Only if we want to get married or die," said Hannibal.

Sam looked at Hannibal and Lei speculatively.

Forty-nine

GRUMBLE GAVE SAM a bear hug that would squeeze sap out of a tree. Then he gave Hannibal an *abrazo* and bowed politely over the hands of Lei and Esperanza.

For sure they were the only ladies in the place. Having no idea where Grumble and Abby might live, and even less where Flat Dog and Julia might have put their lodge, Sam and Hannibal rode downtown to Abby's tavern, casino, and dance hall, The Sailor's Berth. Or maybe she and Grumble still owned it together, or maybe . . .

"Just me," said Grumble. "It's just me now. I have chameleoned myself from con man to respectable businessman. Sometimes I regret it. However, the capital I earned at Yerba Buena bought this establishment for me."

"Yerba Buena" meant the mission on San Francisco Bay, which Grumble had turned into a whorehouse and sold for a nice profit.

"Not that this brothel is so respectable. Excuse my bluntness, ladies," he added.

He expanded a proud arm to show off his premises. He had turned a low dive into a palace. The walls were life-sized paintings of naked ladies (not mere women). The back bar was splendid enough to attract the most highfalutin ship's captain. The liquors on display were imported and expensive, though rotgut was on every table. This place was fancy enough to condone any sin a man wanted to commit.

The cherub had aged well. Grumble was still a rotund, graying man of indeterminate age with an angelic smile and a demonic gleam in his eye. Raised as an orphan by the Bishop of Baltimore, Grumble had learned to live by his extraordinary wits—he'd been the cleverest of con men and had turned the deck of cards (actually, several very special decks) into King Solomon's mines.

"Papa," said Esperanza.

Sam knew. "Sorry, Grumble, but we're in a hurry. Where are Flat Dog and Julia?"

"Look up the hill to the grandest place you can see. That's the hacienda of Don and Señora Strong. Well, their town hacienda. They have another place, an entire estate, in the Salinas River Valley. The former rancho of Don Montalban."

Grumble winked at Sam and Hannibal. In 1828 they'd gotten into a fight with the don while springing Flat Dog from jail. The dustup had left the rancho without owner or heir.

Grumble turned his attention to Esperanza. "Young lady, you don't remember me, but I know you very well. It was I who rescued you and your mother from—"

"Grumble," said Sam. "Later."

"Very well. Go up to the hacienda. Everyone is eager to see you, and Abby will make you very much at home. I will join you for a drink late this afternoon.

"But you may not take a single step away from this establishment without hearing my great news."

They looked at him quizzically.

"You have arrived just in time. Two weeks from Saturday I am getting married."

"To who?" Sam almost shouted.

"I will introduce the lady," said Grumble, "over our afternoon drink."

ABBY AND HER husband were in town doing errands, but a servant showed the new visitors to the guest quarters of the Flat Dog family.

Esperanza threw herself into her mother's arms. Sam was relieved. When they first rescued Esperanza from Kanaka Boy, she seemed to want to crawl onto Sam's lap and suck her thumb, but she never asked to be held and never talked about her abduction. Now the young woman, recently terrified into a girl, found solace.

Julia had hot water brought and gave Esperanza and Lei their first experiences of a bathtub.

Then everybody traded stories. Long journeys afford plenty of them. Julia and Flat Dog were horrified by the episode of Kanaka Boy's trap and how it came out. Azul and Rojo were excited. Sam left out a lot of the blood, danger, and Kanaka Boy's nasty threats. He didn't want to remind Esperanza or give Julia's sons nightmares.

The servant brought them a delicious drink Sam had never seen before, crystals of lemon dissolved in water, and showed Sam, Hannibal, and Lei to their separate rooms so they could rest. Sam loved the lemon drink and thought stretching out on a bed was delicious.

They didn't see Abby until the servant brought everyone onto a wide, lovely tiled terrace for late-afternoon drinks, which was apparently a daily custom. She served watered wine and bowls of the fruits that grew so well in California, avocados and oranges, plus almonds, and a dish entirely new to Sam, artichoke hearts marinated in olive oil.

Azul bit into an artichoke and spat it out. Julia caught the wad in midair and gave her son a talking-to.

Rojo complained that he and his brother were bored and didn't want to be nice and talk to a bunch of adults—they wanted to play.

Flat Dog said he'd get them out of this duty as soon as he could.

"When I say so," said Julia. She hadn't had an opportunity like this for more than a dozen years and no opportunity at all to teach her sons how to behave in a nice social setting.

Hannibal asked Esperanza for her marionette horse, and he and Lei showed the boys more tricks about making it walk and run.

Sam didn't give a damn about any of it. He just got impatient for Abby to appear.

She came alone, wearing a mint green dress, a wide-brimmed hat of canary yellow, and an emerald necklace fit for a duchess. She let a touch of gray show in her hennaed hair. She came straight to Sam, gave him a long hug, a quick kiss on the cheek, and said, "If I wasn't so damned dignified, I'd jump up and make you catch me in your arms."

When Grumble came, he walked down the broad steps holding hands with . . .

At first Sam didn't recognize her, because she'd gotten huge and was crowned with a spectacular blond wig. Though he knew her to be Sicilian, in her embroidered white summer dress with a flaring skirt, plus enough bracelets and necklaces for a Gypsy, and with her olive skin, she could have been a Gypsy. Her hair was pushed high with combs in the Californio style. Her getup said she was the grandest of Californio ladies. Somehow, over the several five years, she had gotten as wide as Grumble and half again more. Her smile said that getting there, and everything else, had been a lot of fun.

"Siciliana," he stammered.

"You knew her by the appellation she worked under," said Grumble smoothly. That had been at The Sailor's Berth, where

Sam knew her intimately. "Now she prefers to be called by her true name. We will start afresh with correct introductions.

"Carlotta, I believe you know my friend Sam Morgan. Sam, Carlotta Casale, who is my madam and soon to be my wife."

The lady turned her smile wicked and did a teasing curtsey.

"And may I introduce further"—Grumble gestured to the sixtyish man and young woman behind him on the steps—"Isabella Grazia, my fiancée's sister, and Don Anthony Strong, your host."

Isabella curtseyed to Sam and gave him her hand. She was wearing a pale aquamarine dress that fit tight enough for Carlotta to wear in her former profession. "Don't worry," she said. "Isabella just borrowed that dress from . . . my friend. She's a *respectable* widow." Carlotta gave a nice curlicue to "respectable."

Sam pulled his eyes away from Isabella to shake hands with Strong, a Brit with an amiable face and a nose that suggested he enjoyed his liquor.

Sam had to force himself not to stare at Isabella. He tried to gauge which of the sisters was older but couldn't tell—both in their midthirties, he supposed, Carlotta round as a walrus, Isabella slender as a the stem of a flower. From their eyes, both of them were endowed with an over-abundance of sass.

"Sam," said Carlotta, "don't look at my sister like that. Her husband died, her son got shot mortally robbing a house, and her daughter married a Greek and went to Olympus or somewhere dumb. She's mad at God, and she's feisty enough to take the Old Man on."

Sam decided to try to be gracious. "She's also lovely." When Carlotta whispered a translation into Isabella's ear, she gave Sam a merry glance.

"Watch out. We Casale sisters don't stand on ceremony around men. You might say our experience, different as it is, has taught us not to." Carlotta's speech still bore an aroma of her native isle.

Grumble pitched in to rescue everyone. "Sam," Grumble interrupted pleasantly, "I formally ask you to be my best man at the great event."

"I don't have any clothes," said Sam.

"That's grand. We shall expect you in your finest buckskins. At our wedding the common shall dance with the aristocratic."

"Long as I'm the bride," said Carlotta, "the common will be conspicuous."

"And Carlotta was about to tell you that Isabella will be her maid of honor—"

"Not that either one of us is maids," said Carlotta, "though only one of us was a bawd."

"When I bought The Sailor's Berth," Grumble said, "I put Carlotta in charge of the ladies of the evening. Now she will be in charge of me."

Carlotta gave him a look that said, *You better believe it.*

Hannibal and Lei brought the boys up and all were introduced.

"So," Grumble rumbled on, "let us all have a grand luncheon at Murphy's tomorrow, that's a fine new eatery in town, and make plans. You two have some work to do. Hannibal and Lei, too."

Sam couldn't bring himself to look straight at Isabella. She seemed to be trying not to laugh at his self-consciousness.

"That's a deal," Sam said, turning away.

"Not so fast," said Carlotta. "You'll have one obstacle putting wedding plans together with Isabella. She doesn't speak English."

Sam gave Carlotta a look that said, *Wha . . . ?*

"I been speaking it since I got here on a boat ten years ago. She just arrived, so I have to translate for her."

"She has about two weeks' worth of Spanish," put in Grumble.

"Let me finish my story, *mio caro.* My family hasn't had anything to do with me since I took up the whoring trade. Only after Isabella took up arms against the Almighty and I sent money for the passage to California did she decide her sister might be worth a visit.

"So if she doesn't say much, don't think she's demure. She's just as brassy as I am. But only in Italian."

Sam found his tongue enough to say, "So what is it you want us to do?"

"Now you're getting into it," said Carlotta. "We have invitations. The printer has them ready now. The engraving is beautiful, I designed it myself. We want the four of you, Sam and Isabella, Hannibal and Lei, to deliver them to everyone who is anybody in town."

"Us?"

"It's a service. Sam, you and Hannibal are acquainted with the people who count—the highfalutin people are the same as when you were here last. Hannibal and Lei can deliver invitations to the couples, Sam and Isabella to the single men. That will give you a chance to introduce my sister to them."

"Enough," Grumble said.

Carlotta didn't even pause for breath. "Isabella needs a new husband. I want her to meet the *comandante* of the presidio, also Mr. Larkin, Captain Cooper, the owners of the French Hotel, everyone who matters. Especially the single gentlemen."

Grumble interrupted louder. "Tomorrow. Now, Sam, I want to talk to Azul. Remember, I aided at his birth."

Sam would never forget that terrible afternoon. Stormy with weather and with violence of man against man, it still produced a new human being.

OUTSIDE MURPHY'S, AFTER the luncheon, which was just an excuse for wine and conviviality, Carlotta handed Sam and Hannibal a carton each of formal invitations. "We'll be on our way," said Sam.

"We will, too," said Julia. "Can you tell us where the shop of the saddle maker is? Flat Dog wants to see it."

Grumble gave directions—Flat Dog and Julia walked that way.

Sam took Isabella first to a shop that bore the sign GIDEON POORBOY, GOLDSMITH in a fancy script.

A teenage boy met them at the front counter. "May I help you?" he asked in Spanish. Sam supposed he was one of Gideon's

Mexican nephews, helping out. He could see his friend the artist bent over and hammering metal against an asphalt block in the back shop. The metal looked like a gold plate.

"Tell Mr. Poorboy," Sam said loudly, "that a Rocky Mountain beaver trapper has come to give him his leg back."

Gideon peg-legged out of the back room as fast as he could, raced around the counter, and embraced Sam. They held on to each other. If you cut and saw off another man's leg, if you take his blood and his life in your hands, you are forever joined. Not to mention riding from the Missouri River to the Pacific Ocean with him.

Sam handed Gideon the invitation, and the goldsmith exclaimed that he would be glad to see all his old friends.

While they traded news she couldn't understand, Isabella looked around at the fine things. In the display cases were many beautiful things made in silver—drinking bowls, spoons, frames for mirrors, and pictures, candlesticks, and plates, some of them with a design raised by embossing. Her family had never been able to dream of such luxuries, although her friend Abby now could and perhaps one day Carlotta could. . . .

In a corner Isabella found liturgical objects. She reached out and touched a silver chalice. She had once been devout, but she thought that the church's money should be given to the poor, not spent on fancy implements for communion or statues for the poor to bend their knees to.

"Señora," said Gideon, "I see you like ze beauty. May I show you some things?"

Isabella spread her hands helplessly.

"She speaks only Italian," said Sam.

"The plate that holds ze wafers," said Gideon, picking it up, "inlaid in niello."

"The black lines against the silver," said Sam, "are really beautiful."

Gideon gave an extravagant Gallic shrug. "I have these church things," he said, "because I had orders from three different missions for them when the government seized all their lands. What a farce. All the mission lands, meant for the Indians but in possession of the *ricos*. Half the Indians are field hands, almost like slaves, and other half, zey went back to their tribes.

"So, I now have these wonderful objects I cannot sell. Neverzeless, my friend, I do very well. The *ricos*, their ladies, sometime a sailor who want a bauble for a woman . . . Very well."

He noticed how Sam and Isabella stood close to each other.

"I t'ink you like zis woman you cannot even talk to. Sometimes it is good, a man can no understand what his woman say. If you decide you like her, or if ze wedding of Grumble, it make you feel sentimental, come back and I give you a small necklace or bracelet as a gift for her. Now I see her coloring, I can pick somet'ing most beautiful."

"I'm not going courting," said Sam. He slapped Gideon on the back, and he and Isabella headed for the homes of a substantial list of single men who might want to meet an attractive and eligible woman from Sicily.

Fifty

SAM, FLAT DOG, Julia, and Esperanza sat in the old mission cemetery. The wooden marker at the head of the grave said:

MEADOWLARK MORGAN
1810?–1827
R.I.P.

"She was sick with you," Julia said to Esperanza.

"Convulsions," said Flat Dog.

Sam found himself unable to speak.

"We brought her in from the trapper camp to Monterey, where the best doctor might be."

Esperanza barely knew what a doctor was.

"There was no doctor," said Flat Dog, "but there was a good midwife, Rosalita. She helped your mother."

"In the end the convulsions were so intense that Rosalita had to cut your mother's belly open with a knife and take you out. This is not uncommon in childbirth. It is a very old practice."

"But the wound may fester," said Flat Dog. "That's what happened. It festered, she got a high fever, and she died."

"I woke up with her cold in my arms," said Sam. He couldn't recognize his own voice, it sounded so pinched.

They all sat and looked at the rich, green grass on Esperanza's mother's grave.

"I was very . . . ," Sam tried to go on. "I went into a kind of black hole."

"Finally we made Papa Sam go away," Julia said, "do something—do anything to jolt him out of his grief."

"I left you with Papa Flat Dog and Julia and went to rendezvous. Damn near died getting there."

"Several months later he came back for you and us," Julia said, "intending to go back to the village to live. But my father had abducted us, both you and me, and taken us to his rancho. Papa Flat Dog and Papa Sam rescued us from him. You know that story."

Actually, she hadn't, not until Grumble told her a couple of days ago.

They all looked at one another across the low mound. Esperanza finally found her voice. "But what was she like?"

"She was the best wife a man could have," said Sam.

"She was a devil," said Flat Dog. "She tortured her little brothers, mainly me."

"She was beautiful and graceful and considerate," said Julia.

Esperanza looked directly at Sam. "Tell me the best thing she ever did for you."

"Love me," said Sam, "and marry me."

"I mean some particular thing she did," said Esperanza.

Sam took a deep breath. He knew the story he had to tell and dreaded it. "Papa Flat Dog and her older brother"——Esperanza knew this meant Blue Medicine Horse and the name of the dead could not be spoken——"her brothers asked me for eight horses for her hand in marriage. I wanted her bad enough to steal a hundred. I took her older brother and Papa Flat Dog on a raid against the Headcutters. At first we got the horses, but some Headcutters caught us and your uncle got killed."

"It wasn't your fault," said Flat Dog, in the tone of a sentence uttered a hundred times.

"I gave a sun dance, Papa Flat Dog and I took revenge on the Headcutters, but that wasn't enough. Your grandparents wouldn't have a thing to do with me.

"So your mother and I ran away together. And while we were there, we talked, for the first time, about me getting her older brother killed. I said some words from the white man's Bible that I remembered: 'Give unto them beauty for ashes, the oil of joy for mourning, and the garment of praise for the spirit of heaviness.' Then she gave me an amazing gift. She forgave me."

The tears flowed openly down Sam's face. He didn't wipe them. "I didn't know . . . about forgiveness."

No one spoke for a while.

"That was the best thing she ever did for me."

"Did she like California?" asked Esperanza.

"She loved it," Sam said. "We came on the expedition because she wanted to see the big-water-everywhere. We camped a few days on a beach near the rancho where Julia lived. All day every day we played in the surf and explored the tide pools."

"I saw some tide pools yesterday."

"She loved the creatures that lived in them, the anemones especially. She would poke the squishy things with her finger and make them squirt. One day we even saw a sea horse."

Then he had to explain what that was.

"I want to see one," said Esperanza.

"We will," said Sam.

Esperanza heaved a big sigh. "If my mother liked California," she said, "maybe I will, too."

* * *

FLAT DOG AND Julia stood at the baptismal font with Rojo and Paloma, the toddler holding Julia's hand. Sam and Abby stood beside them, with Azul, Grumble, and Anthony Strong in the rear flank.

"Flat Dog," said Father Enrique, "this is a great moment for me. I have often thought of the days when I instructed you. Those recollections give me great pleasure, like fingering the beads of my rosary. You were an excellent student, and especially keen to read. How has your reading come along?"

"Well enough, Father."

Actually, Sam had carried children's books in Spanish from Taos to the family, but Flat Dog could only read well enough to make out the signs advertising food and drink on the streets.

"God took your soul to his bosom at that time, and all our hearts soar to see your return with these fine children."

Flat Dog smiled and nodded gently. Thirteen years ago, when Julia's father abducted her and the infant Azul, Flat Dog was thrown into the Monterey jail. Father Enrique got him transferred to the mission prison in order to give him the baptism and instruction that would save his soul. They became friends, and when the time came, the good padre helped Flat Dog escape from jail and head south to rescue his wife and child.

Flat Dog thought Catholicism was a little funny, but his heart was big for the priest.

"Señora Strong, Señor Morgan, you are willing to be the godparents of these children, that is to say, in case of need you pledge yourself to overseeing their spiritual upbringing."

"Yes," said Abby and Sam in chorus. The priest had asked them earlier if they had been baptized Catholics, and Sam had lied. He suspected the priest knew that.

"Then let us proceed." The padre put his hand into the holy water.

"*Ego te baptismo in nomine Patris et Filii et Spiritus Sancti.*" As the priest spoke, he sprinkled the water three times on Rojo's head and three times on Paloma's—Father, Son, and Holy Spirit. Paloma wiped it off her forehead.

The priest said a good many more words, and at last the ceremony ended.

"You well know your duty to these children, Señora Flat Dog."

"Yes, Father. I am so glad to be back in the arms of Mother Church."

"In that case I will hear your confession now, and then Flat Dog's." He reached back and tousled Azul's hair. "And you, young man, I will expect you at catechism class starting Monday."

Azul made a face.

Outside, Grumble said, "I feel smothered by religion. Do you think I might borrow the boys for an hour or two and teach them sleight-of-hand tricks?"

"I'm afraid of what that means," said Julia.

"Picking pockets," said Grumble.

"Grumble!" Julia exclaimed.

Flat Dog laughed and said, "Sure, go to it."

"Every young man needs a way to make a living," said Grumble.

THEY REINED IN the horses at a rise with a spectacular panoramic view of the sea. As they dismounted, Flat Dog took his wife's hand and said to everyone, "I have to tell you something."

He had the attention of Sam and Isabella, Abby and Strong, Esperanza and Hannibal immediately. Even of Lei and Carlotta, who waited in the carriage beside them.

"Yesterday I apprenticed myself to Alano Lopez."

"The saddle maker!" Strong exclaimed.

"Yes," said Flat Dog. "I'm going to learn to make saddles, and all the other gear, for the horses Sam, Hannibal, and Esperanza will train."

Sam said, "That shines."

"Lopez does superb work," said Strong, "the stamping especially."

"I intend to become the best," said Flat Dog.

"This way," said Abby, and the walkers took a score of steps onto a knoll. "This is what we want you to see. This is the spot we recommend."

They looked out across the land of their proposed horse ranch, once part of the Carmel mission and no more than five miles from town.

"It's about what you Americans call two sections of land," said Strong. It was rolling hills, with a good creek angling across the oceanside corner. The grass was summer tawny now, but there was plenty of it and the winter rains would bring it green. In three directions the Pacific swept away toward China, or Japan, or Australia, or whatever was over there. Sam turned and saw Lei looking west out the carriage window, her eyes dreamy. No doubt about what she was dreaming of.

"Come over this way," said Strong. "There are two good building sites together."

The sites were fine, level, pleasant, less than fifty paces from the ocean.

"I love it," Esperanza said.

"We picture the site on this side of the lane for the Flat Dog family, and Mr. Morgan and Mr. MacKye on the other. . . ." The Brit could not bring himself to drop formality.

"And if Hannibal decides to marry," said Abby, "why not a third house over there?"

"Lots of logs to haul," said Sam.

"We've arranged for that," said Strong. "The logs for two dwellings are on the way down from the hills at this moment, and will be on the site in a couple of days."

"We can't afford this," said Sam.

"Oh, but you can," said Abby.

"It's ours," said Strong. "We have more land than we'll ever need. Besides, I intend to make a profit."

"How?" said Sam.

"As your rancho grows, you'll need much more land. And I own the adjoining pieces as well."

"Anthony, don't belittle this. Sam, Anthony and I want to make this land a gift to you, Flat Dog, and Hannibal," Abby said.

She turned to Sam and took both his hands.

"It's a gift of love," she said. "Please accept it."

Sam looked at his partners.

Julia said, "Of course we'll accept it. Thank you, thank you."

"In that case," said Strong, "we'll leave you to look it over at your leisure."

Everyone walked back to the carriage.

Isabella spoke firmly in her language, and her sister translated. "Are you going to put in grapevines? I know you want horses—just like men—but these lands are a natural for grapes."

Sam suppressed a smile.

"Enough talk," said Strong.

As the carriage rolled away, Hannibal said, "I have to tell you, I think this horse ranch will be a rousing success. But I'm not going to be part of it."

"What?" Sam was jolted.

"Lei wants to go to the Sandwich Islands. Hawaii, as she calls them. I'm going to take her."

"And then?" Sam had been afraid of this.

"Probably I'll be back here in a year. But who knows?"

"Maybe succumb to Lei's charms?"

"Maybe. But I am a wanderer."

"Before you go, why don't you give the ranch a name?"

"Easy," said Hannibal. "Vita Luna." Crazy Life.

Fifty-one

CARLOTTA AND GRUMBLE'S wedding ceremony at the mission church was beautiful. The bride and groom created more suppressed smiles than tears, but still it was lovely, and the church was full. Sam dropped the golden band as he tried to hand it to Grumble, and got a good laugh.

Fortunately, The Sailor's Berth was twice as big as the church, and still some of the reception guests had to do their eating and drinking outside. Grumble had laid a feast to satisfy the greediest gourmand and the thirstiest drunk.

Carlotta commandeered the services of her six ladies of the evening to make the rounds with trays and food and drinks, and flirt with the male guests occasionally. They were dressed to the nines. ("But no tricks on my wedding day," she had ordered.)

Monterey turned itself out splendidly. The *comandante* of the presidio was in full uniform, as were all his officers, and Mexicans had a feel for the maximum show of color, brass buttons, epaulets, and braid. Considering himself the representative of his government, the merchant Larkin came in his swallow-tailed coat. The captains of all three ships in port turned up, worthy rivals in their finery to the land-bound military men of the presidio. The merchants of the town, mostly Mexicans but a few Americans, Brits, and Irishmen, outdid themselves. Gideon wore a handsome frock coat and a bejeweled gold earring that drew the envy of the ladies.

Even Father Enrique turned up in his brown robe. Grumble had been afraid the presence of the soiled doves might scare him off. Perhaps the over-sized pectoral cross he wore was a form of protection.

Abby was resplendent and her husband dashing, but that was to be expected.

A half-dozen musicians congregated around the piano, two guitars, a guitarrón, two trumpets, an accordion, and Grumble himself at the piano. Over the years his fingers had apostasized from Mozart to mariachi. For the moment the band sent out a quiet background music, an accompaniment to conversation.

One group of guests was not showy, the Morgan–Flat Dog outfit. Grumble had instructed them strictly not to waste the capital they needed to buy horseflesh on clothes. "Carlotta and I," he insisted, "will have a grand time cavorting among the buckskins."

Against one wall Julia and Flat Dog chatted with Hannibal and Lei. Julia wondered how many days or weeks would pass before she saw these two friends no more. A strange man, Hannibal, in her opinion, ever drifting, a kind of Wandering Jew.

She led her husband toward the bride and groom to say their formal congratulations. Flat Dog looked as out of place, Julia thought, as a sunflower among petunias. He was out of place here, but to her more splendid than any other man. She thought how lucky she was to know he would stay here. She would not wake up some morning to find him fled back to the Yellowstone country. That was because, from the first moment, they had been utterly in love with each other.

Her eyes searched out the three children. Rojo, the most devil-ish, hung around Abby and Anthony Strong. He made a show of conducting an adult conversation with them, which tickled Abby. After a few minutes the boy reached under his hide shirt and of-fered the rich Brit his wallet back. Abby laughed, and Strong pre-tended to.

Azul, the smartest, played poker with men several times his age and consistently lost. Grumble had taught him how to use the deck of marked cards and was bankrolling his losses, the cherub's wedding-day gift to his former victims.

Esperanza talked casually with the young son of one of the rancheros, but her behavior was not at all flirtatious. Kanaka Boy's hideous assault and two heartbreaks in one year—Julia wondered how long it would take her daughter to recover.

Catty-corner across the huge room Sam Morgan and Isabella Grazia stood together and didn't talk. They tried a few phrases in the smidgeon of Spanish she'd picked up, but essentially they only waited for the first dance—which was now.

At Grumble's command the trumpets sounded a fanfare.

"Ladies and gentlemen," he cried, "my new bride and I invite you to join us in a dance."

It was a *Ranchero Valseada*, as Grumble had requested, a waltz in a moderate tempo. The newlyweds led off, as was only proper. When they saw how nimble a plump man and fat woman could be on their dancing feet, the crowd applauded.

"Everyone dance!" cried Grumble.

Sam held his arm out to Isabella, and she took it.

From many *bailes* in Taos and Santa Fe, Sam had a flair for this dance. He felt like he was tossing in a raging river, but he didn't let that show.

He looked down at Isabella. Her face seemed to glow. *All women like to dance*, he told himself.

He liked to dance. A fun-loving partner in Taos had taught how truly to lead a woman in a *valseada*. "It is not done with the hands, or even the feet," she explained. "My hand is on your shoulder. Lead with your chest, and my whole body will move with you."

He did his best leading now and felt how well they flowed together. Then, because she couldn't understand a word, he spoke to her.

"I like spending time with you," he said in English.

She cocked her head a little sideways and the corner of her mouth turned up. *"Che sciocco! Perché non mi tiene vicina?"* Which meant, had Sam been able to understand, "He holds me at a distance, the fool."

This game tickled Sam.

"I make up excuses every day to go to Grumble and Carlotta's house," he said, "just to be near you."

"Scommetto che nemmeno mi bacia. I bet he doesn't even kiss me."

He introduced a tricky new step, flinging her an arm's length.

"You are so much alive."

He used her hand to lead her in a circle and draw her back into his arms.

"Non si rende conto che vuol baciarmi. He doesn't even know he wants to kiss me."

Now the band picked up the tempo, and all the couples whirled faster.

"It's such fun to be around you."

He spun her so that her back was to him.

"Mi sembra di ballare con una verginella. You'd think I was being courted by a virgin."

"I haven't felt this way in a long, long time."

"Carlotta dice che é bravo a letto. Carlotta says he's fun in bed."

"I'm a fool to even let myself dream about you."

"Bravo a letto, un inizio interessante. Fun in bed, that's a good start."

"But I do dream about you."

The music swirled to a climactic ending. Each gentleman (of

the ones that were gentlemen) lifted one of his partner's hands high and bowed his head to her.

Sam spun Isabella an extra time and did the same.

"*Cuore mio, che tristezza, innamorarsi di uno sciocco.* I pity my heart for being enamored of such a fool."

"Thank you for the dance."

"*Baciami, stupido.* Kiss me, you idiot."

They smiled at each other foolishly. Their eyes said what their tongues stumbled over.

Sam waited half-breathless for the music to start again.

Grumble's voice said behind them, "Are you enjoying yourselves, my friend and my dear sister-in-law?"

Sam and Isabella turned to the bridal pair. "Things shine with us," said Sam, "but this day belongs to you."

Isabella looked into Carlotta's merry eyes and said, "*Fammi un favore, appena hai tempo, spiega a questa testadura che farei una moglie perfetta?* Some time soon, very soon, would you tell this thickhead I'll make a damn good wife?"

Author's Note
The Next Decade

The missionaries and colonists were right about the rush of emigrants soon to set out for Oregon. In 1843, just two years after the end of this book, the plains, mountains, and deserts were filled with prairie schooners rolling their way across the Oregon Trail, a tidal wave of people.

Unfortunately, Hannibal MacKye turned out to be right about the Cayuse people coming to despise Marcus and Narcissa Whitman and the other missionaries at Wailatpu. In 1847, because of a measles epidemic they blamed on the whites, the Cayuses killed Dr. and Mrs. Whitman, Joe Meek's daughter Helen Mar, and eleven others and took the remaining sixty people of the colony hostage, to be ransomed one month later by the Hudson's Bay Company.

Hannibal was also right about California becoming a true New World. Discovery of gold at Sutter's Mill in 1848 drew an explosion of people to California from every corner of the globe. San Francisco became one of the world's great cities. California jumbled red, white, black, brown, and yellow together indiscriminately. The chaos did not cohere into a new kind of society for years, and the mixing together did not lead to ideal relationships between the races, as Hannibal hoped. Then or now.

Hannibal's vision of the New World as a second chance for mankind, a beckoning utopia, has been beautifully expressed by Eduardo Galeano in his *Faces and Marks:*

> [Since the discovery of the New World] pursuers of hallucinations have continued heading for the lands of America from every wharf. Protected by a god of navigation and conquest, squeezed into their ships, they cross the immense ocean. Along with shepherds and farmhands whom Europe has not killed by war, plague, or hunger, go captains and merchants and rogues and mystics and adventurers. All seek the miracle. Beyond the ocean, magical ocean that cleanses blood and transfigures destinies, the great promise of all the ages lies open. There, beggars will be avenged. There, nobodies will turn into marquises, scoundrels into saints, gibbet-fodder into founders, and vendors of love will become dowried debutantes.

Though it remains a beguiling illusion, the vision helps to define the American character.

History and This Book

The world of this book is faithful to the time and places it depicts. The state of the fur trade, the situations of the forts and the companies that ran them, the missions and missionaries, the Hawaiian people in the Northwest, traffic on the Oregon and California Trails, the political struggle between the United States and Great Britain for the Oregon country, the relationships between Anglos and Indians in the region—all were just as I have drawn them.

Many of the characters here are historical: Frank Ermatinger, Francois Payette, Dr. John McLoughlin, and other employees of the Hudson's Bay Company; Andrew Drips of American Fur; Joe Meek and Doc Newell (and their adventure in taking the first wagons to Oregon); the four missionaries Doc guided to Fort Hall, and even Father De Smet; Marcus and Narcissa Whitman and their daughter, along with the state of their mission at the time.

Also, the letters attributed here to Narcissa Whitman are ones she actually wrote.

Most of the principal characters—Sam Morgan and his family, the Flat Dog family, Hannibal, all the individual Hawaiians, Grumble and Abby—are the children of my imagination.

Personal Note

The six volumes of the Rendezvous series form one big story. An undertaking like this is a daunting challenge for a writer, and finishing, saying good-bye to characters who have been friends for years, is an emotional experience. I found some eloquent sentences, spoken by the narrator, in a novel by Dean Koontz that speak for me:

> I wrote this to explain life to myself. The mystery. The humor, dark and light, that is the warp and weft of the weave. The absurdity. The terror. The hope. The joy, the grief. The God we never see except by indirection.
> —Dean Koontz, *Life Expectancy*